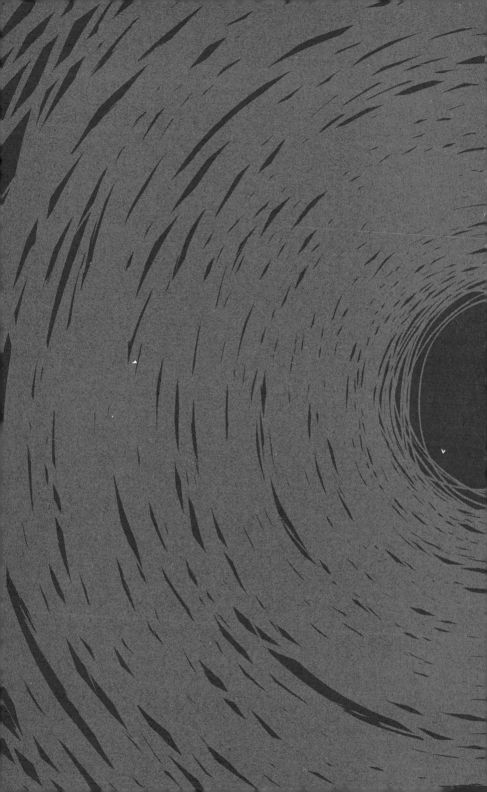

The Grey Land Series

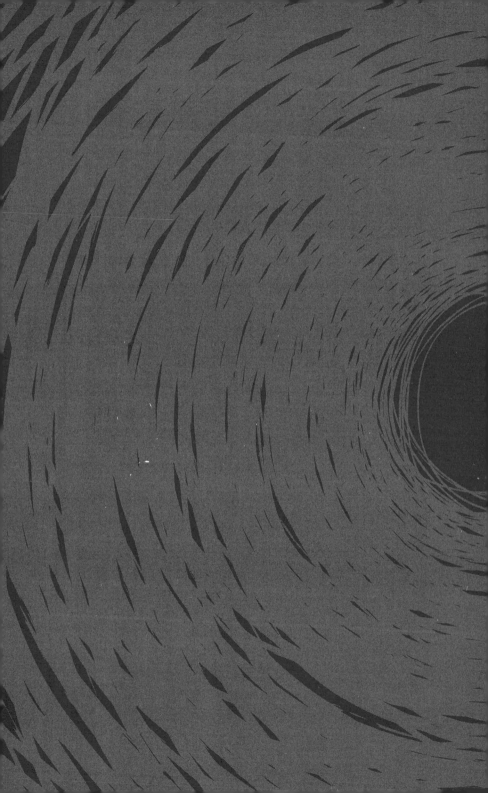

The INVASION

PEADAR O'GUILIN

DAVID FICKLING BOOKS

SCHOLASTIC PRESS · NEW YORK

Library of Congress Cataloging-in-Publication Data available

ISBN 978-1-338-04562-8

10 9 8 7 6 5 4 3 2 1   18 19 20 21 22

Printed in the U.S.A.   23

First edition, April 2018

Book design by Christopher Stengel
Jacket art © 2018 by Jeffrey Alan Love

Do Lúcás—ba chóir duit ceann

acu a léamh, áfach . . .

To part us two is

To part the children of one home

To part the body from the soul

Anonymous, c. 1150. Translated by

Gerard Murphy.

THE GRAVE ROBBERS

Aoife tumbles out of her cot onto an ice-cold floor. *Where am I? am I . . . am I there?*

It comes to her almost as a relief.

However, this is not the Grey Land. Not yet. The palms of her hands find the smooth, familiar walls of the gym. And all around her, Boyle Survival College's last thirty or so students fill the air with sighs and snores, with the smell of rarely washed bodies and the creaks of makeshift beds.

Perhaps she's taken a fever, because she can't get up. Her head is spinning and she bends suddenly, hands over her mouth, as a wave of nausea punches her savagely in the guts.

It eases off when she gets her back against the wall, sweat chilling on her forehead.

"No . . . ," a boy cries in his sleep.

"By Crom, they're eating my face!" says another. It's Krishnan, a thirteen-year-old so lanky that his feet stick out over the end of his mattress. His toes twitch and curl as though they've been stabbed through with pins.

The hackles on Aoife's neck rise as all around her the rest of the children start tossing and turning in their beds, their voices suddenly louder, as if each and every one of them is having the exact same nightmare.

"Get out of here," Aoife tells herself.

Her gorge rises in her throat again. The cold sweat seems to sizzle on her brow.

Out! Out!

But already the sleeping children are settling again.

Plenty of rumors have been flying about ever since the events that saw the Sídhe attack the school. Rumors of how Ireland and the Grey Land are closer to each other than they've been for centuries. Within touching distance, people say.

This is why the enemy appear so much more often now than they used to. And Aoife thinks that the frequency of these episodes of nausea and fear that affect only the young is rising too.

But what do I know?

She decides to get out anyway, hoping the freezing Roscommon air will make her feel better.

She knows the way in the dark, almost as though poor Emma's ghost is pulling her through the night. Once out the door, Aoife passes the shadowy burnt-out dorm building and walks down the alley formed by two long lines of caravans where the investigators and archaeologists now live. They won't allow "civilians" anywhere near the Fairy Fort they've been digging up, but Aoife has seen the dread on their faces at the end of each day's work. Sometimes the last shreds of her curiosity want her to go and find out what they're up to in the forest, but then she remembers what happened last time she did that, and she turns into a sobbing wreck. Emma! Poor Emma!

A dark figure looms suddenly in front of her, and Aoife still cares enough about her life to gasp.

"It's me. Nabil."

"I'm going for a walk," she says, angry at him for frightening her. "You can't stop me anymore."

He sighs, and she knows it was the wrong thing to say, for, of all the instructors, Nabil looks out for the students best and was a major player in saving their lives during the attack.

"Here, my friend," he says. "Take my flashlight. Give it back in the morning."

Now she feels even worse for snapping at him, but manages a small "thank you." Then he's gone and she's free again.

The freezing wind gets her teeth chattering. She's wearing nothing but her tracksuit and a thin raincoat she's been using for a blanket. She used to have Emma to keep her warm and thinks of all the times she told her friend to leave her alone, to let her sleep— as if they were going to have eternity together! As if nothing could ever go wrong! How could she have been so stupid?

Up ahead lies the graveyard. Funerals are never allowed in survival colleges or there'd be little time for anything else. And the bodies of students who die are sent back to the parents. So the few graves on college grounds are mostly for teachers and instructors. People without family or whose families don't want to know them.

And then there's the odd body so horrifically altered by the Sídhe it is deemed better to tell the parents that the scientists in Dublin, having examined it, then mislaid it.

Emma's parents accepted this explanation. They know what it really means and they have another girl back home to worry about.

Aoife moves in among the trees, escaping the wind again. Her once-plump cheeks are so cold they ache. She can't feel the hand that grips the flashlight. And that's when she hears the digging. No animal could make such a rhythmic, metallic sound. Only people. People hacking at the frozen soil of a graveyard in the darkest part of the night.

She stops in her tracks. How can there be somebody out here?

But her second thought is one of fury. *It's souvenir hunters*, she thinks. Dragging Emma's body from its resting place for the pleasure of gawkers. How dare they defile her! How dare they.

She crashes through the undergrowth, blundering out of the woods and into the graveyard proper, the ground slippy and hard as granite. She has come out right beside the heap of earth where Emma is buried, although you wouldn't know it, for there are no markers.

She stops right there, confused to find it undisturbed.

Then the hairs on her neck rise. She swings around, turning on the flashlight by instinct. It's an old windup one. Nobody makes batteries anymore and its light is a pale blue flicker, but it's enough to see the boy in front of her raise his hands to cover his face.

"Who are you?" she cries.

"Dubhtach, I was named." His voice would shame an angel, at once friendly and musical. "For my dark hair. See?"

Aoife is already backing away, her legs like jelly. It's not a boy in front of her, of course, but a little man. She can see now how his skin glitters ever so slightly in the light. How every part of him, from his delicate fingers to the square cut of his jaw, has been sanded to perfection by whatever god or devil created him.

And he's following, walking steadily forward, his grin wide and welcoming.

"Leave the thief alone," says another voice, a woman. "We have what we came for. We must swallow it before we are too small. And this one . . . I feel it. This one we'll be seeing *very* soon."

Aoife flings the flashlight at the little man's head. It knocks him back a pace and she uses the distraction to flee for her life, off into the woods.

When she returns an hour later with Nabil and Taaft, they find the graveyard full of holes and scattered remains. Of the Sídhe themselves no sign is left.

"What did they want with rotted flesh?" asks Taaft. "Are the little scum practicing voodoo now?"

"I never heard of that," Nabil replies. When he speaks English, he sounds so much more French than when he's using Sídhe. "But I do not like it. It's strange of them, no? They will have a reason."

5

"I'm going back to bed," says Aoife. Emma's safe; that's the main thing.

Or is it? The woman Sídhe said they'd be seeing Aoife soon, and she knows what that must mean. It's funny how little she feared the Call only a few hours ago, and how much she trembles now that it is finally reaching out for her. This impression becomes all the stronger when she realizes that, while she was gone, one of the few surviving Year 4s—Andy Scanlon—has turned up in his bunk with flippers for hands and blank skin where he once had a face.

He must have been lying there in the dark, his body cooling, as Aoife was stumbling outside.

NOT SO LUCKY

Nessa sits near the front of the bus, one arm draped around the case beside her, as though it's the dearest of friends. She watches Ireland streaming past the window.

Ivy and weeds push crumbling houses into the earth, and even trees rise in triumph over the corpses of factories and schools. The beauty of it overwhelms any sense of sadness. In winter, the bright green fields are all glamour in their capes of sparkling frost and the distant hills are little more than daubs of white paint against an intense blue sky.

I shouldn't be here to appreciate this, she thinks. Nessa's supposed to be dead. But she's not, she's not! She has paid her dues. No one has ever had to go twice to the Grey Land.

They pass through fading towns where only the old remain, and so rare is the sight of a working bus that all conversations stop and many people wave. Do they know there's a recent survivor on board? They'd make more of a fuss if they did, and Nessa smiles at the thought of it. She smiles at everyone and everything, enjoying even the experience of potholes and roads blocked by cattle and a market at Ardee.

Other children get on there, a group of January-born ten-year-olds heading for a survival college near Balbriggan. She decides she's not going to think about them for now, for ninety percent of them the Sídhe will murder in the next few years. Nessa has survived. She's off to Dublin for the first time in her life, to see Anto, the boy she loves. A fourteen-year-old like herself, who came back from the Grey Land of the enemy with his life and a large chunk of his sanity intact.

She's feeling shy already as rusty road signs tick the miles down. Will his parents be there? Will they mind if she kisses him? Will they care about the delicate twigs she was left with in place of legs after a bout of polio as a child?

They won't mind, she decides. Although they might put up a fight if she tries to steal their son away to Donegal. She grins and her cheeks hurt with it, because she hasn't changed her expression in hours.

And then the bus comes over the suspension bridge near Drogheda to find the Dublin end blocked by a minibus and a government car. It rumbles to a halt with the kids straining their necks to see what's wrong.

The driver, nine-tenths belly, the rest grey mustache, exchanges a few words with an old policewoman before turning to the passengers. "We all have to get off," he shouts. "It won't be for long, all right? Ten minutes."

The pitted surface of the road hosts a group of trench-coat-wearing adults who wouldn't look out of place in a movie.

"Line them up!" says a man at the front. And then, "Wait! Don't bother." He strides ten paces over to Nessa. The Sídhe have been murdering adolescents for the last twenty-five years, which means this tall stranger may just be old enough to have escaped the Call. But no. There is a strain about his movements that suggests he will never relax again. This man has seen the Grey Land. He would have been one of the first, back in a time when nobody understood what was happening. Before the specially trained counselors were around to help with the aftermath.

"This is her, isn't it?" He whispers the words, as though it burns his tongue to do so.

Some of the early survivors used food to cope with the trauma. Some turned to drugs, or immersed themselves in bizarre obsessions. Others faded away to nothing. But this man's muscles stretch his coat to breaking point. He's the type who's been training every day, maybe every minute since his Call.

"Yes, that's her," says a young woman, and Nessa gasps when she catches sight of the beautiful and sad Melanie in the midst of the adults. The girl with a hole in her chest. One of the few students of Boyle Survival College to make it through the school's destruction.

"I don't understand," says Nessa. "Mister . . . ?"

"Detective. Detective Cassidy," the man says. "And I am the one who doesn't understand." He has a hero's square jaw and his

9

blue-eyed gaze is hot enough to melt a glacier. "How . . . ?" he asks. "How did the likes of *you* survive the Grey Land?"

Nessa refuses to flinch. "The same way you did, Detective. I fought the Sídhe and I won."

Cassidy swings around. He pulls the smallest, feeblest of the untrained ten-year-olds out of the crowd. In the cold air, the boy's terrified breathing appears in little puffs of mist, but all the stranger does is whisper in his ear before nudging the little boy toward Nessa.

"What . . . what did he say to you?" asks Nessa. She has never been so confused in her life. She has left her warm jacket on the bus. She badly needs to pee and, above all that, the earlier euphoria of her imminent meeting with Anto is giving way to something more akin to panic.

Out of the blue, the tiny little ten-year-old kicks her bad left leg and down she goes, the frozen ground slamming the air from her chest.

The big man looms over her. "Vanessa Doherty," he says, his voice stiff with loathing, "you couldn't have escaped the Sídhe. You can't even beat this little child. I am placing you under arrest for treason." She feels handcuffs on her wrists and can't understand what's happening. What about Anto? She needs to see him! "The Nation will survive," he says. "I doubt you'll be so lucky."

THE NEW RECRUIT

The bus station stinks of greenhouse tobacco and the damp warmth of a hundred people fighting for tickets on the rare remaining routes. But no matter what their errand, everybody finds time to stop and stare at Anto. It's that freakish outsized arm of his. The Sídhe gave it to him, of course, and none of those staring will ever understand the pain he suffered at the fairy woman's hands.

That trauma follows him wherever he goes. It wants to smother him, to leach the world of joy. Yet Anto grins. Nessa won't let that happen. Somewhere a bus is bringing her closer to him, with that smile of hers that's too bright, too intense for any shadow of the Grey Land to withstand. He can't wait to show her Dublin. He wants her hand in his, her head on his shoulder like the night she risked her life to climb into his bedroom. He can already feel the warmth of her cheek against his neck.

But now he shivers. A pair of policewomen are approaching him and his family with purpose. *Please*, he thinks, *don't let this be about Nessa.*

His parents have brought him here to meet her. He's thought of little else for days, suffering the teasing of his nine-year-old sister and embarrassing maternal comments such as, "She'll be sleeping in the spare room. I'll be watching to make sure you keep your paws off!"

But Ma has seen the guards approaching too, and she's the one to squeeze his shoulder. *You can deal with it, son.* That's what she's saying. And she's right. Nessa's had a lifetime of stares, hasn't she? Anto won't let her down, so he straightens his back, always sore from the extra weight of the giant arm.

"Oho!" says Anto's dad. "They must be coming to give you another medal for all those Sídhe you battered up in Boyle."

"Please, Da. I don't wanna talk about that." Anto remembers the crunch of bones. Their screams, their laughter.

The guards take one look at the boy's left side and nod. They don't bother getting him to confirm his identity, but the younger one—still in her fifties—can't seem to keep herself from mouthing, "Holy God!"

The other is more businesslike. "The State needs your service, Mr. Lawlor."

"You don't mean me, I take it," Da says, and the guards ignore him.

"We need you to come with us."

"I don't understand," Anto says. He can barely squeeze the words from his throat. "We're here to meet my, uh, my friend, I—"

"Vanessa Doherty won't be arriving, son. I'm told she's been given a mission of her own."

Anto hasn't seen Nessa since she went home to give her Testimony and be with her family. He finds it hard to cope with the dreams, and none of the counselors can help him the way she does just by sitting near him, by being so . . . serene. Is that the word? Nothing gets to her. Except him, and only in good ways that make her smile and talk about her strange interest in lost poems and songs.

"Are you saying my boy has a mission, guard?" asks Da, puffing up his chest.

He's oblivious to Anto's shattering disappointment, but Ma can feel the quick rise and fall of his breathing under her fingers.

"We're not allowed to talk about it, sir. But he *must* come with us. We have a car waiting."

"A car!" Da is delighted. Thrilled. "You hear that, son? A *car!*"

"I don't want to go," says Anto. He doesn't like the sound of the word "mission." He needs to find a school now, a real school where the pupils aren't murdered. He's supposed to learn a trade and to have time to get to know the girl he loves. Da pushes him gently toward the women, but he resists.

"You want to get us in trouble, son?" asks the older guard. "And remember, your friend's not coming today. You're not missing out on anything." Her face is beginning to harden. They could arrest him, or even his parents. The Nation will do anything to survive.

What choice does he have?

For the first time in Anto's life, he gets to travel by car. The journey takes them up the old M1 before they turn onto narrower roads, barely fit for purpose anymore, with the sea on their right.

One of the policewomen is sitting beside him in the back seat.

"Beautiful, isn't it? Wales used to be out there somewhere."

Now the horizon just fades to mist. He doesn't like to look at it. He's heard stories of boats heading out to sea, only to drift back to shore empty of human life.

The policewoman must be thinking the same thing. "Where do the passengers disappear to?" she muses. But she has to know the answer is hell. The Grey Land. At least that's what everybody says. A trip in a boat would be worse even than the Call, because there is no coming home again, alive or dead.

"That's where we send them all these days," she says. "We put them in rafts or dinghies and let the current take them into the mist."

"Who?" Anto asks.

"Oh, you know." She shrugs, as if the answer doesn't matter. "Criminals. Traitors."

PRISON

The cell door is open, but Nessa stays where she is, lying on a mattress made of hard lumps. Damp stains splotch the ceiling and a thousand names and dates crowd each other on the walls, layer upon layer of them. "Effie took the boat." "Remember Cathy—not one bit sorry." "This here picture is the warden and a sheep."

Outside, a woman screams. *That's how I feel*, Nessa thinks. *That's it exactly.*

Yet she's not dead, is she? Not waking to the horror of the Grey Land either. Instead they have brought her to the women's wing of what appears to be a prison. She never knew such a place existed. The Nation has no resources for criminals, does it?

She growls. "I didn't do *anything*." But nobody's listening. Nobody cares that she should be celebrated as a survivor, that she should be burying her face in Anto's neck and teaching him to laugh again. No. Beyond the cell it's all just shouting and jeers while somebody weeps.

"Doughnut!" a woman cries, winning applause. "Doughnut!" The sobbing that follows is breathless, desperate, full of whispered pleading that Nessa can't quite hear.

She throws off a thin blanket and walks gingerly to the doorway. The scene is like something out of a movie—an old one, from the time before prisons had automated doors. Two stories of cells form a square around a central area containing what might be a table-tennis table. It's hard to tell with such a thick crowd of women surrounding it, jostling, angry, laughing, while others hang back.

"What's going on?" Nessa asks a pudgy grey-haired woman. "Aren't there guards? Isn't this a prison?" But then the crowd parts to reveal Melanie, the only familiar face here, lying weeping on the table. She is naked from the waist up; the denim shirt everyone else wears has been ripped away to reveal a hole in her torso the size of two fists. She tries to lie down, but two burly women force her shoulders up while others take turns to put their hands right through her chest. They wave and make faces. Someone tries to stick her entire head through and Melanie screams with the pain of it.

"My heart!" she cries. "The doctors! Call me a doctor!"

Sturdy wooden chairs line the walls between the cells. Nessa helps herself to one, raises it above her head, and smashes it across the wall, leaving her with a splintered leg. The *crack* brings sudden silence.

"By the Cauldron," she cries, "you'll kill her!"

The pair of large women who were holding Melanie drop her and push their way through the crowd. The girl flops back like a doll, and what worries Nessa is that she makes no effort to cover her deformity.

But Nessa should be more worried about herself.

Almost everybody here has at some point been trained to kill. They have survived horrors beyond human imagination and, for some, the experience has taught them the worthlessness of life. Two of the strongest are facing Nessa now: a red-haired brute of a woman with a scar right across her nose, and a younger pale-skinned girl, her hair bleached and spiked, her bare left forearm deformed by the handprint of a Sídhe.

"By Lugh, Mary." The spiky-haired woman is speaking the language of the enemy. "It's strange the cripple should defend that little twist, isn't it? Considering it was Doughnut who got her locked up here."

"What do you mean?" Nessa asks.

"That's right, Ciara," says the redheaded Mary, grinning at Nessa's confusion. "Doughnut made a deal with the Sídhe to cure her, and only when that fell through, she confessed. Says there are a lot more like her. Traitors. People who *claimed* to survive the Call."

"Only they didn't survive, did they, Mary?"

"Not really, Ciara, not really at all." She looks pointedly at Nessa's legs. "Some of them *couldn't* have made it through. Not without doing a deal with the enemy. There's no other explanation, is there?"

And now they're both looking at Nessa, grinning. Their shoulders tense, and this is a mistake, because how stupid of them! To signal their intention to fight like that. Nessa has never needed to wind up before delivering a punch; never needed to think it through. She simply acts.

Ciara goes down right away, with a chair leg in the side of her spiky-haired head. It's enough to upset Nessa's balance, but she saves herself by grabbing Mary's shoulders and head-butting her hard on her scarred nose. Both of them fall together and when Ciara tries to rise, Nessa reaches over and uses every ounce of her considerable strength to squeeze the girl's Sídhe-marked arm. The sound she makes shows just how much that hurts.

Finally there are guards everywhere, sharing out kicks and spraying jets of something that has women screaming and grabbing for their eyes.

Two men drag Nessa to her feet and hurry her down to the end of the hall and out through a security gate. She is breathing hard and not really paying attention to where they're taking her. Instead she's thinking about what those two bullies told her. How Melanie made a deal with the Sídhe. Nessa can't believe it! That anybody would do such a thing. *But Conor did, didn't he? How many others can there be?*

It's a terrifying thought that the country could be brimful of people ready to betray their friends and families to the pitiless enemy. And then Nessa, normally so controlled, cries out loud enough that her two guards skid to a halt.

"What's wrong with her?" one asks.

What's wrong is that it's only now coming home to her how suspicious her own survival must look. She gasps, her legs going suddenly loose, and it's all she can do not to heave up bile from her empty stomach.

"There, missy," one of them says. For all the gentleness of his tone, he never relaxes his grip on her arm. "Come on now. We'll be there in a minute, all right?"

Her throat constricts as though squeezed by a fist. It's not just that everybody expected her to die. It's far, far worse than that. Because the enemy, the Sídhe, actually helped her. They *helped* her! You could count on one hand the number of people altered in a positive way over the past twenty-five years.

Nessa will never be able to prove that they made her fireproof only to keep their promise to their ally, Conor. They saved her from the flames so that he alone would have the joy of killing her. Of course people think she's a traitor! Everybody must be thinking it.

The guards drag her along like an empty sack, until Nessa, with every drop of willpower she has left, forces the fear from her face. She'll figure it out. First though, she needs her self-control back. "I'm all right," she says. "I'll stand."

"Good on ya, missy, but we're here anyway."

A door opens and Nessa finds herself in an office with a haggard old man behind a desk. He waves her to a halt. Then he smiles, but he has a phone pressed to his ear and whatever he's hearing gets him frowning again.

"Try to restart her heart," he says. Every word rises and falls in the singsong accent of Cork. White tufts of hair grow from the ear she can see, and there's more peeping out of each nostril. "I don't care what it costs! For the love of God, boy, she's fourteen! Just a girl . . . What? . . . I'm not accusing anyone of anything. But you think of it this way: She's the only witness we have, and the minister will put both of us on boats if she dies."

He replaces the receiver and covers his eyes for a moment with the other hand. The hair in his nose rises and falls, rises and falls. Then he forces a smile onto his face and looks up.

"Well," he says, "quite a splash you've made, girl." He coughs into a tissue, and the younger men who are still holding Nessa's arms tighten their grip, forcing her to hide a wince. "Not so hard, lads, please!"

"With respect, sir," one of the men replies, "you don't know the training they've had. They're always dangerous . . ."

"I know, I know. But don't hurt her. I mean, it's not like . . ." His eyes stray to Nessa's legs, but to his credit he says nothing except, "Wait outside, lads. Please."

"Well," the old man continues when they're alone, "I know who you are, so let me introduce myself. I'm the warden. Mr. Barry. As you can see, I'm in charge here. Running the last prison in the Nation." He waits, and Nessa waits too, but she's better at this than he is and after no more than a few heartbeats he adds, "Normally they ask."

"Ask what, sir?"

"Why this is the last prison."

"I didn't think there were supposed to be any prisons at all, sir.

They're . . . uh, I heard rumors." She swallows. "Criminals are sent away in boats." *And traitors too.*

He nods slowly. "It doesn't have to happen to you, you know."

She stares, her mouth dry, not daring to reply.

"You're so young," he continues. "Of course you wanted to live! And in a gentler age, that's exactly what you'd have been allowed to do. Nobody can blame you for . . . for any *compromises* you had to make."

"I didn't betray the Nation, sir."

But it's her useless legs he's looking at rather than her eyes, and when next he speaks, she has to lean forward to hear him.

"You're somebody's daughter," he says, "and I can tell you, sure as God is in heaven, I miss my own and I wouldn't have cared what she did if only she had come back alive. I would like to keep you alive too, Ms. Doherty."

"You . . . you can do that?"

"Our country has changed so much since my youth, girl. But there's no point in looking back, is there? Because we live in a hard, hard place now. The Nation is desperate to live. Just like you were during your Call. And like you, it will cut any deal or any throat, just to get out of this intact. The sick? Useless mouths! Family pets? A source of food. Every beautiful tree cut down for fuel and every statue used as rubble for the roads.

"And then there's this prison, where thieves and wastrels are sent to . . . to . . . ." He wipes his brow. "Well, you know where they're sent." At last he looks up and forces the smile back onto his face. "But there's more to this prison than that, girl. We're a second chance too. If anyone who comes through our doors can prove her worth, she'll get to stay. Anybody! Why, the worst murderer in Irish history lives within these walls—a scientist. Unfortunately, she's a . . . a . . ." Nessa can see him biting his own tongue to stop what he's about to say next. "It doesn't matter what she is. That's the point. What matters is her genius, that she's the country's leading expert on the Sídhe. She's killed, and God forgive me, I'm sure she'll kill again. But because we need her . . . Well, if we allow the likes of her to live, then why not a child who had no choice in the crime she committed?"

"Do I have to be a genius too, sir? To . . . to live?"

"No, girl." He smiles. "For you, it will be much easier than that. All we need is information about the enemy. Tell us about the deal you made with them and I swear to you, for every nugget of information you give us, the ministry will allow you to stay here an extra week. I'll fight them for more too! I don't want to see you hurt."

"Sir . . ." Nessa draws a deep breath. Her whole life is in the balance, but surely here she has found a reasonable and compassionate man. "There's . . . there's just one problem with that. I . . . I have no secrets to share with you because I am not a traitor. I would have died before, only—"

"Please don't do this," he says, visibly distressed. "Please . . . Look. Look, you have a few days' grace to think about it. I'll . . . I'll do my best for you, Ms. Doherty, that's a promise."

"But, sir"—her voice cracks—"it's the truth, sir!"

"But it's not!" he cries. "If only you could be honest. Don't you want to live?"

She stumbles forward, stretching out to him, because he cares, she can see that, the distress clear in every line of his aging face.

"Get back!" he says. "Guards! I've heard enough lying for one day. Guards!"

The two men arrive to drag her out the door.

INFESTATION

Anto doesn't know what he's doing in the countryside. Only a few hours ago, he was waiting at the bus station for his girlfriend. But the guards who drove him out of the city have just pushed him through the door of a long, low building. It's warm inside and damp with the exhalations of two dozen . . . soldiers. That's what they are. Men and women hurriedly checking weapons and stuffing duffel bags.

Once, before the age of ten, the whole scene would have excited him. But he's past that. All that matters now is that Nessa isn't here. His arms, made to fight for her, to hold her, hang uselessly.

The draft of his entrance hits the soldiers. As one, they look up. The noise of their preparations, the hum of their chatter, comes to a sudden stop. His cheeks grow hot under their scrutiny.

Anto has seen soldiers before. They're not supposed to wear their hair long like this lot, or to stuff their belts with so many wicked-looking knives. In his experience, they're pudgy old men going to seed guarding warehouses; trudging alongside convoys of food, making their way into the fading cities. But while many in the room have long seen the back of their thirtieth birthday—sporting scars, missing fingers or even ears—they look as trim as any teenager. They seem both frightening *and* frightened. How strange. The Call did its worst to them long ago. What could possibly worry them now?

They wear tattered uniforms of mottled green, and every one of them has a stag's head on the shoulder. At least it resembles a stag, although Anto has never heard of deer with blazing red eyes and long, sharp teeth.

A woman at the nearest table looks up and sighs dramatically. "Oh, my poor sweetheart, were you looking for the playground?"

She stalks over to him. Her middle-aged frame has more than its share of muscle, and her dark-skinned face is hard too, totally at odds with the way she speaks, for her voice, her accent, surely belong to a white woman in petticoats, playing cards and sipping tea while her husband administers an empire.

She makes as if to shoo him toward the door, but then her eyes reach his left arm and widen.

"Well, well," she whispers. "You *are* an odd little gentleman. Corless!" The last word is a bark that makes Anto jump. It summons a hulking, scary-looking man with a charcoal cross drawn or maybe carved onto his forehead.

"Sergeant?" he rumbles.

"Do let the good captain know that we have received a . . . a *boy*. By mistake."

He lumbers off, utterly obedient to her ridiculously genteel demand. When she turns back to Anto, he spots three words tattooed in a column under her left eye. He's heard of this custom, but never seen it. They'll be the names of her children. The ones who didn't come home. He forces himself to look away; he doesn't want to read what's written there.

Her dark eyes bore into him. "You dear little thing," she mutters. "You can't be more than fifteen."

"Sixteen," he lies, and has no idea why he did that. Maybe because she's so beautiful and scary at the same time. Like the Sídhe are, but the opposite of them too, for she is clearly aging.

"You've been trained to run, little boy," she continues, "and how delightful for you! Yet here . . ." She has been speaking English up to this point, but switches now to Sídhe. ". . . here we hunt a different type of boar. Here we—"

"Leave him alone, Karim!"

A new man, tall enough for his head to scrape the low roof, has arrived. Old enough that sagging eyebrows threaten to blind him. Everybody moves out of his way though. Everybody except Sergeant Karim. He doesn't seem to notice and steps around her as he would a particularly jagged piece of furniture.

"The new recruit," he says.

"A recruit, Captain? Surely not. He *claims* he's sixteen. The infestation squad is no place for tiny children, however delightful they may be."

"What's that to you, Sergeant?" She grates on him—Anto can see that. "What's that to any of us? Orders say he's coming along tonight."

"But he's staying in the truck, Captain."

"Of course. The boy can be the new mascot for all I care."

The captain points Anto to an empty bench. "You sit there, son, until we're ready to leave."

"I . . . I was told I had a mission."

"Were you, by God? A mission? Fair play to you, son. Stay the feck out of the way and do exactly what you're told. That can be your mission. Understand?"

No. Anto doesn't understand, but he does obey. He can't make head nor tail of anything here. Not the gleaming weapons or the nerves. Not his presence either, because what Karim said is true. He doesn't belong here, not for many years yet. His youth is an incredibly valuable resource in a dying country that can't afford to waste anything.

He should be learning mechanics or farming. He should be getting married and having as many children as possible—or so the State would like. That's what it normally demands, and the pressure it brings to bear to ensure such behavior can be considerable. Not that anybody would have to pressure Anto! Now that he has found Nessa, he wants to do all those things.

The only purpose he could serve in a place like this is to get in the way. Sergeant Karim has made that very clear.

"All right!" the captain calls now.

And everybody except Anto knows what he means. Faces grim, they troop out the doors and into three trucks, each decorated with the disturbingly red-eyed stag. Engines sputter into life and the fried-food smell of biodiesel clogs the air.

"Come along, boy," says Sergeant Karim.

Anto is pushed into the last truck and shoved along like baggage until he's right up behind the driver's cab. He can hear the captain's voice coming in over the radio. "Move out!"

And then, it's off into the night. The soldiers whisper to each other in a bizarre mix of English and Sídhe and made-up words of their own. One of them, a skinny man with the twitching manner of a rat, pokes Anto in his massive left shoulder. "Did it hurt?"

Anto nods. It felt like his arm was being ripped off, not just once, but for the entire time the Sídhe woman was touching him. Her smile grew as she tortured him, and she whispered, "How marvelous! A giant! How I have longed for a giant of my own!" Those are the words he hears in his dreams, and more than once he has woken in the stink of his own urine.

He doesn't want to say any of that to the skinny man, but he doesn't have to.

"I'm Ryan," the soldier says. "Look." He bends over in the crowded space to show two spurs sticking out of his shoulder blades. They twitch as though they have a life of their own. Anto feels that way about his arm—that it's not really his; that it doesn't belong in this world at all.

"They were going to make me into a bird, but I got away." The man shudders and twitches, although the event must be two decades in his past by now. "Doctors couldn't cut them out without killing me. Have to sleep on my front."

Ryan covers up again and they shake hands. "Thank you," Anto says. And he means it, because however useless he may feel, now he belongs.

They clatter over roads, passing the lights of farm dorms that Anto can see only in flashes through the open flap at the back of the truck. He hasn't eaten in hours and nobody thinks to offer him anything.

"Where are we?" asks a hoarse voice. It's Corless, the hulking man with the cross on his forehead and gleaming, sweaty skin.

"Meath," says Ryan.

"The worst ones are always in Meath." Corless rubs at the cross.

"The worst what?" Anto wants to know.

"That should be obvious," says Karim. "Infestations, of course. But don't you worry, dear. You shall have the big, big job of minding the truck. Don't let anybody siphon off the diesel."

Anto hangs his head.

"She's not so bad," Ryan whispers in his ear. "Honestly. You'll see. She's great." The soldier has no chance to say more. He's interrupted by the captain's voice coming in over the radio. "We're pulling in by the field on the right. Everybody exit the vehicles. Extinguish all lights. It's time for a hike."

A moment later the truck swings over beside the two others.

"Off we pop," says Karim, and as everybody rushes to obey, she turns back to Anto. "Stay put," she warns him. "We may be all night."

"OK."

"And let there be no sneaking after us. Some of the boys and girls are a little flighty and might shoot you. We'd all be *devastated* by the mistake of course."

"Uh, of course."

Anto's not the sort to sneak. Not like poor Squeaky Emma or Megan. He'll hang out all night in the hopes that in the morning they'll send him home again, or at least let him know where Nessa went. *Oh, where is she?* He's hardly had a second to think of her all day.

The soldiers pile out of the truck and not one of them is speaking now, apart from the odd muttered prayer. Anto slides down the empty seats to look out of the flap. A full moon shows him moss-covered drystone walls with men and women clambering over them, ripping themselves free from brambles without so much as a curse.

What could possibly be out here? he wonders.

Time passes. Enough for the moon to rise a finger in the sky. He's starving.

Since . . . since his *experience*, he needs so much more food than he used to. His arm needs it. Or so the doctors tell him. He's hungry enough to eat the wooden benches, to chew on the leather straps, for all that he's a vegetarian. But in the end what drives him outside is the shivering. The truck was never meant to stay warm, and the soldiers didn't think to leave him so much as a blanket.

He jumps up and down a few times on the gritty ice of the roadside. He windmills his normal arm and does some of the back exercises the doctors gave him while his breath forms clouds through chattering teeth. The only distraction is the sight of a rabbit, and then another, running through a gap in the wall and sprinting across the road.

Anto laughs aloud. Are rabbits even nocturnal? Nessa would know, being from the country. He adds that question to the growing list of jokes and endearments he's been saving up for her. But then the rabbits fall right to the back of the queue as another pair of shadows expose themselves to the moonlight. "Badgers!" he cries. "By Crom! By Danú!"

And now a whole flood of animals are squeezing themselves past the wall: field mice, a fox, more rabbits, something that might be a weasel or a pine marten or Crom knows what. Above him are crows and bats and birds of every size and shape, and slowly, slowly, Anto's delight fades.

The infestation squad. Was it named for all these animals? Certainly, the wildlife of the countryside thrives now that both Ireland's population and its industry are dying. But even a city boy like Anto knows something is terribly wrong here.

In the distance, far across the fields, a great *crump* sounds. Two more follow, each accompanied by a flash on the horizon. Next come tiny pops and cracks, like the snapping of twigs. And now the ground shakes through the thin soles of Anto's shoes. It's a rhythm, somehow familiar: the pounding, panicked heartbeat of a dying land. And in the moonlight Anto sees it: an inkblot that grows enormously quickly even as the tremors intensify.

It's just another fleeing animal, he thinks. What else could it be? But then it reaches the edge of the field, and the drystone wall explodes. Rocks bigger than his head smash through the cab of the nearest truck, ripping apart the shrieking metal, shaking it on its axles. Other stones hurtle over the icy ground as though shot by a cannon, spraying splinters as they skip across the road.

And then silence.

Except for the *breathing*. A great bellows.

Anto finds himself on hands and knees with no memory of falling. Blood drips from his scalp and he realizes then that a stone must have clipped him. He crawls over to the wreckage, pulls himself up, and looks round the edge of it.

The first truck stands completely unharmed, but the second has been thrown right into the next field. Anto doesn't spare it a thought—how can he?—because all his attention is taken up by the bull. Its mighty boulder of a head whips from side to side in what must be fury, while thick mucus dribbles from nostrils that could hold a man's fist.

The boy has seen minibuses that are smaller.

Moonlight glitters off its hide. Some of that is sweat, and some of it is darker, pooling on the ground beside it. It takes one step—away from Anto, thank God!—and then another. Limping. But a shot comes out of the darkness of the field and Anto fancies he can see where it hits the creature in the buttock. The bull roars. Anto cries out at the sound of it, stumbling backward even as the beast whirls around and sees him there.

It charges: a tank of flesh. Its twisted horns are longer than he is. It barges through the wreckage to get to him even as he flings himself out of its path and scrambles away. The monster skids on the icy surface; makes ruins of another wall before wheeling around to take a second run at him. More shots come, worse than the sting of any horsefly, each creating its own geyser of blood so that the monster roars and spins in search of the enemy, finding none except, again, the boy.

"It's not me," Anto says to it. He's used to terror, yet that's not what he feels as it moves toward him again. The bull isn't charging now because it can't. But it's not giving up.

Bullets ripple against its hide. Its breath bubbles and it must be thinking—if such a beast can think at all—*I'll take one; I'll take just one down with me.* And Anto weeps to see its bravery and its pain, for how is it any different from a child that is hunted in the Grey Land? And he feels a kinship with it. Of course he does! Because a bull this size is no natural thing. No more natural than he is himself. Twisted by cruel hands to become a monster. Turned violent and dangerous.

It bellows suddenly, a sound of pain, betrayal, fury. Then it lunges, its head thrusting forward with the weight and power of a wrecking ball. Anto gets his huge arm in the way and is flung toward the drystone walls of the field from which the monster emerged.

His clothes shred against the frosty ground. He's bleeding everywhere. But just as Nabil would have wanted, he rolls immediately onto his feet, facing the poor beast.

It staggers after him, leaving a dark river behind it. More fluid leaks from sad, fist-sized eyes.

"Boy," somebody says. Karim, he thinks. She's speaking calmly and quietly. "Be so kind as to get out of the way. Slowly, yes? No sudden movements. Just . . . step aside and we'll do the rest."

"No," he says. Instead of getting out of the way, he walks *toward* the bull, his big arm held in front, but not as a threat. He wants to show it something. *I'm you. I'm like you.*

"Boy!" Karim's voice has anger in it. Menace too. "We'll have to shoot. By Crom, I mean it!" And she does. All his senses are hyperaware. He can hear even the sounds of rifle stocks fitting into shoulders. The shifting of leather straps.

The monster pauses to consider Anto's arm, caught between goring him and turning aside. Its eyes, its huge eyes, are pools of pain and madness and fading hope.

Then, like an enormous sack, it simply settles to the ground, emitting a long, slow moan. Even now, it clings to life. One eye swivels to follow Anto as he kneels next to the head.

"I'm sorry," he says, stroking it. "I'm so, so sorry."

In the field behind him, one of the women laughs. "By all the saints! If he wants a pet, let him get himself a dog."

They take him back in the only working truck, leaving most of the soldiers to start walking.

"Never get in our way again!" Karim says. "I ought to break your darling little face for you." She looks like she could. Like she's had practice. Then she snorts. "You're shivering. Corless, give him your jacket."

"But he's still bleeding!"

"That, my dear, is why he's not getting mine. Now hand it over."

Corless opens his mouth to object further, but then he slides across to place the jacket around the boy's shoulders himself. "I hate Meath," he grumbles. "It always goes to pot up here."

The jacket is warm enough to smother the shivers. Anto thinks it strange that the only two sergeants he's ever met have been women. Taaft and Karim. Both quite short; both harsh of tongue. But Karim's manner is a necessary shell, he thinks, that surrounds a core of genuine love. It also serves to keep the madness of her visit to the Grey Land at bay, and maybe also the sadness from the loss of her children. Taaft's cynicism, he suspects, is all real.

But for now, all Anto wants to talk about is the bull. "How . . . how did it get that way? Are animals Called too?"

It's Ryan who answers. "It was grazing, that's all, lad." He shrugs his narrow shoulders, careful not to brush his wing stubs against the back of the bench. "There must have been a Fairy Fort in those fields. Maybe nobody recognized it because it blended in with the landscape. Or maybe the farmers here didn't report it during the surveys. Probably trying to keep their land from confiscation."

"But . . . but if there was a Fairy Fort there, other animals must have eaten the grass too at some stage."

"Sure. I suppose so." Ryan twitches, biting his lips with small, straight teeth. He reminds Anto of something, but the boy can't put his finger on it. "I mean, yeah, Crom knows a lot of animals must have been exposed. But it's all very random. The one thing I can tell you is this: We get sent out every single month now. I mean, it used to be only once or twice a year."

Corless nods. "Well, you'd know why it's increasing if you read the Testimonies."

"Oh!" Ryan waves his skinny hands. "You shouldn't read those, my friend. They always make you depressed."

"Well, if *you'd* read them, Ryan, you'd see how the Sídhe keep boasting about the two worlds getting closer all the time. And if you ask me, the closer they get, the more the evil of the Grey Land leaks into Ireland to mess it up. *That's* what I think."

"But the bull wasn't evil," says Anto. "He didn't want to hurt anyone. He was just afraid."

"I don't want to hurt anyone either," says Corless. "But you shouldn't have protected it. We're at war, lad. We're clinging on for our lives." And then, bizarrely, the big man ruffles Anto's hair.

"Rest assured, my dears," says Karim. "Next time that child indulges his sweet nature, it will be my pleasure to put a bump in that perfect nose of his. But I still don't know why he was sent here. I don't think even our great captain knows. It's all too ridiculous."

"Anto's brave though," says Ryan. He never seems to look at Karim directly. "You gotta give him that, Sergeant. Standing between the squad and its prey."

"Brave is no use to me," she says, "if he hasn't got the pluck to hurt a fly."

Anto hangs his head. He wants their admiration, longs to boast about the Sídhe he killed when he thought Nessa had died. But his whole body convulses with revulsion at the thought of it. He closes his eyes, looking for an image of Nessa to help him relax for the rest of the journey.

THE PROFESSOR

Nessa wakes to the smell of stale teeth, a weight on her chest. A face presses right up against hers. "I could hurt you," says a squeaky voice. A white tongue moistens cracked lips and for a moment it's as though Nessa is in the Grey Land again, with one of its creatures perched on her belly. A head-butt might be the best thing now, the easiest way out, except she has no room to swing back. And her arms are pinned at the wrist.

"But you're right, sweetie," the stranger says. A woman. "Why would I fight *you*?" She climbs away from Nessa. "You and Annie's going to be best friends, aren't we?"

"You're . . . you're Annie?"

The woman grins, and squeezes a pair of ample breasts. "Well, I'm hardly Jeremy or Michael with these beauties, am I?" She's about forty years old and Nessa spots three separate gaps in her teeth. Her every breath comes with a slight wheeze.

"They brought me in an hour ago. You slept so sweet, baby, and they told me to turn out the light, but I didn't."

"What . . . what time is it?" asks Nessa in English. This woman comes from an era when almost no Sídhe was spoken in the country, when the enemy's language was still being pieced together and barely three in a hundred teenagers made it to adulthood.

"We're to share *everything*, you and Annie. We're to be *best* friends."

Best friends? Nessa wants to laugh at the thought. Her best friend is Megan—*was* Megan. A redheaded terror. An absolute joy to be around. Or she would have been, if Nessa didn't spend half her time worrying what she might do next. At school Nessa never said anything bad about anybody. She didn't have to, because Megan always got in there first, her tongue like a whip soaked in acid. But funny too; she was always funny.

And when the girl was lost to the Call, Nessa had Anto to turn to. Quiet after his time in the Grey Land, but still charming underneath it, still adoring and protective, although it was really Nessa who looked after him. And she still can look after him. She knows she can. Oh, Crom! Her throat constricts.

"That's right," the older woman says, misunderstanding. "You'll be safe with Annie."

Nessa wonders whether any guards have seen the light through the little square grate on their cell door, but nobody comes, just as they didn't come when Melanie was practically the center of a riot.

They really don't care about us. The thought brings a shiver as she remembers the warden's threat.

The strange woman has no intention of letting Nessa get back to sleep. "Annie woke you up, sweet thing, because she thought you'd want to see the midnight visits."

"The what?"

"You ain't been here before." The woman grins. "But Annie has seen it all, so she has. So now I'm gonna turn off the light, OK? We have a few minutes to train our eyes to see what they must see. But not a word, baby. Not a word from now on, OK?"

Nessa nods. The room goes completely black and the only sound is the wheezing of Annie's breath.

How long do they wait like this? Nessa can't tell. It might be an hour or even two. Yet those who have trained to be hunted have learned endless patience for the times when predators fumble for them in the dark.

She hears the rattling of keys first and sneaks over to the door. Annie's wheezing and bad breath follow along.

"Not a word," Annie whispers.

Flashlights appear down at the main corridor. Dark figures approach one of the cells with a cylinder on wheels. They insinuate a tube in through the grille and twirl a knob. The hissing of gas follows.

Moments later, two limp bodies are carried out of the cell before the door is closed again.

"Where are they taking them?" asks Nessa, fearing the worst.

"Oh, some are released back to their families. Like Annie was last time. But then they say I messed up again, even though anybody would have taken that bicycle. They left it right out in the open with no lock! In the *open!*" She's not bothering to whisper anymore, and from another cell a sleepy voice growls a command in Sídhe to shut up.

"What about the others? The ones who don't go home?"

"Expelled," says Annie. "They're tied to a boat and it's sent drifting out to sea. Sometimes it comes back empty. Sometimes it doesn't come back at all."

Nessa tries to suppress a shiver.

She thought she'd never sleep after that, but now a truncheon against the door has both her and Annie leaping up in painful surprise. "Malley! Stay in bed. Not a foot outside of the blankets or it gets broken. Doherty, you're coming to the professor."

"The what?"

Annie yawns, already going back to sleep. "Whatever you do, baby," she mutters, "don't touch anything."

Nessa dresses and finds herself in a group of six. There's the spiky-haired young woman she fought yesterday. Ciara? Was that her name? Whoever she is, she's glaring and rubbing her sore arm as though in memory of the pain Nessa caused her. There's another woman in her twenties with sallow skin and a plain face. She looks utterly, utterly normal, except Nessa can't help staring and neither can several of the others. What is it about her? She's at least ten years older than Nessa's fourteen, but her uncertain smile is all so . . . so *innocent.*

A line of armored guards herd the prisoners along between them. They carry truncheons. They keep alert. Nessa knows they have to. Nobody over the age of ten and under the age of forty is harmless these days. The guards keep their distance and drive their charges through a series of bewildering turns until the group arrives at a huge metal door, scarred, scratched, etched with acid, and, in several places, badly scorched. One of the men speaks into a tattered walkie-talkie. "Where is she?"

The reply comes hissing and crackling: "Behind her desk. I can see her on the screen."

"You're sure she's not faking the images again?"

"I haven't taken my eyes off her."

The guard bites his lip. "All right, lads. Gas masks at the ready in case she tries to get funny again."

They nod and grip truncheons while one of them pulls back the bolts and slides open the heavy door as quickly as he can.

What's inside? Nessa wonders, her heart beating fast. And then she remembers what the warden told her, about how the worst murderer in Irish history lives within the prison. What was it he said? "She's killed, and God forgive me, I'm sure she'll kill again." *Are we to be murdered?* she wonders.

The guards herd them into a large space crowded with equipment and chairs and sharp metal objects. Nessa scans the room for a monster, but all she sees is a frail little woman, her white hair in a sloppy bun.

The doors slam shut. Not one of the guards has come inside.

"Sit down, ladies," the woman says pleasantly. "Wherever it's convenient."

"Who by Lugh's greasy spear are you?" Ciara asks in Sídhe.

"I won't be having any of that funny talk. Speak English in this room. Or German if ye must."

"What's German?" The spiky-haired girl is mystified.

"It's a country beside England," another prisoner replies. "They had a war, I think."

"No," says Ciara, rolling her eyes. "No, by Crom—everybody knows it's Spain that's beside England."

Nessa looks around the long rectangular room that's half scrap yard and half laboratory. Machines lie everywhere, their innards exposed. Dust covers mugs on shelves, spoons stuck to them with old honey. The only clean objects Nessa can see are a collection of skulls. All were human once—she can tell that much. But a short time before they died, the Sídhe got their hands on them. Now some are shaped like crocodiles, some like cows or snakes or baboons. One still looks completely human, except for an indented spiral, drawn idly with a lazy finger. Nessa has to swallow hard when she sees that one, wondering how much it must have hurt. Wondering at the terror, the hopelessness of the victim's final minutes.

Meanwhile, the strangely innocent woman with the sallow skin wanders over to one of the tables. She picks up a box. And then, a *crack* sounds, loud enough to make everybody jump, while the girl herself flies backward to land in a heap on the floor.

The old woman stifles a yawn. She doesn't look like a murderer. "I suggest ye don't touch anything. Now"—she clears her throat as the victim groans, vomits, and climbs up onto her knees—"ye may call me Professor Farrell. Or just Professor will do." She has been standing behind a desk and she limps around to the front of it, a feeble creature, her bones probably brittle, her hair wild.

Warden Barry said she was the Nation's leading expert on the Sídhe. A resource so valuable that any crime she commits can and must be overlooked.

The professor pokes the woman on the floor with a metal walking stick.

"Name?"

"Uh . . . uh, Fonseca, miss. Angela Fonseca."

Professor Farrell's eyes widen. "Oh! You're that one. Just as well you weren't killed just now. Sit then. All of ye must sit!"

"Why should we?"

"Name?"

"Ciara. Not that it's your business, by Crom." Her entire mouth is made for snarling. "I'm sick of orders. Sick of it. Sick of that sack of a husband and the screaming little Sídhe-twisted puppy I bore for the Nation."

"How lovely for you. Do what you're told, Ciara."

"Why?" She stands, muscular, imposing, glaring down at the diminutive professor. "Why do you old ones get to give all the orders?"

A fine mist sprays from the end of Professor Farrell's cane. The front of one of the girl's prison shoes simply melts and Ciara falls back screaming and grabbing for her foot.

"This is the only question of yours I will answer," says Professor Farrell, as Ciara writhes on the floor. "The old are in charge because we are the only ones who know anything. For example, how to make acid from sodium bisulfate and table salt. The rest of ye are taught only to survive and have babies, and ye're not even very good at that!"

"You . . ." Ciara isn't quite ready to give up, although tears stream down her face. "You wouldn't talk like that if . . . if *you'd* seen the Grey Land."

"Yes, I believe it can be unpleasant. Now, here's what's going to happen. Ye're all unusual in some way, and since the attacks on the survival colleges in Mallow, Bangor, and Boyle, ye're suspected of treachery to the Nation."

Other than Nessa, watching carefully, and Angela Fonseca, still on the floor, everyone protests loudly.

"I don't care," the professor says. "Save yeer moans for when they're sending ye out to sea. But I'll tell ye this: Every woman who cooperates with me has a chance of being cleared of treason. At the very least, Warden Barry'll give ye another week before getting rid of ye."

She takes the names of the remaining prisoners. When the professor reaches Nessa, however, she pauses. "Little twig legs," she says. "I know who *you* are. I'll get to you soon."

One at a time, she invites the others over to a desk where medical and scientific junk fight for space, and there she examines them, none too gently. Ciara screams as the professor probes the Sídhe handprint on her arm. "Wait by the door," the old woman says afterward. "You're nothing but an accident."

The next woman claims her eyes changed color in the Grey Land. The professor shoves needles into her until she weeps and then studies her tears. But she too is dismissed and told to wait by the door. In the end only Nessa and Angela remain unexamined.

"You're next, polio girl. I've been looking forward to this." The old woman has an evil witch's grin, but Nessa will not give her the satisfaction of seeing her flinch. *I don't like you*, she thinks, and this too she keeps from her face, fighting not to pull back when samples of skin and blood are taken with more gusto than necessary. But Professor Farrell is merely going through the motions. Her eyes don't really light up until she produces a Bunsen burner and sets it aflame.

"For your sake, girl, I hope you were telling the truth in your Testimony."

"I was." Mostly. Nessa left out the part about how Conor died. Her account stops right at the moment she walked naked from the burning dorm, and, as with most Testimonies, nobody cares too much about the aftermath. Let the counselors deal with that.

"Put your hand over the flame, girl."

Nessa does, leaving it there, feeling no pain except for a gentle, ticklish warmth.

"By God! That's twelve hundred degrees right there. They must have loved you, those Sídhe, to give you such a gift."

"They did not."

"Don't move your hand, we're not done. Now, girl, answer me this. Where does the heat go?"

Into Nessa's bones is the answer, gently, gently, spreading evenly throughout her whole skeleton. She can release it anytime she wishes. Or hold it in. She could spit it into the professor's face if she were that kind of person, but of course she is not.

"I don't know," she lies. She has to speak around a thermometer stuck in her mouth. The mercury hasn't budged. "Into the air?"

"Don't be a fool! I'm measuring the temperature around you. You think I wouldn't have planned for that when I knew you were coming? No, no, it's not the air. You must answer me, or it's the boats for you, girl."

"I told you, I don't know, Professor. For all I care it goes to the sky, or the Grey Land, or—"

"Stop!" Professor Farrell's eyes bulge, her breathing suddenly quick. "The Grey Land! Now that would be some trick! It goes to the Grey Land!"

And Nessa realizes she has something the professor really wants: a mystery. The woman may be a monster, but she loves her work to the point of obsession. As long as Nessa can keep her intrigued, she will get to stay away from the boats that may or may not take her back to hell. But the heat is filling her bones now, and the evenly distributed warmth is turning hot. She might have to release it soon, and what good is her mystery then?

"My hand is tired," she says, doing her best to sound bored. "Can I take it down?"

Professor Farrell nods and extinguishes the gas.

"I'll call the guards to take the rest of them back to the cells. But you two"—she means Nessa and Angela—"ye're coming with me. I'll introduce ye to His Excellency, the ambassador." Her eyes gleam and she even rubs the palms of her hands together like the villain in a movie. "Yes, always an interesting first step . . . I can't wait to see what he makes of you!"

She picks up an ancient telephone—it even has a dial!—and mutters into it for a few minutes. Moments later, the metal door slides open. The others are taken away, and that seems to be the end of it. The three of them are left alone, with the old woman murmuring to herself, taking notes with the filthy chewed stub of a pencil.

"That's pretty amazing," Angela says to Nessa. She has the little voice of a mouse, husky and squeaky at the same time. Her eyes never quite meet those of the younger girl. "That thing you do with the fire."

Nessa smiles. Angela has spoken in Sídhe, but the professor no longer seems to notice them so Nessa responds in kind. "I know it is. But why didn't she test you?"

The young woman smiles sadly. Her face is so ordinary, yet Nessa still can't shake the feeling that something is deeply wrong with her. She has dark, sorrowful eyes, and she moves like a lost chick, so full of uncertainty, of worry and yearning.

She takes a deep, ragged breath. "I . . . I've told people this a host of times and I'm sure you won't believe me any more than they did. But . . . I haven't been Called."

Nessa can feel her mouth hanging open and forces it shut. Questions rush up her throat, but like the fire that still lies coiled in her bones she holds them back. *Everybody* gets Called during their teens. Everybody. A few famous cases have made it beyond their eighteenth birthday before it happened to them, but they are always the ones who have it worst. Waiting and waiting, the tension rising day after day as the odds of it happening grow ever higher. It's driven a few of these hangers-on to suicide, despite the extra counseling they get telling them to keep training, to hold their nerve . . .

"I'm twenty-five," Angela says, and all Nessa can do is blink at her. "Nobody will marry me. There's no . . . there's no legal mechanism, you see. Nobody will take me as an apprentice. The Nation won't pay for education. Either I'm lying about the Call or . . . or it may still be waiting for me. They can't believe a word that comes out of my mouth."

Nessa's not a hugger, but she wants to hug this girl. "I believe you, Angela" is the best she can manage. And she does. There's a look the Called have, and it's nothing like the innocence on this young woman's face. "Don't cry," she says. "It might never happen now. You're past the age, after all."

Their conversation is interrupted by a loud buzzer. A voice comes over a speaker in the ceiling. "Professor, it's Warden Barry. I hear you want to take these two to see His Excellency."

"I do. I will learn so much."

"Well then, please stay away from the exit. You know the drill."

The doors open again, just long enough for a few lengths of chain to be thrown inside.

The warden continues. "All three of you ladies will secure yourselves in the handcuffs provided. We will be watching you on the camera. Closely. Professor, you will use a cane the guards will provide. Do not attempt to take the metal one with you."

Professor Farrell snorts. "What makes you even think I want to escape? I came back the other times of my own accord."

"People died those other times. They had families."

"A great achievement on their part, no doubt." The professor yawns. "Very well, girls. Let ye put on your manacles. Ye're about to learn one of the Nation's great secrets. As if the enemy don't already know! Come on."

THE NIGHTMARE

Anto wakes when a glass of water is thrown over his face. It drips down his cheeks in the pitch darkness. "You were screaming," says a voice. "Keeping us all awake." But there's no anger in the words. All of Ireland has long since learned to deal with the likes of him.

"Thanks," Anto whispers. He's panting. His throat feels raw and the sheets cling to his sweaty skin. He wants to scream again, because his arm is throbbing in the exact spot where first *she* touched him, the Sídhe woman. So beautiful, she was. He can see her gorgeous face painted on the darkness. A goddess, an absolute goddess. It's all he can do not to whimper.

His arm grew under her touch. But how? It's not as if the rest of his body became smaller to compensate. The substance came from elsewhere. From the Grey Land itself, a colony of evil at home in his flesh.

Nessa should be here. With him. But even the thought of her helps. It pushes aside that other woman and slows his breathing back to normal. Nessa has drawn so many lovely pictures for him. Of a house with a dog. Of clean air and no strangers to gawp at his disfigurement. Already his eyes begin to droop. Nessa. She anchors him so that no storm of the Sídhe can tear him away from happiness.

He starts to drift again, but then he sits up, gasping. Nessa! Of course! She's in trouble. That's why he's here; that's why! The State wants him out of the way, but if the most important person in his life needs him, then "out of the way" is the *last* place he should be.

Don't be a fool! part of him says. There'll be another explanation. He spends the rest of the night trying to find one.

———

Anto gets to the cafeteria later than everybody else. It's not so very different from the refectory at school, except there are a lot more men here than women, and Anto has no idea where he's supposed to sit. He balances his tray awkwardly with his normal hand and looks around for a familiar face. Lots of people are staring at him for some reason.

He spots dark Karim, looking so much older in the morning light than she did yesterday. She sits forehead to forehead with another woman, their heated conversation leaving no place for a mere boy. But as he passes, Karim's friend turns to him and he recognizes the mocking voice from the night before that suggested he get a pet.

"Well," she says, her face glittering with almost as many piercings as Anto's granny had, "can't believe you didn't shoot the boy for that stunt with the bull, Sergeant. And then you gave him my seat on the truck!"

"Look at him, Ellie," Karim says. "He's simply too delicious to kill." Ellie winks, and with that the two women lower their heads, leaving him alone in the middle of the floor.

A few of the men at a nearby table are grinning. Others shake their heads or roll their eyes. Some nudge each other.

"Hey, Bullboy, you can sit over here!"

It's Ryan, slurping from a big bowl of porridge, although he has to hunch over in his chair for the sake of his sensitive wing stubs and every spoonful raised loses half its cargo when he twitches. He's tired-looking too, like everybody here. And old. None of that stops him from grinning. Anto slides in between him and stocky Byrne, who, despite the Irish surname, looks wholly Chinese and mutters a Sídhe greeting in a strong northern accent.

"We're just hearin' now," Ryan says, "that you were from that school that was burnt down in Roscommon?"

That explains the stares. Anto nods, remembering screams and deadly Sídhe attackers no larger than toddlers.

"You must know this already," Ryan says, "but the rest of us are just hearin' that the whole school was a nest of traitors." Ryan misinterprets the look on Anto's face. "Oh, not you! We know *you're* not one, lad, or they'd have sent you off in a boat, right, Byrnie?"

"Right," Byrne says, although he doesn't look quite so sure.

Three men on the far side of the table make no pretense of having any conversation of their own. One is Corless, whose enormous jacket Anto bled on the night before.

"A nest . . . ?" Anto says. Anybody who spends time in a survival college knows how rumors can grow out of all proportion from their modest beginnings. He shakes his head. "There was only one traitor. Conor Geary. He was in my year. They . . . they made him king so he could revoke the treaty that banished the Sídhe to the Grey Land. It's the only thing keeping them out of Ireland."

"Right!" says Ryan. Anto still can't figure out what the man reminds him of. "Terrifying. But it makes sense there'd be more than one traitor. The Sídhe catch people in the Grey Land. Hurt them—you and me know how bad that can get, right? And then, the only way to stop the pain is if you agree to work for them." His garbled mix of English and Sídhe can be hard to follow, so Anto almost misses his next words. "And now they're saying that there was a girl traitor too. From your school. Workin' with that Conor. The cook heard it from his cousin up there."

Corless nods emphatically from the far side of the table. "I bet there're spies everywhere!"

"Right," says Ryan. "I mean, who knows what really happens to us when we're in the Grey Land? We've no witnesses to say we stayed loyal. But you we can trust, Anto. Everybody in that school owes you their lives. That's what we heard this mornin', right, Byrnie?"

"Right."

Byrne—Byrnie—looks uncomfortable with the conversation and gulps down his food as quickly as he can. Then, without another word, he's gone. "He's a decent fella," Ryan says. "It's the talkin' that puts him off, not you." But then he notices the worry on Anto's face. "You OK, Bullboy?"

Anto's not sure he is OK. His mind is swirling with the thought that there was a girl traitor too. Of course it wasn't Nessa! She wouldn't. She couldn't! But people will be suspicious of how she escaped when her legs are so weak. They'll be wondering why, when the Sídhe altered her, they made changes to her body that ensured her survival. When has that ever happened before? Unless you count the poor boy with the holes in his head who claimed to see the future. Or a freak like Anto himself.

Feeling sick, he forces food down his throat. It doesn't want to go though. The muscles in his neck squeeze it back out and his entire stomach has turned into a burning-hot stone.

Nessa. He's here because of Nessa. He worked that out last night. With Megan dead, nobody knows her the way he does. Others called her "stuck-up" at school because she hid her emotions. But Anto has felt her heart quicken, has heard her breath speed up when they kiss. There's a real girl under the reserve, not some kind of monster.

Nobody pays any more attention to his discomfort. But Ryan must be aware of it, because he hangs around, reminiscing about the caravan he was born in and his old, deaf father, who still breeds workhorses to replace tractors all over the country.

Anto is not listening. *I need to get out of here. I need to find her.*

He could steal a car if he knew how to drive or if his enormous arm wouldn't get in the way, which it would. A bike would be better, but where should he go? In the whole wide country, he wouldn't know how to begin a search or even who to ask for help.

A bugle blares over the speakers set up next to the main door of the cafeteria.

"That's the assembly," says Ryan. "You might as well come. The captain'll tell you if you're not needed."

The tired soldiers gather in front of the one working truck, which had to do relays last night to pick them all up. The captain, his breath clouding the air in front of his face, stands up on the tailgate.

"So," he says, "seems like last night wasn't a fluke. Our comrades in Kerry, Antrim, and Waterford all had callouts, and that makes twenty for the month—ten in the last week alone, by God."

"Holy Danú!" Ryan whispers. He's not the only one, and the captain nods his head.

"Yeah, that's right, lads. That's right. Word is getting out among the civilians. Farmers going missing and the like. But it, uh . . ." He pauses, and even Anto, who only met the man yesterday, can see he doesn't believe what he's about to tell the members of his squad. "Well, we won't be getting any more callouts. I'm told . . ." He clears his throat. "I'm told we'll be handing our duties and this barracks over to the local gardaí." He almost spits the last two words.

"The police are taking our jobs?" This from Karim, who's right up at the front. "But whatever is to happen to us?"

"There's a bigger problem for us to deal with," the captain says. "In Sligo. We have to go there and sort it out."

"No way!" a woman shouts. "My mother can't move across the country to be near me. What about the Donegal lads? They're right next door! Let them fix it."

"Enough!" says the captain. "The Donegal squad *will* be fixing it. They're going too, fair play to them. Every squad in the country is going. I need you to pack your bags. I don't know what's behind all this myself, but there's to be no communication with your mammies, or whoever the hell you've got left. I do know that this is big though, you understand me? People up in headquarters are afraid, really afraid." He clears his throat—he does this a lot. "Now," he says, "one hour. There's a bus coming for us. The truck will take our bags."

Anto grabs Ryan by the arm. "You're going to Sligo?"

"*We're* going, lad. That includes you. And no, before you ask, I have no idea why. The captain though . . . he looks panicked. It's the only word for it."

Anto nods. "I'll get my stuff," he says. Not that he has any stuff to get. He's thinking he can use the chaos of everybody leaving to get away and go looking for Nessa. Yet he still doesn't know where, or even how to start.

But Ryan is still talking to him. "You'll know the area anyway, won't you, lad? It's not that far from your old school."

The boy stops dead. It's true—Sligo town lies no more than an hour up the potholed roads from the college that taught him to survive the Grey Land. Alanna Breen, who literally wrote the book on the Sídhe and who knows government ministers by their first names, is still up there.

Anto has somewhere to go after all, somewhere to begin his search. But first he'd better go back and finish his breakfast. He'll need his strength for what comes next.

THE AMBASSADOR

The guards part to reveal the strangest door Nessa has ever expected to see. It's like something out of an old book of peasant stories—and Nessa has read more than a few of those. Her teachers insisted on it.

Horseshoes hang nailed to gnarled wood, each touching its neighbor without a gap. Ribbons are jammed into cracks between the boards and somebody has taped a handwritten prayer to St. Brigid right up at the top.

Professor Farrell snorts. "Superstitious peasants," she says. Scorn drips from her words, but beneath it all is excitement. She must think she is going to learn something today, and she's not the type to care who pays for it. "Only the iron is important here," she adds.

As if to prove her point, the door opens to a room made entirely of shiny metal, with an exit of the same material right in front of them. Guards push the three women inside, squeezing them together so they can fit. *It's like a coffin*, Nessa thinks, an impression made all the stronger when the door swings shut to leave them in total darkness.

"What's happening?" asks Angela, a hint of panic in her high little voice.

Nessa feels the same way. She struggles to keep from leaking any of the flame out of her bones, if only to have a bit of light, to confirm she hasn't died. But mere seconds later the inner door heaves open and they pass blinking into a much larger space, where Warden Barry and four more guards are waiting for them. The warden smiles reassuringly, but Nessa notices that he makes no effort to approach and that he steps back slightly as the old woman hobbles in.

One entire wall is made up of a mirror, faced by four chairs. *How strange*, Nessa thinks. She sees her own tired features looking back at her, her hair grown to the length of a finger for the first time in years.

"What you are about to see," says Warden Barry, "is a state secret. Am I clear, ladies? If ever you are released into the public again, you will say nothing of it, even to your mothers. I doubt this nation of ours would hesitate to send both you and them out in a boat. You understand?"

Nessa and Angela both nod, but it's not enough for Warden Barry. "I need you to speak the words, ladies."

"I understand," they chorus.

"Good." He rubs at the grey hairs under his nose, his face solemn. "In a moment I'll turn off the lights in here and the mirror will become a window into the cell of another prisoner. The person on the other side cannot see you. No matter what he may claim. It's one-way only. And he cannot hear you either unless we turn on the speaker system. Again, you must ignore anything he may say to the contrary." He turns to the professor. "Are you sure we need to do this?"

"I need to learn," she says. "It's your job to let me."

The guards, all young men, sit the prisoners in chairs against the wall farthest away from the mirror. They are particularly careful not to touch the professor, merely pointing the way with truncheons. She obeys readily enough and surrenders the wooden cane without complaint. She even grins, her eyes eager, excited. "I want him to speak to the subjects," she says. "But not straight away."

"All right," says Warden Barry. "It's your show."

One of the guards twists a knob and the room fades into twilight. And, just like that, they can see him. The other prisoner.

His skin folds into a thousand wrinkles and cracked lines. His legs are knotted arthritic sticks and a wattled neck bends backward as though he is looking all the way up through his metal prison into heaven. Slowly, although he can't possibly know anybody is watching, his chin comes down again and he is facing them. Every muscle in Nessa's body jerks into life; she bangs her head on the wall behind her. Her jaw is clenched hard enough to hurt and her eyes blink and blink again. She needs to get out of here! She needs a weapon. She feels fire in her throat.

When finally she can talk she says, "That . . . that man is a Sídhe."

There's no mistaking those eyes, the skin that glitters slightly under the lamps in his cell.

"So kind of you to point that out," says Professor Farrell.

"But he's *old*!"

"You really must have been top of your class."

It's Angela who stands. Angela who approaches the mirror. Nobody tries to stop her. On the contrary, the professor leans forward, an expression on her face that could be greed or lust. The monster, the Sídhe, cocks his head to one side.

"Wonderful!" Professor Farrell whispers. "He feels her presence." And indeed he must, because he too stands and walks forward to the mirror. He raises his hands—but no!—only the stumps of his wrists remain.

"So cruel," whispers Warden Barry. His sadness seems genuine.

"A waste," the professor agrees. "We could have learned so much by keeping his hands . . ."

The stumps press up against the glass, exactly opposite where Angela's hands now lie.

"Get away from him!" Nessa cries.

"Don't be absurd," says Professor Farrell. "Even if he could touch her, what harm can he do now? You. Warden. Turn on the speakers. One-way only for now."

Nessa pushes herself upright and reaches for the back of Angela's uniform. "Don't talk to him!" she says.

Warden Barry hesitates, narrowing his eyes to look at her. But then he says, "Speakers on."

And here now is the voice of the enemy. "Oh, you *are* special," he says to Angela. His words crackle and hiss with age. "Is it that you can't hear us," he wonders, "or that we can't see you? Yet there you are and here am I. I can *feel* you through this stone."

And now Nessa realizes something else.

"He's speaking English," she says.

They called him "the ambassador," didn't they? She wonders how long he's been a prisoner. How the professor caught him, if she really did. Or if he came here once upon a time of his own volition to . . . to negotiate?

Nessa shakes herself free of the spell and takes Angela's hand to pull her away. No sooner are the two girls in contact than the Sídhe covers his mouth as though in horror. "No!" he gasps. He pounds the glass with the stumps of his wrists. "No! A broken promise! Oh, no!" He staggers back, a look of pure nausea on his face. Then he masters himself. And forces a smile such as the ones his comrades seem to wear at all times in the Grey Land.

"Little one," he says, his eyes focusing exactly on the spot where Angela is standing, "tell me what you want." He starts coughing and has to fight to speak again. "Tell me what you dream above all else. Keeping a promise to you may allow us to fix the uncompleted one. The goddess has shown me the way. I feel it."

Angela, fascinated, opens her mouth to reply, but Nessa silences her. "You mustn't talk to him!" she hisses.

"That's right," says Professor Farrell, "because he can't hear you yet."

"You mustn't," says Nessa, grabbing Angela's wrist to pull her away, "because he—"

She never gets a chance to finish that sentence. Somehow the old lady has freed herself of the handcuffs. Now she swings them hard enough at Nessa's head to knock her from her feet and leave her barely conscious on the floor.

Warden Barry cries in outrage, yet his guards hurriedly obey when the professor says, "Turn on our speakers too."

"Tell me what you long for," says the cracked Sídhe voice again, and Angela, as though hypnotized, responds.

"I wish," she says, "I wish I survived the Call."

"No . . . ," Nessa murmurs. Her vision is swimming. She must stand. Never stay down! A tiny flame escapes from between her lips, but nobody is looking, not even the warden. And nobody hears her when she says, "Don't talk to him . . ."

"You wish to return from the Grey Land alive?" The Sídhe ambassador is pressed right up against the partition.

"Oh, yes!"

"Then it is yours, little one." He seems to suppress another cough. "It is a promise. And keeping it will allow us to mend the other that is broken." And Nessa knows he's talking about her. Because the Sídhe had sworn to let Conor take her life, yet he was the one to die instead.

"You never tell me why ye Sídhe are so obsessed with promises," says the professor.

The ambassador laughs at her. "Dear thief, it is simply that you refuse to believe the answer."

"Because it's nonsense!" she cries, enraged. "Superstitious nonsense like the horseshoes on the door. There's an explanation. There's *always* an explanation!"

He's coughing too much to say any more, sliding back against the far wall.

"He won't last another year," mutters Warden Barry. Then he remembers Nessa. "Help the poor child up, somebody!" Two guards lift Nessa to her feet as the lights come up. Her head is beginning to clear, although warm blood drips down one side of her face from where the professor struck her.

"Well," says the old woman, eyes shining, "I bet you found that interesting."

It's all Nessa can do not to burn the hag to a cinder. But she's not one to give in to spite, especially not when her survival is at stake.

On the way back, new handcuffs are found for Professor Farrell. The two girls walk along beside each other and have a chance to talk again. Angela is smiling as though a great weight has been lifted from her shoulders.

"You shouldn't have drawn attention to yourself," says Nessa. She's sweating. The heat won't be happy to lie curled in her bones much longer. It wants out. It wants out now, but there's nowhere safe for it to go.

"What do you mean?"

"I want you to do something for me, Angela. I want you to promise that if you find yourself waking up in the Grey Land, you'll run for all you're worth."

"Run? What for? I'm not sure I'll ever be Called, but if I am, he promised I'd survive it, didn't he? And he's, well, you know, an ambassador."

Nessa takes her by the elbow, squeezing hard with her powerful hands. "He said you'd *survive*. He didn't say what condition you'd be in when you came home. With the Sídhe, you need to be clear, you always need to specify—"

"Oh, Crom!" Horror blossoms on Angela's face as she understands what she has done. "But I'm not fit," she breathes. "I haven't trained in over two years."

"Listen," Nessa says. "You can do what I did. Threaten to kill yourself. They fear breaking a promise more than they fear missing out on their fun with you. It's the worst possible thing in the world for them."

"But . . . but why?"

"How should I know? Even the professor hasn't got a clue—you heard her! The ambassador, he was . . . *disgusted* when he sensed me there. I should be dead, but I'm not. So he wants that fixed now."

Angela covers her mouth with both handcuffed hands. "Have I . . . have I gotten you in trouble? You said to keep away from him, but I couldn't. I *couldn't*. Even when the window was a mirror, he was pulling me to him, like I had a hook in my belly. I *wanted* to go though. And now . . . now . . . I've . . ."

Yes, Nessa thinks. *You've agreed to be Called. You've asked for it. How could anyone ask for it?*

"Maybe," she says aloud, "maybe they won't Call you at all, right? You're an adult now. You're past all that." But she doesn't believe her own words. And also, as they lead her back to her cell where Annie sleeps noisily on the other bunk, she can't help wondering what the ambassador intends for her.

THE BATTLE
KINGDOM

The last of Boyle Survival College's students are out running in the fields, all years mixed together. "Pick it up!" Taaft cries. Lena Peekya takes the lead, though she's only twelve. Aoife, never the best athlete, is barely ten steps ahead of the three tiny Year 1s. And at her side, not even breathing hard, Liz Sweeney lopes along.

"Diseased little cow," Liz Sweeney whispers—it's worse by far in Sídhe than it sounds in English. "You souring udder."

"It's . . ." Aoife can barely speak. ". . . got . . . nothing . . . to do with . . . you."

"I have a right to be angry," Liz Sweeney says. "I mean, it's not that I like you." As if there could be any doubt! "But you're deserting us. Every student that leaves bleeds the school a little more."

"I'm . . . done for . . . anyway . . ."

"Pick it up, Aoife!" Taaft screams. "Pick it uuuuuup!"

The school is already dead, as far as Aoife can see. It can only be a matter of days before the remaining students are parceled out to other colleges. Anybody can see that. If it weren't for the investigators wanting to keep the subjects of their inquiries all in one place, it would have happened already.

But Aoife isn't going to wait for that. Her Call is coming soon—the Sídhe in the graveyard told her so. She knows she won't survive it. By Crom and Danú, she can barely stay ahead of twelve-year-old Mitch Cohen with his tiny legs! Or the bumbling, tree-high Krishnan, who can trip over thin air if no rocks or shoelaces are handy.

She has decided to find a way to kill herself the moment she sees the spirals in the sky above her. Or before would be even better. She won't risk being caught, and if the rumors about Melanie are true, well, she refuses to become a traitor too, murdering friends and family for a life that doesn't include Emma anymore.

"Leaving is cowardice," Liz Sweeney says.

They're coming up to the edge of the trees now. The frigid air tears at Aoife's lungs. The bare soles of her feet slap against the numbing frost of the grass. She wants to go home. If all she has left is a day or a week, she refuses to spend it here under Taaft's sadistic instruction and Liz Sweeney's needling. She'll sit in her stepdad's old chair for a night or two, and then, when Mam is out on an errand, she'll visit the doctor and ask for the pill to which any child over the age of twelve is entitled.

Emma, she thinks, *I'll join you soon. I'll—*

Up ahead, Lena Peekya cries out and skids to a halt. Her rival, Bianconi the Boar, runs right into the back of her and both go tumbling to the ground.

Taaft is furious at their clumsiness. Alone of all of them, the ex-Marine gets to wear boots, although these ones are literally patches of mismatched leather held together with string.

"There'd better be a good reason for this!" she cries, but even she stops speaking, her jaw agape, at what lies before her.

Some women have walked out of the trees. Strangers. Something is wrong with them that Aoife can't identify at first, because her eyes are watering from the cold air. But her stomach knows, yes it does, and it clenches hard.

Bianconi the Boar whimpers and crawls backward on hands and knees, but Lena Peekya allows her curiosity to take her forward.

"Stay away, child!" Taaft calls. "Stay away from . . . from *them*."

But there is no "them." Not really. Aoife's breath is like the mist of an overworked steam train in front of her face. Her shoulder aches with the grip of Liz Sweeney's fingers.

She sees only one woman here, her skin as dark as Krishnan's.

But unlike the gangly Year 4 student, this . . . this person has three heads. All are bowed. Aoife can see that one is an old man of African descent; the middle one is a pudgy, Chinese-looking woman, while the third head comes from a red-haired child, maybe eight years old.

Aoife can't close her mouth. She can't blink or breathe or think. Because this . . . this is a thing of the Grey Land and it doesn't belong here. Not among the trees, not with the sharp brilliant white of frost and the garish berries of a nearby holly. Impossible! Terrible and wrong!

"I want everyone to lie down," Taaft says. "You hear me, Peekya?"

The creature's three pairs of eyes turn to fix upon the twelve-year-old at the front, and no two irises are the same color.

"They call it art," Liz Sweeney whispers.

And the Sídhe do think of it that way. Aoife can see how the pale skin of the child's head blends seamlessly into the darker complexion of the body below. The old man's wrinkles form patterns: delicate whorls and breaking waves. The enemy care about such details and imagine them to be beautiful.

"I'm going to shoot it," Taaft says. "Lie down, Peekya. That's an order. Lie down!"

Used to obeying the whip of Taaft's voice, the girl lays herself flat on the ground.

The sergeant creeps forward, all horror replaced by the dispassionate mask of a trained killer. The heads look at her with neither fear nor curiosity.

Then the mouths open and something like magic occurs: The three voices speak, all at once, and in perfect synchronicity. But it's more than that, because the timbre of each has been chosen so that together they form as perfect a chord as any played on guitar or piano. The body too adds to the message with fine, long-fingered hands that gesture and punctuate every phrase.

"I am the Herald of Peace," says the magnificent voice in Sídhe.

"What . . . what is it saying?" asks Taaft, but none of the students can bring themselves to translate. Still, she lowers the gun and takes tiny Cohen aside. "Get Nabil. Get anybody you can find and tell them I want weapons here. Go!"

Aoife surprises herself. She is the only student brave enough to speak. Maybe it's because she has already decided to end her own life, or maybe it's because she feels pity for the woman, the *thing*, in front of her.

"What do you want?" she asks it.

Three mouths smile.

"My masters have restored the Kingdom of the Battles, on whose border your settlement now lies." Over the centuries, Ireland has been home to hundreds of ancient kingdoms, some with names far stranger than this. "We have given it a new ruler. A human king—"

"A traitor!" Aoife says.

"A king. Chosen by the humans who serve us. A king! Without whom the People of the Goddess could not return! The treaty has been repudiated and already the Many-Colored Land rejoices to the arrival of my masters!"

"Let them come back all they like!" says Liz Sweeney. Of all of them, she has stood closest to the Fairy Realm. She came within touching distance the day she climbed the mound with Nessa. She hasn't been fully herself since. "When your masters shrink we will stamp on them like cockroaches."

Three mouths smile. "Those who shrink do so because they are not fully in this world. But the ways have opened now. The time of the Milesians, those you call 'Irish,' is at an end. Many of Danú's people have passed through the proper door, and more arrive by the hour. At last! At last they can age again and hope for death sur-rounded by the beauty of their stolen home.

"From now on, the borders of the Kingdom of the Battles will grow until all the land returns to its rightful owners. In sweet cele-bration, my masters make you this offer: Any who wish to go under the mounds of their own free will shall not be harmed."

"What is it saying?" Taaft demands again. Cohen is already off in the distance, almost back to the gym and the burnt-out remains of the college.

Liz Sweeney laughs. "You think any of us would willingly go to the Grey Land? That we would swap your world for ours?"

Aoife feels sick at the thought. She wishes she could see the doctors right now and get that pill.

"If you stay here," sing the heads, "my sweet masters will make you as beautiful as they have made me."

Aoife shudders. She's not the only one. Taaft alone looks puzzled, wanting to kill something, but still unsure.

"You have not answered," say the heads.

"Oh, we're going to answer!" cries Liz Sweeney. She makes to step forward, but Aoife grabs her arm. "Don't! Don't!"

"We'll answer, all right! And the answer is no! The answer is never! The answer is—"

In the forest a horn sounds. Not one of the assembled children has ever heard it before. They've prepared for it their whole lives of course. It's just that they never expected to feel that deep despairing note while they stand paralyzed in their own world.

"Back!" Taaft shouts, just as something comes slithering out of the trees. "Back to the school! Run, you shits! Run!"

And they do, all except for two—there's Aoife, frozen in place by the sound of the hunting horn, and Lena Peekya at the front.

A snake is coming. It has white human skin and the face of a man with weeping eyes. The Year 3 hops to her feet, as she's been trained to do, but no sooner is her right foot in the air than the "snake's" head darts forward and bites once. The girl screams, but she's the fastest student remaining in the college and she keeps running.

Aoife turns to follow, finding a speed she never knew she possessed. Why, she even overtakes Lena! A line of guards and instructors waits just ahead with automatic weapons and Aoife almost weeps with relief when she sees it.

Nabil is there, his eyes wide with horror, and this makes Aoife run all the harder, terrified at what must be behind her. But the only thing there is another human. Lena Peekya, her pale skin riddled with silver threads of poison, her limbs inflating like balloons. Luckily for Aoife, she is facing the wrong way to see them burst.

VISITORS

During the day, cell doors yawn open into the communal area. Women play table tennis with a dented ball older than most of them, while the country's last radio station fills the air with Elvis and Lisa Hannigan, jazz and rap, hip-hop and metal and all the rest. And then Emmett Tinley comes on, his soaring miraculous voice singing about love in lost Chicago.

Annie crows along, murdering the high notes, drowning those lower down in asthmatic wheezes. But before she can entirely ruin the song for Nessa, the music skips once. Then again and again. The presenter's mic is still on for some reason, and he whispers, "Come on, come on. Oh, for the love of God!" Then he sobs. "It's the last copy. The very last copy." And he screams and weeps, smashing at something until abruptly he is cut off.

Spiky-headed Ciara breaks the stillness that follows with a braying laugh. "Another one for the loony bin, eh, girls? Bloody old people. Fragile as eggs, every one of them. You'd swear they were the ones had the Grey Land waiting for them, you really would!"

Sitting by herself, in the corner, Angela Fonseca ducks her head, as though ashamed.

Nessa misses the radio already. She has no poetry here to distract her from the heat in her bones. No Megan to make her laugh. Oh, Crom! She was never the type to feel lonely before, but it's almost all she can think about. Even her body feels it: longing for the exercise of school and the buckets of appalling but nourishing slop that fueled it.

She was the one who'd insisted on going to a survival college. She refused the poison doctors offered to girls like her—the hopeless ones, the doomed. No! No, Nessa was determined to live. And she won, didn't she? She conquered the Grey Land against all the odds.

But her very success is now all the evidence people need to believe that she has betrayed the Nation. If she can't find a way to make herself useful, Warden Barry will put her in a boat and send her right back to what might be . . . what *must* be the Grey Land, never to leave it again.

How? she wonders. How could anybody who has read the Testimonies send another human being to that place on purpose? And that's when she spots Melanie peeking from the door of her cell, not daring to come out.

Nessa feels her breath speed up and the warmth stored in her bones flushes her skin enough to bead sweat on her forehead. Melanie. It's Melanie who put her here, who has sentenced her to death instead of happiness in Anto's arms.

"You OK, girl?" asks Annie, but all Nessa sees is a tunnel with Melanie at the other end.

"Where you goin'?"

She limps across the common area. Her clothes are steaming now and women fall back from the heat of her body.

"What's wrong with her? By Lugh, is it contagious?"

Melanie holds her ground and raises her chin, almost as though offering her neck. She is a beautiful girl—or was, anyway. Now, she's more like a model from the old magazines, her bones and skull barely disguised by a thin scraping of flesh.

Fire has no place in a human body and holding it there has taken a toll on Nessa. It wants out, and if anybody deserves to feel the force of it, it is the traitorous Melanie.

"Do what you want," says Melanie. "I'm sick of it now. I'm sick of the heart attacks. I won't survive another one anyway . . ."

But all Nessa does is push past her, the girl who has destroyed her life. "Shut the door!" she gasps. "Shut . . . the . . . door."

The older girl obeys, blocking the view of those outside, who hoot with disappointment at the expected confrontation. Nessa falls to her knees, shoves her hand into the filthy toilet in the corner, and flashes the water it holds to steam.

"By the Cauldron!" cries Melanie. The room is like a sauna from the movies and Nessa lies like a rag doll against the far wall.

"Why?" asks Nessa.

Melanie thinks she understands what's being asked. She shuffles over to sit on the lower bunk. "What I did was wrong," she says. "Cooperating with the Sídhe. I knew that all along. But I wanted to live. Same as you. You must understand that. But later, at the school, when I saw how they almost won. With *my* help. When I saw how they were killing everybody. Oh, Crom! Oh, Dagda! They would have destroyed us. All of us! All of us!"

"Except you?"

"Except a few thousand, I think. They were going to heal me and leave me to live out my life. But I knew . . . I knew all along they'd have killed Daddy. Everyone. It was wrong what I did; I had to confess. I had to warn them about . . . about me. About people like me. About you." She stands straight, doing that thing with her neck again. "I don't care if you kill me, Nessa. A fly could do it now. But at least I got *you* caught. I finally did the right thing."

Nessa doesn't even know where to begin with this. She wants to scream her innocence at this girl, but what good will it do when even now the walls are dripping with the results of enemy magic? Nobody will believe she isn't guilty. Nobody can believe her and if she doesn't get out of here in the next few days, or if she doesn't invent a few believable lies of her own to extend the deadline, they'll send her back to the Grey Land, and this time it'll be forever.

A shout comes from outside in the common area. Have they seen the steam? Does this mean she's been caught? But then Ciara's harsh voice is braying out for a watch to be found, and another woman, just outside, is saying, "What's the rush? We'll have our answer in three minutes anyway."

Somebody has been Called. And there's only one person in the whole of the women's prison who might be.

ANGELA

Angela has been sitting against the warm wall of the prison. Her eyes are closed, and when her chair disappears her first thought—it lasts barely a second—is that one of the usual bullies has yanked it away. But then her buttocks are in the freezing mud, and she finds herself sliding and then rolling down three yards into a soft mosslike plant that cushions her fall and replaces the chill of the mud with the warm towel-like texture of its tiny fronds. Now she opens her eyes and learns the truth. A squeak emerges from her throat, no more than that. She is a mouse, after all. Only prey.

"I've got to move," she says to herself. She hasn't so much as gone for a jog in the last two years. She hasn't sparred with anyone, and even when she did that sort of thing, her squeamishness, her slow reaction times, had the instructors shaking their heads and marking her down as lost.

Yet two things make it worth Angela's while to get up and run. First of all is the part that luck plays in survival—the Testimonies have demonstrated this again and again. Second is the sacred promise of the Sídhe ambassador. Yes, they will want to hurt her. Of course they will. But it's something to hold over them, isn't it? It's got to be.

She has rolled into a hollow. Above her are the famous swirls of silver light. Rarely in her life has she ever felt so comfortable, and if it wasn't for the acrid air, for the hunters that even now must be on their way, she might easily sleep here. But no. No. Time to get up! Time to move.

The moss beneath her has other ideas. It sticks to Angela's naked flesh wherever she touches it. She jerks one arm free and cries out in horror, for tiny, tiny tendrils have burrowed into her skin to sip at her blood. She weeps as she frees the rest of her body, although there is no pain yet, for the plant numbed her skin before it started to feed.

Angela crawls out of the hollow—it's full of bones, she sees now: human skulls on four-legged bodies.

From the top of the little hill, she gets her first proper glimpse of the Grey Land. She sees an ivory-white forest off to her right, the trees lumpy as though plagued with boils. To her left lies a plain with animals of some kind, blaring defiance at each other. She can't make out what shape they are exactly, and this is a good thing.

But then another sound rips through the air, a hunting horn. This world's vile masters know she's here. They are oh-so-desperately eager to welcome their new playmate in person.

With another squeak, Angela flies in the opposite direction, off toward the trees.

Between leaving school and being adopted by the remains of the prison system, Angela had moved home with her Italian-born father. Nobody ever asked for her as an apprentice, and what little money she earned came from allowing aging experts to poke at her and shake their heads over her survival.

"What do your friends say?" asked one scientist, her face crusted with flaking makeup.

"They're all dead," Angela replied, before apologizing through noisy tears. She was nothing. She was nobody, and her life had seemed of less use than a bag of air.

Now, as she leaves a trail of blood behind her in the freezing mud of the Grey Land, she longs for the paradise of her father's decaying kitchen with the photos of Mammy and all her murdered siblings, each of them fitter at the time of their Call than she would ever be.

Ahead of her, she notices that the bone-white trees are even stranger than they first appeared. They are little more than lumpy columns of wood rising straight out of the ground. None has branches or leaves, but they do vary in height from two to seven yards. They sway in the wind, and moisture glistens on their lumpy trunks, as if to warn her off any attempt at climbing. She stumbles to a halt, all of her senses screaming in alarm.

"Don't be a fool, Fonseca," she scolds herself, while heaving for breath. "Of course it feels wrong. This is the Grey Land. It's *all* wrong." Then the hunting horn sounds again. She dares to look over her shoulder and there they are! No more than a few hundred yards behind her, a score of figures making far better time than she has. Their every step is graceful and the breeze carries happy, childlike laughter right to her ears. But she's already exhausted! How on earth is she supposed to escape them? Angela's knees threaten to buckle, but then she remembers Nessa's words. What she needs, in order to save herself, is a high place from which she can threaten to jump, thus breaking the promise of their ambassador.

Or I can find something sharp, she thinks. *Something to cut myself with.*

She throws herself back toward the trees, only a hundred paces away now. The ground booms like a drum beneath her feet as immature spider bushes snatch at her and flecks of ash twirl down through the air like black snowflakes.

It's only when she finds herself in among the trunks that she realizes the lumps under the bark are pulsing and that the trees themselves have begun to sway farther than before, curving all along their lengths. And this without any increase in the wind!

And then a "tree" right ahead, three times her height, whips its top toward her. There's a mouth at the tip! She sees this in a flash as it arcs down. Glossy and red, flecks of drool spraying from it. At lightning speed a tongue shoots out. She screams, but her old training throws her aside just in time. And then another of the "trees" crashes its body against the first, allowing a third to lean over and lash at her with its rasping tongue.

She totters backward. One of the trunks is right before her, the lump under its bark writhing, and she cries out in horror as she recognizes human hands pushing at the surface as though desperate to break free. She dodges behind that awful trunk as another tongue whips toward her face. Vomit burns the back of her throat. Her breath is all gasps and panic. But she still has enough air in her lungs to scream when her ankles are ensnared and she is yanked off her feet so that her face smacks into the ground.

Angela grabs at the moist bark in front of her. "God save me. Holy God, save me. Danú! Crom! Jesus!"

At least one of the deities is listening, for the grip on her ankles is loosened at once and a warm liquid sprays over her legs.

A grinning Sídhe stands just behind her, a man with huge beautiful eyes and glinting skin.

"Welcome, thief!" he says, before a tongue curls around his neck. He doesn't get to say another word. The tongue yanks him, fast as an arrow, into the slimy red gullet of a tree. The monster's success only seems to inflame the hunger of the rest of the forest. They all want Angela—every white neck curves toward her, buzzing with urgent need.

But now the cavalry are here. A Sídhe princess of impossible loveliness throws herself at the wall of tongues coming for Angela. "Run, thief!" she cries, laughing, even as her body is literally ripped apart. The human obeys, going back the way she came rather than deeper among the trees. Every step of the way, there are Sídhe who give their lives to save hers, chopping at the tongues with knives of bone, grinning and dying and crying out with joy.

Their sacrifice might not be enough: The moss from earlier in the day has robbed Angela of both blood and energy; terror has done the rest, wringing her dry.

But, bizarrely, it is not for her own life that she struggles now. It is for the heroic Sídhe, her enemies. The tragedy that such beauty must perish for the sake of a useless lump like herself is too much for her conscience to bear. So Angela pushes herself harder than she ever did in the survival college at Ballinasloe. She totters out from between the last of the "trees" and falls to her knees before a lone Sídhe male.

"You cannot rest, thief," he cries. He has the chiseled jaw of a movie star. "Up! Up!"

Her head is swimming too much for her to understand his meaning. She doesn't realize that she hasn't moved far enough out of range.

The Sídhe leaps straight at her, knocking her aside, and once again a tongue that tried to take her captures one of the fair folk in her place. But before he can be yanked away from her, she grabs hold of his fine wrists, anchoring her feet around a few rocks.

"It is a big tree," the Sídhe tells her gently. He is right. It is a monster, several feet taller than any of the others, its tongue as wide as the red carpet that used to usher celebrities into one paradise or another in the world of her parents. It wraps right around the man's torso and gives him a python squeeze strong enough to pop ribs like matchsticks.

She gazes into her savior's eyes and finds both joy and pain there. *Why do we hate them?* she wonders. She knows the answer of course, just not in those few seconds, not when so many heroes of the enemy have died in her stead.

"You are not strong enough for this place," he whispers as the tongue gets a tighter grip and his whole torso shrinks and creaks. Blood dribbles from between his perfect lips. "Most of the day remains, but . . . urgh . . . ha ha! Urgh . . . But you can leave here earlier if you . . . if you find the exact place you came in . . . Oh, Danú! The glory!"

He yanks himself free of her grip and disappears as fast as a frog-caught fly. And she's alone, weeping for those who would make her kind extinct. But the tears don't stop her crawling back the way she came. "You can leave earlier," her savior said. Earlier. No need to spend a full day. Can that be right?

For all their murderous ways, nobody thinks of the Sídhe as liars. And isn't this just what the ambassador promised? That she would return home alive?

Angela stops, breathing hard, her naked body crusted with blood and tree saliva. Should she have allowed herself to die back there? It would mean not one but two broken promises for the Sídhe, and wasn't that a good thing for the future of the Nation? And what about Nessa? Angela's survival will somehow allow the enemy to threaten that nice girl in some way.

But then she thinks of the red tongues. Of the horrible gullets. Of the writhing lumps, slowly digesting in the bone-white trunks. And she weeps with the horror of what almost happened to her. She will help Nessa any way she can. Yes, she will. But not *that* way. She will help by living.

"On your feet, Fonseca."

Her mam, God rest her, used to speak to herself in exactly the same way, and it's always her voice Angela hears when she orders herself about. It helps. It gets her upright so that she can follow her own tracks and those of her rescuers across the mud. She is puzzled at first, for the little hill she rolled off when she first arrived in the Grey Land has doubled in size. But as she approaches she sees that the compact earth has been replaced by massive piles of loose soil, as though an entire army has been digging here, and indeed, when she clambers over the spoils, she finds that her original little hill has been replaced by a narrow tunnel leading down into total darkness.

"You can leave here earlier," she's been told, "if you find the exact place you came in . . ." And here, in the exact place, is a tunnel.

Who dug it in the short time she's been away? They must still be down there, still digging. But why are no more spoils coming up to the surface, then?

She ponders staying here to wait out the rest of her day in the Grey Land, but in the distance a pair of lion-sized creatures are loping toward her. She hasn't the strength to take on a fly right now, and there's no way she can hide with the trail of blood she's left behind her, so down she goes, Angela Fonseca, into the smothering dark.

Far better had she faced the lions.

THE GREAT
SLAUGHTER

I t's morning. Anto squeezes into a rickety bus with forty-three
men and eight women. The interior stinks of fried food and
when fumes shoot out the back they obscure the other dozen members of the North Leinster Infestation Squad, who'll be taking the
surviving truck.

All around him, everybody speculates about why they're being
sent to the far end of the country. Never before have all the island's
infestation squads gathered together, and more than once along the
road they cross paths with ragtag convoys heading in the same direction. Anto loves the mascots they paint on their trucks. He spots
horned pigs, cows with spiders' legs, a whole variety of unnatural
animals that make the toothy red-eyed stag of his own new comrades
look positively tame.

"I hear the Sídhe have found a way in," Ryan says. "I hear that's
what it's about. An invasion."

Anto shudders. He knows what this means. "They've found
another king," he says.

"A what, lad? A king? We have no kings in this country."

"But . . . but we used to. Back when the treaty was made that kept the Sídhe *there*. In that place. We had dozens of kingdoms on the island. Maybe hundreds. The Sídhe just need a traitor to make himself ruler of one of them so the treaty can be revoked."

Even now Anto finds it hard to believe that some human could be ruthless enough to set the enemy loose. Certainly under the pain of torture a person might promise anything, but afterward, to actually go ahead with it, they would have to be an utter monster.

"Ha!" says Ryan. "Is that so? Well, I hope that treaty *has* been revoked because I can't wait!"

"You can't?" Anto asks. "Aren't . . . aren't you afraid?" He and Ryan have both felt the touch of the enemy's hands. Even the thought of it . . .

Ryan guesses what's on the boy's mind, but he just grins. "Listen, lad, here's the thing. Those sour udders have been gone two thousand years or more. They've missed out on a few bits and pieces, yeah? Those hands of theirs might be dangerous, but they can't fire seven hundred rounds a minute like we can!"

"Your gun can hold seven hundred rounds?"

"Well, ha ha, no. More like thirty, but you get the point, right? And they'll get it too, believe me, lad. Thirty rounds will be more than enough."

Enough for what? Anto wonders. He remembers the *thud* of bullets into the body of the poor bull, and he has felt bones crunch against the massive knuckles of his left hand. He's struggling to accept any of that as a good thing. And yet a part of him thrills at the thought. As though it *wants* to hurt and smash.

"Uh, Ryan . . . Do you think when the Sídhe caught you in the Grey Land, when they touched you . . . ?"

"Lad?"

"Do you think it made you more . . . violent?"

Ryan shrugs and winces as his wing stubs brush the seat behind him. "Maybe it did. Or maybe it was the loss of three children that did it to me."

"I'm . . . I'm sorry."

"Thanks, lad. Let me just say this though, to answer your question. Plenty come back from the Grey Land with a taste for blood. But any kind of horror will do that for you. It takes decades to breed a war out of a people that went through it."

Anto nods unhappily.

Still, though. Still. If the Sídhe could be defeated here, once and for all, there'd be no need to keep Nessa detained any longer, would there? The Call would stop forever. The Nation would be saved!

He can see it in his mind's eye, like one of those movies with dancing in the streets and fireworks. He imagines Nessa, hand in hand with him. A kiss of shared excitement while, all around, soldiers grin at the hopeless, lovestruck teens. *Lovestruck.* Yes, that's the word and that's the truth too!

Spirits are high as the bus crawls along past overgrown houses and bare-branched trees. Somebody starts singing the drunkennights song and while Anto joins in with the chorus his eyes track the long line of vehicles taking soldiers north. He can't help feeling afraid, because when has the crumbling state of Ireland ever made such an effort before? And is there a link with Nessa's disappearance? It seems like such a coincidence that she should be gone at the same time as this.

He distracts himself by staring out the window: at the overgrown houses and the icy fields; at untamed woodlands and Norman towers. Who lived in all these places? Will they ever be homes again?

The column trundles on.

The army has barely made it into County Leitrim when Corless, near the front of the bus, interrupts the singing to say, "Will you look at that? That certainly wasn't there when I was on my way to my father's funeral . . ."

"What's he on about?" Ryan wants to know. But Anto, who has often traveled this way to school, immediately spots it. The road rises here with views of rich fields on all sides. Why is there a hill now just to the north? A *new* hill. Warm muck covers all two stories of it and there's not so much as a sapling growing there, nor a single blade of grass. And where is the layer of frost that covers everything else?

The driver, a tall, skeletal man, brings the bus to a stop, ignoring the angry horns of the vehicles behind.

"Everybody out," Karim says. Her voice is quiet. As calm as somebody suggesting a Sunday walk. "Get the weapons down."

And then the hill disintegrates. Soil explodes in all directions, blackening the windows, cracking glass, rocking the bus so that Anto falls hard against Ryan.

They tumble outside, through front door and back, but once on the road all they can do is stare slack-jawed at the thing that was hiding under the hill, that *was* the hill. Nobody can look away.

The monster stands the height of a building. The four seemingly delicate, many-jointed limbs that support it must each be as thick as a dozen welded girders. But it's human beings that make up the entirety of its flesh. Thousands of them melted together, all still alive, all moaning and screaming and begging.

Right at the top, a tiny distant Sídhe balances. Anto sees it point at the slow-moving vehicles a hundred yards ahead of him, and at this command its terrible mount rushes for the road.

Two steps suffice to reach the convoy. The first of its "feet" flattens a bus. A truck is delicately kicked, barely a tap it seems from this distance, but it's enough to send the vehicle flying off into the far fields.

"Shoot!" Karim screams. "Shoot that thing!" Her voice wakes the infestation squad from their trance. They're used to monsters, are they not? Of all the Nation's defenders, this fight couldn't have fallen to a better group. They kneel and point and fire. A hail of bullets tears into the monster's legs and the underside of its torso. Many of the individual men and women that make up the creature's body die in horrific explosions of blood. Some are "merely" wounded, their screams horrible, their agonized writhing obvious, as the Sídhe driver, having destroyed a dozen irreplaceable trucks, urges his mount around to face his assailants.

Karim grabs Anto by his normal, right, wrist. "Get off the road, child. You don't belong. Go!"

He obeys at once, for he has no gun and knows himself to be useless here. And he's afraid too, no doubt about that. But if there's one good thing the survival schools of Ireland have taught the young, it's that cowardice bears no shame. Above all, you must stay alive. Leave your guilty feelings for the counselors to deal with after you make it home.

He has barely scrambled over a ditch and into the gorse bushes when the creature arrives. So large is it that it can't fit all four limbs onto the road, and one stamps down mere yards from where he crouches in the muck. Everybody who made up the base of that leg is dead, squashed against the frozen earth. Others have been shot by the infestation squad: men and women, little boys and girls, their bodies hanging limp like pieces of flayed skin. But none of that is the worst. What horrifies Anto are the agonized looks on the faces of the living. Every one of them moans and cries. So many are weeping that, with the spider's great body hanging overhead, Anto is bathed in a salty mist of tears and blood.

"Oh, Crom!" he shouts. "Oh, Lugh!" He is sickened. Racked by fear and pity; shame and horror. Why can't he help them? He has to look away, back toward the road. And he thinks that somewhere in Sligo is a man or woman who revoked the treaty and allowed this to happen. Somebody, a traitor, worse than the Sídhe themselves, because they can't help what they have become.

The gunfire has intensified. One of the legs begins to wobble, but it's not enough to save the squad, for the limb nearest Anto sweeps past him, rips through the gorse to crash into the men and women on the road. A dozen are gone in a heartbeat. The return sweep scatters twenty more. Byrne is down. Ryan drags him away. Karim and Ellie are firing their weapons straight up into the belly. The captain screams what might be an order to retreat just as the leg comes back and flattens him.

The squad dissolves in panic.

But Karim is still there, in the very center of the road, her whole face a snarl. She keeps firing and reloading, even as one of the feet smashes down right beside her.

The Sídhe up top goads his mount along the road to where the next few units are already abandoning their vehicles and running for their lives.

"Shoot the rider!" cries Karim. "Somebody shoot him!" She's trying herself, but the enemy has lain down flat in the middle of his monster's back and nobody can hit him from here. The beast charges the unfortunate units behind.

The infestation squad regroups.

"Grenades," Karim says. In the heat of the moment, her accent had slipped, but it's right back now. "If we can cut even one of those legs, the whole thing will fall. Then we'll have a jolly time with the scoundrel on top."

They jog back down the road, digging into pockets and bandoliers. Anto is following along for some reason. He can't help himself. They hop over bodies and run around the crushed wreckage of a tractor. The supply trailer it was pulling has overturned so that tins of food are rolling everywhere, and Anto thinks there can't be a single truck left to the Irish army. Maybe the army itself is gone by now, lost in one battle. The thought sickens him. He's struggling to keep up with the soldiers, for although he has a big advantage in age, none has to carry half their own weight in the form of a Sídhe-twisted limb.

The squad pulls away from him. His friend Ryan runs in a crouch. Karim and Ellie and Corless, and two brothers called Murphy, take the lead.

Only the top of the monster can be seen around a curve in the road, but he can hear explosions ahead. The tarmac shakes under the soles of his clumsy boots.

And then the enemy is staggering back toward them, spewing gore from rocket-torn holes in its torso. It moves more awkwardly than before, with one of the legs shorter than it used to be. But this damaged limb is now to prove the final undoing of the squad. The Murphys disappear under one bloody foot. Another man is kicked clear across the fields, like a soccer ball. The return sweep brushes Karim off to one side, where she lies curled over an injury. And Anto knows, as sure as he knows his own name, as sure as he knows Nessa's face, that the onrushing hind legs are going to obliterate the sergeant as though she had never been.

The boy runs faster than he has ever run in his life. He dives, his massive arm bouncing off the surface of the road like a skipped stone. But he catches Karim on the way past and the two of them roll off to the side before he has time to register the pain. Even as that's beginning to hit him, Karim, her face like a map made entirely of scratches, presses something into his good hand. A grenade.

"Jush . . . jush . . . pull the pin, little boy . . . pull, and throw."

He obeys. It's straightforward enough. The pin comes free. His giant's arm, torn and bloody, takes aim and fires it off. It arcs high and through the air.

"Supposhed to aim at . . . at its legs . . . ," Karim manages.

But her complaints die when the Sídhe driver is blown from the monster's back. The few remaining squad members stand around, their jaws agape.

"By Crom!" says Corless. "That throw must have been sixty yards!" Not to mention the added height needed to reach the top of the monster.

"Impossible!" somebody else whispers.

And the creature, riderless now and lame, bashes off through the fields toward the bog that lies beyond.

Anto watches for a minute, but then Ryan cries out. The bird-like man has only now realized that his sergeant has been injured and he comes running over. She stops him in his tracks with a murderous look that wrinkles the tattooed names of her children on her cheek. Then she turns to Anto. "Here," she wheezes. "Come here, boy."

He winces as she grabs his face in her rough hands. But all she does is pull him down to plant a kiss on his forehead. Then she's out cold.

"You're one of us now," says Corless, who's standing nearby. "She does that with all the new recruits. You're in."

But in what? The infestation squad?

Not without Nessa. He needs to find her more urgently than ever.

Ryan still stands where Karim stopped him as twitches ripple throughout his body. Other squad members lie smashed and scattered across the surface of the road.

And there's a dead Sídhe lying there too, his body shredded by the grenade. Did Anto do this? Did his arm do it?

But there's something else to think about here. He's only half a day's walk from the school. Nobody is in any state to stop him from leaving. Yet his own legs refuse to cooperate.

He can't move at all until Corless takes him by the shoulders.

"That was some throw, boy. But come on. You need stitches on that shoulder and a good long sleep."

"Yes," the boy mumbles. They'll all have to sleep, won't they? That's when he'll make his escape.

FINGERS

Three minutes and four seconds. That's how long the Called are missing. Then they come back, living or dead; twisted into hideous shapes or bewildered and whole. But return they always do.

Or at least they used to.

Nessa makes it to the door of Melanie's cell to find Annie standing there, listening to the countdown. Ciara has the watch she was calling for earlier and she cries out the last few seconds: "Three . . . two . . . one . . ."

The count must be wrong, because there's no sign of Angela. But more minutes pass and a great clamor rises up among the prisoners, because now there can be no doubt. Angela was Called—what else can it be when somebody disappears like that in front of so many witnesses, their clothing in a heap on the floor? She was Called, but she has not returned.

"Get back! Everybody to your cells! NOW!"

Guards have come through in a wedge of shields, their truncheons and sprays at the ready. But this isn't a riot and nobody resists them.

"She was too old," Annie says. "The little sweetheart! That's why they didn't give her back. It's never happened before."

Nessa's not so sure. Despite twenty-five years of Testimonies, holes and mysteries abound.

Annie hangs by the cell door, her breath wheezing, her eyes pressed to the hatch. "Oh, look at them now!" she says.

Nessa steps up to join her. She barely knew Angela, but she's feeling terribly uneasy all the same. "What's that?"

"A vacuum cleaner of course. You not seen one of them before?"

"Only in movies. We don't get a lot of electricity in Donegal anymore." The machine moans like a tortured giant.

Oh, poor Angela. They think the Sídhe have turned you into a puff of dust and now they can just suck you out of the air.

But Nessa is sure the explanation must be otherwise.

"You all right, sweetheart?" Annie asks her.

"Fine," Nessa says. But she has to force the words out through jaws that are almost locked together. Every muscle in her body is tense, ready to fight, despite the absence of a visible threat. She knows Angela's failure to return is all part of a plan whose intended outcome is her own destruction. Something that will make her envy anybody who ends up as a mere cloud of dust. It's been promised, hasn't it?

"Annie," she whispers. "The ground . . . Is the ground trembling?"

"No, babe. No. Annie feels nothing like that." But then the woman cries, "Oh, sacred heart!" and falls back, for a guard has appeared right at the door of their cell.

"You. Doherty. Come with me. Annie, get to your bunk and stay there."

"Annie doesn't like being locked in with nobody to talk to."

"Well, read a book for a change." They both know there are no books.

The guards don't bother handcuffing Nessa this time. There are five of them and a fourteen-year-old who has to limp to keep up, but who refuses to complain when they walk too fast.

The last time she visited Warden Barry, the guards came into the office with her—he's not stupid, after all. But today they wave her ahead and close the door behind her. The warden has his own bodyguard with him, and Nessa's blood boils with fury when she sees who it is: the same tall, muscle-bound detective who arrested her off the bus that was supposed to bring her to Anto.

His startling blue eyes never blink as they bore into her skull. He needs a shave and a wash. His trench coat looks like he slept in it a week running and ate his dinner off it too. The whole room reeks with his sweat and, like her, he has a look of anger about him.

"Detective Cassidy"—Warden Barry mops his brow—"I believe you already know—"

"Doherty!" the detective says. "Doherty. They haven't put you in the boat yet?"

"She has two days left to confess," the warden says. He is tall enough to look the detective in the eye, but he keeps the heavy desk between them and grips it with both hands. "That poor girl has been informed how to earn an extension to her life. She—"

The detective takes two strides to stand right in front of Nessa, who refuses to move out of his path. Perhaps he intends to pick her up by the neck? He'll lose an eye if he does, because she's not the kind of girl to waste time trying to loosen his grip, or to kick feebly like a puppet. Not that kind of girl at all. Already she's planning the best ways to hurt this giant.

Luckily for him, he doesn't make the mistake of touching her.

"The Nation doesn't have two days to wait for your confession," he says. "All over the country, traitors are rotting us from within. This week alone we uncovered three. The first was a veteran in a college, if you can believe it! He returned from the Grey Land unharmed and he was making his own digitalis to poison the students. The other two had no orders yet. But one, the filth! He had a contact. An old woman with an actual Sídhe living inside her . . ."

Like Frankenstein, Nessa thinks, *from school.* The poor woman had become little more than a covering of flesh over a Sídhe spy. The detective nods at the recognition on her face.

"I don't have the warden's patience," he says. "If you won't tell me who your contact is right now, I'll snap your neck."

Warden Barry slaps at his desk. "You will not!"

"I will."

"The . . . the Nation . . . The professor! The professor is interested in this one."

"Oh, I'm sure she is! Yet another traitor we're wasting resources on! But the professor's not the only one interested in her, is she?" Detective Cassidy swings his intimidating, unpredictable bulk back toward the desk. "You said the ambassador spoke to this girl too. Specifically spoke to her. What did he say?"

"It was . . . it was too quiet. The equipment never picks up his words."

"Well, traitor?" Cassidy is facing Nessa again. "What did the ambassador say to you?"

"He wants me dead. Like you do."

"How convenient that nobody heard it!"

"The professor must have heard it. Angela too . . ."

"Angela who is gone? Called and never returned!" Cassidy turns to Warden Barry. He waves his mighty right fist in some random direction. "It's time you put that professor in a boat. Time you let me have the so-called ambassador for questioning. We can waste no more resources on this entire prison. Things are becoming crazy out there."

The warden mutters, "I believe infestations are intensifying somewhat."

"Somewhat? Somewhat!" The detective's voice drips with scorn. One massive finger points at the warden, hunching behind his desk as though it is the wall of a fortress. "I will question this traitor. Here. Now. I will break her bones until she tells the truth."

"You will not!"

Nessa looks around the room for a weapon and sees plenty of them, but they're all on the warden's desk—paperweights, letter openers, pencils, an inkwell. Too far for her to reach.

"This is madness," she says. She's good at controlling her voice, but can't prevent the damp patches forming under her arms, or the light sheen she knows is on her forehead. "You think I betrayed my own people in the Grey Land to save my life? If I'm cowardly enough to do that, surely I'd tell you everything now, wouldn't I? I'd have told you the day I came in."

"These traitors are clever!" the detective says. "They'll say anything."

"So why amn't I saying anything, then?" Nessa asks. "Why don't I just make stuff up?" And she pauses, in confusion, because it's true. Why doesn't she just invent something? By Crom, how she wants to live! Her close encounter with the horrors of the Grey Land has only confirmed that.

She shouldn't have allowed herself to be distracted, for in that instant Cassidy grabs her by the neck and pulls her close. "What strange skin they left you with, your Sídhe masters." Of course she goes for his eyes, fast as a whip. And he, just as quick, avoids her scrabbling fingers before she can draw more than a single drop of blood.

Here is a man, after all, who survived the horrors of the Grey Land in a time when nobody was prepared for them. He twists her around, one massive arm pressed against her neck, her left hand enveloped in his.

"We are not animals!" cries the warden, but Cassidy ignores him.

"Who is your contact?" the detective growls, his hand squeezing down on hers. "I just want a name. Who is it?"

He's done this before. The pressure is gentle at first, increasing in tiny increments. "It'll be an old person," he says. "They're always old. Their tongue might be grey. They'll sweat a lot, as you're doing now, and sometimes they forget for a little while who they're supposed to be. You know one of these, don't you?"

Nessa gasps—she can't help herself—the bones of her left hand are rubbing together, the pain suddenly so intense it's almost all she can think about. *Give him a name. Give him a name.*

"The . . . warden," she cries, "Warden Barry!" as the man himself sputters in outrage.

"Nice try. He's a fool, but not quite doddery enough."

"The . . . professor . . ."

"Listen, girl." She can't help but listen, because he's whispering right in her ear. "I'm going to break your little finger now, understand? You have betrayed our nation, you have—"

She swings her head with all her might, smashing him in the face, but he doesn't let go. He curses, his voice thick and shaken. "Nishe move, girl." He spits blood. Then he carries out his threat. She hears the *snap* three long heartbeats before the pain registers.

"Don't lie to me. We burn them, you see? Old men, old women. If you give us a name, we have to burn them to be sure. Don't add murder to your other crimes."

"You what?" Tears are streaming down her face. "You do what to them?"

"Give me a name." He squeezes her broken finger. Her eyelids flutter; her jaw comes close to dislocating with the pain.

"A name, girl."

"For . . . for you to burn . . . ? No! No!" And then she panics, years of control giving way as he takes a firm grip on her ring finger; "Please! I don't know—" *Snap!*

"A name. Just one. Any one. I'll have to stop hurting you to check them out. It'll be a break for you. Just one name."

A pistol appears. Warden Barry is the one holding it, pointing it right at Cassidy's head. "You will stop this now, Detective. I'll . . . I'll shoot."

"He won't," Cassidy tells Nessa. "He's not like you and me. He hasn't seen it and never will. Unless it's where weak old men go when they die." He takes hold of her middle finger. He says, "I'm not going to break this one. I'm going to wrench it right out of its socket."

"Cassidy!" wails the warden, and everybody knows he won't pull the trigger, that he doesn't know how and the only voice that matters here, the only one, whispers right in Nessa's ear. "Say good-bye to the finger. Say good-bye."

"Please," she says. She can remember no other English words. "Please. Please."

He speaks so, so gently. "A name, and I swear I'll stop."

Oh, how she wants to obey him! She knows a few likely candidates. That crotchety farmer back home who threatens to set his dogs on Dad for Crom-knows-what distant offense. Ms. Breen from school. The ticket seller at the bus station in Letterkenny. The half-deaf shop owner at Devenny's. Any one of them uttered aloud will put an end to this, and if she thought Cassidy would find some harmless way to test them, their names would fly from her mouth. But the madman will kill them. She knows it. She knows he will burn them alive for the survival of the Nation. That's the sort he is; the sort that's running things these days.

"Please . . ."

And remarkably, the pressure eases and she finds her face against the chill floor, the agony in her two broken fingers coming like a knife with every rapid beat of her heart. The ground is vibrating too, as though in sympathy with her pain, as though a giant keeps hitting it with a hammer.

"She's innocent," says Cassidy. And he laughs. "Holy shit! There's no other explanation. What she said earlier is true: They're all cowards, the traitors. That's why they betray us in the first place." He tightens the belt on his coat. "All right. I'm off to the next one. You can release the Doherty girl. I'm done with her."

"I can't release her," says the warden miserably. "The professor . . . the ambassador . . ."

Cassidy spits. He actually spits.

Then his boots are standing right next to Nessa's face.

"Well done, girl," he says. "Keep serving the Nation, and perhaps we'll meet again. I have more survivors to interview. All over the country."

He's gone in a puff of foul air, replaced sometime later by Warden Barry and the prison doctor. "Want me to give her something for the pain? I have some ibuprofen. It's out of date of course . . ."

"Please." Barry's voice. "Give her anything we can afford. She . . . she didn't deserve this. That monster's gone off on his motorbike to torture somebody else."

Nessa closes her eyes and tears spill onto the floor. But like all good students of Boyle Survival College, she knows that to stay down is to die and she fights waves of agony to get to her feet again.

She is light-headed. She has the strangest feeling that no amount of broken bones can shake. A feeling that Angela isn't lost at all, but is on her way home right now, and getting closer all the time.

THE TUNNEL

The doctor does as he's told and patches Nessa up—two fingers on awkward splints. She feels feverish. She stumbles as the guards escort her from the warden's office back toward the women's cell block.

"You all right, missy?" one of the men asks.

"Speak English!" one of the others warns him. "Or they'll think you're conspiring with her."

"Oh, for Crom's sake!"

She doesn't answer. The doctor didn't give her the pills in the end. Instead it was willow tea, bitter enough to make her gag. It has helped a little with the pain, but her fingers still throb, and her head too. It feels like an army is trapped in her skull and they're smashing their way out.

Nessa is all but senseless when they throw her on her bed. "Easy!" says the friendly guard. "She has broken fingers!"

Annie's there too. "Is it over?" the woman asks the guard. "Can I go now? I've done my bit." Her voice turns to a whisper.

She probably thinks Nessa is unconscious. "I told you everything she said, didn't I? Annie doesn't belong here anymore. Hardly my fault nothin' important was said, is it?"

"Take it up with the warden."

Then the door swings shut, with Annie using all the old sexual curse words that used to shock members of her parents' generation.

Perhaps she shrugs—Nessa can't see—but minutes later she is crouching by Nessa's side, bathing the girl's forehead with a damp cloth, her breath a wheezy, pungent cloud. The cloth feels wonderful and Nessa manages to open her eyes to thank her.

"I don't understand, babe," the woman says. "Annie don't speak none of that Fairy language."

"Sorry." Nessa is feeling more herself. "It was Irish, not Sídhe. For a moment . . ." For a moment she thought she was home with her mother.

"Used to know some of that," says Annie. "From school, like. They was always gettin' us to write about going to the beach and picnics. What a joke! When Annie was a kid, she screamed if her mam tried to drag her from her headset to go to the beach. Little did I know!"

Nessa is only half listening, because most of her attention is on something else.

"Annie," she says. "Annie, can you feel it? Can you feel the . . . the thudding? The pounding?"

"Don't be silly, babe. All that's wrong with you is a fever. Annie'll probably catch it from you and then where'll she be? They don't waste medicine on an aul' one like me! Now that my kids are gone an' they don't trust me fixin' engines anymore, they'd rather I took myself off for a swim."

"Annie, we have to get out of here." The words all slur together. "We have to . . . go . . . now."

"It's what I've been tellin' them, pet. But will they listen? Stuck in this place for the sake of a stupid old bike!"

Nessa fights the wave that's dragging her away from the world. "Please, Annie," she says, but she's speaking Irish again as she sinks back into the pillow.

More pounding. Hammering too. It's loud, loud, loud. The pain in her broken fingers doesn't want her to rest either and grabs attention by shooting lightning all up the length of her left arm. By the Cauldron but it's bad! And there's nausea too, of a particular type that Nessa recognizes. But from where?

She uses her good arm to sit up in the darkness, her forehead dripping with sweat, her heart hammering with fear. She can hear Annie snoring in the bed next to hers.

Her vision spins. The back of her throat burns, and in her mind's eye she sees it now, the Fairy Fort in Boyle, and remembers herself and Liz Sweeney crawling up the path toward it. The farther they went, the sicker they became, getting closer and closer to that great stone door. And what was on the other side of it? The Grey Land of course. She has no doubt of that now.

Nessa, who hates to show fear, whimpers in the night and pulls blankets away with her working hand. "I've got to get out of here. Annie? Annie, wake up! Wake up!"

"What, babe? What is it?"

Nessa hobbles toward her. The cool tiles are vibrating beneath her feet. How can Annie not notice? The very walls of the room are trembling. She must see it, she must! "I need to call the guards. Tell me how to call them."

"I—"

There's a noise like an explosion, a mighty *crack*—as though the whole world is being split in two, which perhaps it is. Right behind Nessa's bed, the floor collapses, swallowing it whole. The ceiling drops by a yard, causing the iron-reinforced door to crumple and shoot out into the common area beyond.

Nessa grabs Annie by the scruff of the neck.

"Out," she says. "We're getting out."

Emergency lights flicker on, almost useless amid the clouds of dust and the shouts of confusion and fear from nearby cells.

"Ow! You're strong, girl," says Annie. "There's no need to be so rough. There's—"

They hear the laughter then, from almost right below them. From the hole in their cell that took Nessa's bed away. It has an innocent joyous quality about it and that sound, that sweet sound, turns all Annie's protests into a cry of pure terror. She needs no further urging, but pushes Nessa ahead of her into the common area.

Already, behind them, pale hands are grabbing at the edges of the hole in the floor of their cell.

Alarms sound as all the other cell doors spring open automatically. The prisoners would be safer locked inside, Nessa thinks.

But it's too late. Everybody is rushing into the common area. They seem to think it's a fire or a bomb or a drill. They think they can escape, when really, if they knew, if they really knew what was coming, they'd be hiding under beds or cutting their own throats with whatever came to hand.

A sweet voice calls out from inside Nessa's cell: "I see her!"

She staggers forward to the main door that leads from the common area to the rest of the prison. Despite the alarm, it's still locked. Of course it is.

"Open up!" she cries. "You've got to open it up!"

"We're trying," a voice comes back. "The automatic system hasn't been used in years, it's—oh, by Crom! Holy Danú!"

He has seen something behind her, and when Nessa turns she sees it too. A dozen stunningly beautiful men and women, their clothing a bizarre mix of human skin and natural fibers—if anything from the Grey Land can be described as "natural."

"Get down!" says the guard. He's struggling with a pistol at his belt, but Nessa knows he can't kill all of them and that they won't stop in any case.

"Enough!" she shouts at him. "Forget that. I need you to find a way to open this door!"

Even if he does, it will be far too late for herself and Annie. But he obeys anyway. Glad, maybe, not to see what's about to happen here. Not to have the horror of his Call brought back to him.

All the other prisoners have pushed themselves up against the walls, expressions of horror on their faces. "Get back to your cells!"

Nessa calls. Or tries to, because her voice is faltering, breaking. "It's me . . . it's me they're here for." And the Sídhe, no more than a dozen yards away, spreading out—a full score of them, by Crom!—smile at her, as though they feel nothing but love. Perhaps that's even true.

At the front of the pack walks a prince, his hair like red silk, his huge eyes sparkling and grey, his limbs armored with bloodred wood. "All will see how we keep our promises! Our people to yours, binding us together, one to the other!"

They stalk forward. Annie is sobbing, but she straightens her back all the same.

Then the thug, Ciara, emerges from her cell holding one leg of her bed like a metal club. "Come oooooooooooon!" she shouts. "They'll kill us anyway! You know they will! Come ooooooon!"

Nobody here likes Ciara. Maybe they don't like anyone. They're criminals, aren't they? The useless leeches who grow fat on the Nation's desperate, ailing body. Thieves; unloving mothers; murderers; resource hogs: everything that Ireland hates. Yet they bring their pathetic weapons and come running to answer Ciara's challenge. Women fling shoes and hairbrushes. The younger ones, trained for combat, kick at knees or even faces, so that a few of the Sídhe go down.

"How marvelous!" says the red-haired prince. He laughs and his people are laughing too. They launch themselves into the fight and it's not long until the screaming begins. Human flesh is like putty to them. Even as Nessa watches, a Sídhe beauty grabs old Ellen O'Brien by the neck and melts her windpipe shut. Ellen's cellmate, Caoimhe, is already on the floor, her skull half the size it used to be, while other women totter around on limbs that have grown too long or that bend the wrong way entirely.

From one of the cells a voice howls out in perfect agony. It's Melanie.

The prince is lapping it up, but now, maybe, he wants to join in himself. "You were right, delightful thief," he says to Nessa. "I'm here for you. Of course I am."

And he does something completely unexpected: He removes a knife from inside his cloak. It is white, made of ivory or wood of some kind. Does he really mean to attack her with that little thing? It's not that the Sídhe don't have weapons. They have been known to bring down their human prey with arrows or spears.

Nessa feels a growl rise in her throat. "I'm no easy meat," she tells him.

"But I have not come to hurt you," he says. "I would *never* hurt you. None of us here would do so."

A *bang* sounds behind Nessa and the red-haired prince staggers back, blood blooming in his shoulder. The guard is there, his pistol sticking between the bars.

"Thanks," Nessa manages, but then she takes a step back, because the gun is now pointed at her.

"You're next, traitor!"

"What? I don't—"

A figure lunges in from the left, knocks her aside. The gun goes off again, hitting the Sídhe woman who has jumped in between

Nessa and the guard. The victim lies bleeding on the ground. Now five or six of the enemy rush forward, trampling their fallen comrade, as though they actually want to protect Nessa. The gun fires again and again. Blood spatters everywhere. Big pools of it form, streaked with footprints from both the Sídhe and the human prisoners. The invaders grunt and laugh every time they're hit, reaching through the bars to grab at the guard. Annie is somewhere in that scrum too, screaming and begging.

Nessa slips on the wet floor and goes down.

"See what we do to keep our word?" says the wounded prince. He has come to kneel beside her, his shoulder still oozing blood. "Do you see? We have promised not to kill you. And we won't."

Then he stabs at her, the ivory knife streaking toward her face. Nessa knocks his arm aside with her good hand. The other she jams into his shoulder wound, and she's screaming more than he is as her broken fingers are bent backward all over again. But neither of them gives up the struggle, fighting for control of the knife.

There's smoke in the air now, a smell of ozone and burning.

The Sídhe prince's face twists, flashing between mirth, agony, and determination. He leans down on Nessa's injured hand with all his weight.

Abruptly she stops trying to push him away and pulls instead, so that his nose flies toward her forehead, smashing itself to a pulp, even as her whole vision goes white. He falls away, limp as one of her old teddies.

Smoke is flooding the room now. Nessa feels woozy from the impact, but she manages to crawl a few steps through the fog. Her hand doesn't hurt anymore, she thinks. Nothing does. She finds her cheek on the tiles in a pool of somebody else's blood, her eyes too heavy to stay open.

"Get up!" she tells herself, and then she's out cold.

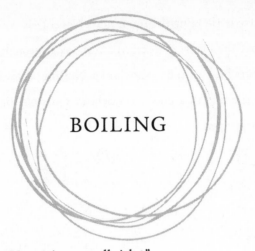

BOILING

Nessa? Nessa! Are you all right?"

Maybe. But she feels sick. Her eyes sting and the world lurches and blurs in her vision. Somebody supports her head in their lap. What if it's Anto? All dangers have passed. He'll lean down, so he will, his lips against hers.

But that's Professor Farrell shouting nearby, and Nessa knows Anto doesn't belong in the same world as that witch. "I demand you let me in there right now! Without my gas, ye would never have taken them alive!"

"You . . . you shouldn't have had that gas," the warden says. He's standing right above her. His voice is shaking, maybe even shocked, but he plunges on. "You shouldn't have known anything was going on here and you certainly shouldn't have been able to get out of your room. We have an agreement."

"My instruments were going haywire, you idiot warden. What an opportunity. Every second you delay costs me knowledge.

You think your rules matter one jot compared to this? And Melanie! They killed her, you say?"

"They fixed her up first. Plugged the . . . the hole in her."

"Of course they did," the professor says. "They were keeping their promise. I know them. This is all wonderful."

The voices begin to fade out, but the girl holding Nessa shakes her awake again. "Is . . . is that you, Megan?" Nessa mumbles.

"It's Angela. Angela Fonseca." Hearing that name fills Nessa with urgency and she fights to get her eyes open. That black hair, those same dark eyes, although they have lost their innocence. "They gassed you," the girl says, "but . . . but it's cleared up pretty quickly."

Only half the fluorescent lights of the common area still work, and many of them flicker. But it's enough to show Nessa a room filled with bodies. Women are groaning or weeping.

"I'm a monster," somebody cries. "Oh, Lugh! Oh, Crom! I'm . . . I'm a *twist*."

People in white overalls stalk the room with cameras, recording everything. But none of it is as bizarre as Angela's presence. The young woman wears nothing but a frayed prison blanket. She has cuts on her face, but seems otherwise unharmed.

"How?" Nessa manages.

"I didn't come back the normal way," Angela says. "I was . . . I was so unfit. And the trees! Oh, Lugh! The *trees*. The lions." She fights to keep from losing the contents of her stomach. Tears roll off her face to land on Nessa's bruised forehead. "The Sídhe gave their lives for me, and let me follow them through that tunnel they made."

"A tunnel?"

"It . . . it came out here. I climbed right out into your cell and saw all the fighting and the guns. And then the gas came. But most of the Sídhe were dead by then."

"I want those two." The professor has made it into the common area after all.

"You won't hurt them?" the warden asks. He keeps wary guards between his own lanky frame and the little old woman at all times. "Ms. Doherty? Nessa? Do you need patching up first? Were you shot?"

"No, but my fingers—"

"I'm sorry about that. I'm sorry. But the Nation . . . Cassidy . . ." He coughs and the white hair in his nostrils visibly flutters. "Please don't keep them too long, Professor. They've had a terrible time."

"I'll keep them as long as I need them," the professor says, and the warden affects not to hear her.

Angela is pulled away and handcuffed first. There's something strange about her that Nessa can't quite articulate. Never mind. She has problems of her own. She's lying on something hard. The knife, she realizes, the one the Sídhe tried to stab her with. A little thing, no longer than her hand, white as bone, jagged and sharp. It's the most natural thing in the world for her to slip it in under the dressing on her injured hand. She pays for that with a wave of intense pain that beads her face with sweat.

And then two guards are there for her, pulling her upright, examining her bloodstained clothing for cuts to her person.

"They didn't touch her," one of them says, his tone outraged. "She's the only one here they didn't try to kill. If anything they were keeping her alive."

They're rougher with her after that. Handcuffs are tight enough to make her eyes water. Then a gang of them escorts her and Angela out the door and down the same corridors they took the first time they went to the professor's lair.

She's still not sure what's bothering her about Angela. The girl seems whole and healthy, completely unharmed by the Sídhe. No doubt her mind will have been horribly affected by her experience, but that's not it. It's something physical that Nessa can't quite put her finger on.

The guards give her no time to reflect. As before, they set a pace that's too fast for her malformed legs, dragging her whenever she slows or trips. But the way is long and soon they tire of the game.

"How did that Crom-twisted madwoman get out of her room this time?" one of the men asks.

"Same gas she used on the Sídhe," says another. "Barney McD was out cold on the floor. She smashed his monitor too for good measure."

"Don't see what good it does to watch her anyway," says the first. "That sour udder always goes where she wants. And when the likes of us get damaged along the way, they never make her suffer for it. It would only be self-defense if a bullet made a home in her face."

"Hush!" one says now in English. "For God's sake, don't let the swimmers hear you!"

Swimmers, Nessa thinks. *They mean me and Angela.* A good name for women they plan to send to their deaths in a boat.

But now, at last, she has a chance to study her companion again. Yes, she's sure of it—something is definitely wrong with the girl. But what?

"Angela," she says.

"No talking there, if you want to keep the rest of those fingers."

Angela looks up anyway and Nessa has to clench her jaw to keep from crying out, because last time they came this way together and talked, the other girl didn't have to look up to meet Nessa's eyes. Which means she's shorter than she was a few days ago.

She's shrinking!

It's a horrible realization that makes Nessa's whole body go cold. *Does she even know it's happening to her? Or is she one of* them *in disguise?*

Her thoughts roil with these ideas, but confusing though they are, it's better than thinking about how close the red-haired prince came to stabbing her with the knife she now carries.

Moments later they reach the scorched and pitted double doorway to the laboratory. Are these the results of the old woman's previous experiments? Men and women are just fuel to her thirst for knowledge, Nessa thinks. And the Nation is so desperate it panders to her whims.

The doors swing open and a brutal push in the small of her back sends Nessa sprawling inside with no way to protect her face from smacking down onto the floor.

"I'll have the keys to their handcuffs!" the professor calls out.

"Like you even need them!" says one of the guards, and the door slams shut.

"Pah," the old woman says. "They waste my time. Doherty, show me your wrists." She fiddles at the lock with a wire for a few seconds until the cuffs spring open. "Now you, Fonseca."

"Wait!" Nessa says. Back in her survival-college days, squealing was considered the worst thing you could do to another student, but Nessa is way beyond any of that childish stuff now. "She . . . *Angela* . . . is shorter than she was before."

"What?" The other girl has no idea what's going on. The confusion in her eyes leaves Nessa feeling sick.

But the professor grasps the implications in the time it takes to blink. "You're sure?"

Nessa nods.

"What are you two talking about?" Angela hasn't got a clue, she really doesn't.

"How . . . ," the professor asks her, "*how* did you come back here, girl, after your Call?"

"It was the tunnel. I . . . I followed the Sídhe into it."

"You didn't serve out your time in the Grey Land, then? It's supposed to feel like a full day."

"It . . . it can't have been more than an hour . . . The . . . the lumps in the trunk . . . I . . . I don't know how anybody lasts longer than that. You . . . you have *no* idea."

Nessa does, but why contradict her? Everybody's horror is their own.

"Well," says the professor, "you're going back to the Grey Land. That's what the shrinking is. It's your body returning to where it belongs."

"But I belong here."

"Yes. And you'll come back here too, I don't doubt. By the *correct* route. There are rules, you little eejit. What makes you think you're the one who'll get to break them? Our worlds are tangled up in each other. A hundred ways in and a hundred ways out. You were Called. That's one path to the Grey Land and it has its own rules, and those rules are that when you go, you stay there for a day. Not a piddling little hour! A day. And your presence *there* gives them a way to come here. It's like a cultural exchange program, do you see?"

Angela might not, but Nessa remembers hearing how Liz Sweeney's brother returned from his Call only to find his school destroyed by the Sídhe.

"But the Sídhe can't hide from the Grey Land for long. It summons them back and they shrink and shrink——"

"Unless," Nessa says, fascinated, "they can get inside one of us."

"Exactly!" The old woman's eyes glitter. She loves this stuff. It's all she loves. "When they are small enough—no larger than a speck of dust—they crawl up to your face, hoping you'll breathe them in. A little parasite that grows and grows inside you until—"

Angela shrieks, "Stop! Stop! I can't go back there! You can't make me go back!"

"Well," says the professor, "I could hold you in the ambassador's iron room. There's no point though. You've been Called and what made you special is gone. But you . . ." She turns to Nessa. "Oh, you! You're the one they really want. They only took her so they could get at you."

"They were trying to kill me." By now Nessa has pulled herself upright.

"No they weren't. The guard who speaks their primitive language heard one of them say that none of them would hurt you. They actually put themselves between you and the bullets."

"He was lying," says Nessa. "I mean, one of the Sídhe did say that, but then he attacked me!"

"Really? When we all know that lying is the one thing the Sídhe don't do?" Then the professor is staring at Angela, as if something is terribly wrong. It's just a ruse, because when Nessa follows the old woman's gaze, she finds herself back on the floor with no idea of how she got there.

"You electrocuted her," says Angela.

"Only a little. You want to go back to the Grey Land?"

"No!"

"You're barely taller than I am now, girl. But I have a place I can put you if you help me get her into a chair. I'm not as strong as I used to be. I'll make sure she stays asleep until we get her comfortable."

A damp cloth stinking of alcohol is placed over Nessa's face. She tries to rise, to fight against it—she's seen the movies, after all— but her arms won't move and all she sees is the red-haired prince and the white knife sweeping down toward her face. It's true what the professor said: They don't lie. They never lie. So why did he attack her?

Sweat rolls down Nessa's face. "Mam?" she asks. It's the flu, and soon there'll be a cool cloth and honeyed apple tea for her throat.

But it'll take more than that—this is the worst fever Nessa's ever had. That anybody has ever had! Even her bones are boiling over with it. She imagines steam leaking from under her eyelids and that her tongue is a slab of hot leather in her mouth.

"Mam?" she asks again. "I don't want the tea. Cold water, Mam, please."

But when she opens her eyes it's only the professor's wrinkled face looking back at her, full of contempt.

"Do I look like I can speak Irish, girl? German, I told you. English. Latin. Something with a bit of science in it. Oh, and you're getting hot, by the way. So much for the heat going to the Grey Land!" She grins. "You tried to waste my time, but I'll find everything out. I can't wait for what comes next."

Nessa is lying on a table with her arms stretched out to either side. A Bunsen burner fires away at full blast into the back of each hand. She has no idea how long she's been trapped here, but her body tells her she's reached her limits and that any second now she must surely erupt like a volcano. Already her prison uniform has begun to steam. Who knows where it will go from there?

I'll spit out the fire, she thinks. *I'll torch that Crom-twisted witch.*

And then what? Will the Bunsen burners keep going? Will the whole prison burn down around her as happened back in school?

Oh, Lugh, the heat! Is her blood boiling? *Can* it boil? Did the Sídhe fix that too?

The professor has turned her back for a few moments, adjusting some kind of machinery. Nessa looks around the cluttered shelves for a way out of this and her eyes pass over a little girl weeping on a chair in the corner.

"Angela?" She's half the size she was. She's disappearing into the prison blanket she's been using to cover herself.

"You said you'd put me in an iron room," Angela says.

"Oh, I will," replies the professor. She waves what looks like a metal thermos cup, not much larger than her hand. "I have it here. I'm just waiting until you can fit. I'll need to find a way to get you oxygen too . . . Oh! And some fiber optics, so I can observe you eating and defecating and so on. Might get some use out of you after all."

Then, somewhere, a phone rings and the professor curses. She flicks a switch. "What is it, Barry?"

His voice comes out on a speaker. "*Warden* Barry. I do you the courtesy of—"

"Show your hurt feelings to the vet, Barry. I'm busy."

"That's too bad, *Professor.*" The warden is speaking through his teeth. "Because I've had a call from the justice minister herself. And . . . well, it's a terrible thing, but the . . . the Doherty girl has to go."

"Are you a fool? She's mine! Another week and I'll know how she works. I *need* to know."

"We've no choice in the matter. The enemy could come for her again at any time. You saw that. The ministry says she's too dangerous now."

"*I* am the dangerous one, you fool. It's why my lab is in a prison, after all. But the Nation needs me. And I need the girl. The Sídhe only got in here by using a Call, so—"

"She's important to them; they'll find a way!"

"You don't know what you're talking about, Barry. You're not getting her until I've finished. Now, leave me to my work."

"I thought you'd say that," says the warden, sounding strained. "I don't want you to get hurt, but we're taking her. We'll do our duty and you can't stop us."

"Who's this 'we,' you eejit? Your pathetic guards won't dare lay a finger on me. I know all their faces."

The double doors at the far end of the laboratory explode open—literally. A dozen soldiers pour inside wearing ancient gas masks and real army uniforms. There's not a prison guard among them.

"She's mine," the professor mutters. "She's mine." Her stick fingers fly over buttons. Glass balls drop from the ceiling, and where they strike, liquid sprays and soldiers scream, tearing at their clothing.

The survivors scatter. Then a book explodes by the old woman's head. "That's it!" she screeches. "Ye've pushed me to this! Ye've pushed me too far!"

Balls of acid continue to fall from the ceiling; holes open in the floor; electricity arcs between seemingly unrelated objects when men and women try to pass through. Nessa would feel sorry for the attackers, except she knows they're here to see her dead.

And she has her own problems: a body that feels like it consists of nothing but searing flame. She's got to get out of here.

Nessa concentrates. Her flesh steams, though her skin feels as dry now as old cork. Bullets ricochet around the room, pinging, clattering, and smashing everything they touch.

But she squeezes her eyes shut. She directs the heat toward her wrists until, with a *whoosh*, the dressing on her injured hand bursts into flame.

The handcuffs turn red, then searing white. She jerks herself free.

But her triumph lasts barely a second. Something has cut her thumb. She whips her hand away from the source of it, but it's only a tiny thing really: a knife no larger than her little finger. It's the weapon the red-haired prince brought from the Grey Land, and it must have been shrinking ever since.

"Nessa!" Angela cries. "They're shooting at you!"

They're shooting at everything really. Glass explodes. Distorted skulls topple from their shelves. So Nessa ducks down beside Angela.

I don't want to die yet, she thinks. *I don't want to die at all.*

But better a bullet than to be Angela. The girl has shrunk to the size of a toddler. Those tear-reddened eyes know they'll see the Grey Land again in a few more hours and that the Sídhe will be queuing up to welcome her.

"No!" cries the professor. "Don't shoot at that! Please! It's the last one on the whole rotten island! Stop it!"

And then, a few moments later, her voice rises to a screech. "All right! You can have her. But it's a waste, you hear me? Such a waste."

A man shouts, his voice muffled but clear enough. "Send her out, then. The Doherty one."

"Oh, for another hour," mutters the professor.

Nessa ignores her. "I'm coming," she calls. And then, to Angela: "Stay well back—I may have to burn my way free." She crawls out from under the bench, standing with great difficulty on legs barely worthy of the name.

Groaning bodies lie scattered about the laboratory, but four men and a woman remain standing no more than three yards from Nessa, rifles pointed right at her face.

The fire still seethes in her flesh and, oh, how it longs to be free! "Please," she says, "I don't want to hurt you."

"Likewise." The man's voice is surprisingly gentle behind the gas mask. "I don't care if the enemy turned you traitor, girl. What I saw in the Grey Land . . . Well, nobody could be blamed for giving in to that. But I've a young daughter of my own now. Just learning to talk. I'll do what I have to. The Nation must survive."

"Please," Nessa says again. She curls a fist and allows it to grow hot.

"I'm sure you're strong," says the woman. "I'm sure you're a good fighter—"

"It's not that," hisses the professor, watching from safety. Nessa can hear the grin in her voice, the anticipation of what is to come. "Our girl has a special skill, don't you, Doherty? You think I haven't figured it out by now? I saw your clothes smoking. I can see the remains of the handcuffs." She hobbles out from behind her desk, her deadly metal cane ringing with each step.

"What are you talking about?" the man says.

Heat, Nessa thinks. Enough heat to melt the flesh from the soldiers' bones. To cook the very brains in their skulls!

"Burn them," the professor says. "Burn them to smithereens and I'll take you out of here with me. I swear it."

Out! Oh, to be free again! Oh, to live! To hope! She raises her hand. Can't they see it? Can't the soldiers see it glowing?

"What use are these fools anyway?" continues the professor. She's right at Nessa's shoulder. "To the likes of us? Just let me study you and I'll get you away. Burn them, I say! Burn them!"

And Nessa can't. She can't do it. Not to the man with the toddler at home. Not to the lone female warrior who fought her way into a man's world. Not to any of them.

"Ex-excuse me," she says to the nearest soldier.

"I'm sorry," he says. "My orders—"

Nessa whips around and punches the professor hard in the face. The old woman crashes to the ground, her cane spinning away.

Nessa feels dizzy. Her knuckles sting from the impact, but somewhere inside her brain Megan's ghost is jubilant: *Brilliant, Ness! That wrinkly cow won't be picking her nose again for a while!*

The soldiers stand frozen, as though shocked by what she has done to somebody so frail, or perhaps guilty for what they themselves are about to do to a teenager.

There's still a chance, Megan whispers. *There's enough heat to turn them to ash.*

Instead, with a sob, Nessa allows most of the heat to hiss away into the air, her own sweat rising from her as steam. She sags, dropping back against the desk, as the soldiers quietly, kindly, bear her up and take her out past their own wounded and into the corridor beyond.

THE BOAT

They don't send people out on windy days, or so one of the guards tells her. "And lucky for you, miss!" he adds, showing her a mouth only half filled with sagging teeth. "It's like a pond out there right now. You'll be back with your fairy friends before you know it."

Nessa and her two guards stand on a quay in a place called Loughshinny. All around them lie the rotting hulks of fishing boats, for who would brave the oceans now?

"Sometimes we strip the prisoners," the guard says conversationally. "If their clothing's any good. Nation needs it more than you do, right? You can keep yours though. It's half burnt to bits!"

Nessa pays him no heed. She's too busy fighting to conceal the shivering in her body, the chattering of her teeth. They'll think it's fear rather than the cold, and that will bring them joy. Well, they won't have it! Not from her! Nor, by Crom, will they see her cry.

She looks up and out to sea, as though merely interested.

Nine waves from shore is where it begins. Or at least that's what people say, referring to that ancient line in *The Book of Conquests* . . . It's more like a mile though. That's where the horizon fades away, melting into a fog that hasn't shifted in twenty-five years.

"The boat will go in," the man says. "And you . . . you will simply be gone."

He and a guard she thinks of as "Tobacco Breath" lead her down seaweed-slimed steps and sit her in the boat. She could struggle, she thinks. She's far stronger than they expect her to be, and she could fling one or both of them into the water and maybe make it back to the top of the pier to where the other men are only half paying attention.

But Nessa doesn't know how to drive the rusty prison van they've left in the empty parking lot. And besides, there is a small hope that she shares with all of the other prisoners who were ever tied into the little rowboat before her: Maybe, she thinks, just maybe she's not going to the Grey Land at all.

Certainly she will be gone from here and the boat will come back empty. But what if she wakes up on a beach in Wales? There has to be a chance, doesn't there? Or the Isle of Man? Like most young people's these days, her geography is sketchy, but she knows those places weren't too far away from Ireland once upon a time.

Tobacco Breath sees that dreamy look on her face and shakes his head.

"I'd give that thought up, if I were you, miss. Wales wasn't in swimming distance in the old days. If the Sídhe don't get you, it'll be the crabs. Anyway, it's in the Testimonies, isn't it? At least twice people have been recognized in the Grey Land, though they'd been made into monsters or animals."

Nessa shrugs. She's read the Testimonies too. "Thank you," she says to the man.

"Sarcastic, eh? I like your spirit."

But Nessa isn't being sarcastic at all. They sit her on the little wooden thwart in the center of the boat. They tie her hands with thick rope, but not so tightly it causes her splinted fingers to ache. She's thanked the old man because he has taken away that stupid false hope of reaching Wales. And that frees her up for what she knows she must do. So she sits calmly until she has been fully secured.

"You've been told about the last requests?" This is from the nastier of the two guards, the half-toothless one. He has a pen and paper ready. "I'm not going to stay more than ten minutes. Too bloody cold. So give me the address and keep the message short."

Now at last Nessa feels something she cannot hide, and a lump almost too large to permit speech pushes up into her throat.

"I . . . I have parents and a boyfriend."

"Had," the man says with a grin.

"I don't want them to know what's happened to me."

"That's not a message!"

"That's a request, mister. My final request. Nobody is to know."

He looks unhappy, but nods. He snaps the notebook shut.

Two other old men appear now in a dinghy with an outboard motor. Neither of them looks at her as they tow her rowboat away from the pier and out toward the mist. She can cry now in perfect safety. She will never see her parents again. She will never marry Anto or have the little farm with chickens and dogs and all sorts.

But the Sídhe aren't going to get her either, of that she's certain.

The two boats pass out of the small harbor and into the open sea. She can feel the difference. For all that the day is calm, the swell raises and lowers her gently in the palm of its giant watery hand. "You'll be safe with me," it seems to say.

"Are we in the current?" one of the men asks his comrade, who nods.

Still not looking at her, they unhook their boat from hers and head back toward the shore as quickly as they can. Nessa is no longer moving so fast now. But move she does, slowly and surely, farther and farther from the quay. The current has her, and she knows she doesn't have much time, no more than five or ten minutes before it carries her into the mist and the boat somehow drifts back home again somewhere down the coast.

She tests the knots around her wrists. As she expected, the gap-toothed man knew his business and not even Nessa's strength will free her. "All right," she says. The words emerge more as a sob than speech, but with nobody around to hear, she doesn't mind so much. She stands, her arms held back by the rope. Then she throws her weight to one side. She fully intends to flip the boat over, to drown herself, because she knows for a fact it's better than whatever will happen to her in the Grey Land.

What she doesn't expect, however, is that the boat is less enthusiastic about sinking than she is. Gently it stabilizes, as though she's done nothing at all. She tries once more, pushing all of her weight to the right, only to fail again, but this time, as she falls to the other side, she realizes that it's just like being on the swings as a child. She needs to make a rocking motion that grows stronger with every cycle. So, she pulls her weight left, then right. The boat rises significantly out of the water. Cold spray drenches her, chills her to the bone . . . Then her weaker left leg gives way and she's on the floor with her two arms stretched painfully behind her. "By Crom!" she cries. Her voice turns to a squeak when she looks up, because the edge of the mist is only a few hundred yards away now. How did it get so close? She pushes herself upright.

"They won't have me!" she shouts. And Nessa starts the rocking all over again, locking her legs at the end of each swing to keep them as strong as possible. She curses and groans like a madwoman, refusing to waste more time looking ahead. She will not be distracted. She will not!

The boat tips enough to take on water. It hangs almost vertically and Nessa heaves one last time at it, hard enough that her shoulder feels like it's coming out of its socket . . .

And down she goes! Feet first! Arms twisted painfully behind her. Down with the whole boat!

I'm going to drown! Oh, Crom! Oh, Lugh! Anto! Anto, get me out of here! Dad! Dad!

But this is what you wanted, isn't it?

Several seconds pass before she realizes she hasn't swallowed any water at all. Air surrounds her in the bottom of the boat. She didn't expect that. And she has a new dilemma now as the horrendous freezing chill of the water numbs her body and squeezes her hard enough to gulp down precious oxygen faster than she ought to. She must choose whether to wait for the air to run out and suffocate, or whether to try to drown herself by forcing her face into the water. She suspects the latter won't work at all, because even now her idiot heart dreams of life.

Her legs are starting to feel warmer and she imagines this is simply the first sign of another of the many deaths fighting for the privilege of finishing her off: hypothermia.

Perhaps there'll be hallucinations next. And right on cue, here they come! The ropes turn insubstantial. The wood of the boat fades in her vision like glass and then . . . then it's gone altogether! The boat is gone! And Nessa is free. The air forms itself into a huge bubble and she just has time to take a last gulp of it before it flies off up and away from her.

The water has turned as black and viscous as oil. It hates Nessa; it expels her; she's shooting up to the surface after the bubble of air. And when the girl's face finally breaks free of the sea, it's not the Irish sky that greets her at all, but slow, slow moving spirals of dull silver.

THE LIE

Anto has no memory of falling asleep. He opens his eyes and cries out in terror to find himself in darkness. He stumbles to his feet, ready to run, but something weighs him down. A giant arm! What has happened to his arm? And slowly the boy realizes that this can't be the Grey Land, but a tent.

He pants for a bit, starting to shiver as the air chills his sweaty brow. He wants to weep with relief, but there's no time for that. He's supposed to be leaving. Running away to the school to quiz Alanna Breen about Nessa.

He reaches around in the dark for the pack he prepared earlier. He's got food—mostly jars of beans and raw potatoes, although he doesn't know the first thing about cooking them. He took grenades from the body of one of the infestation squad, but left the rifle behind, knowing its theft would be too obvious. Besides, he has never learned to shoot.

And out he goes into the freezing night under a million twinkling stars. He's not alone in the darkness. Over by the road, a large silhouette that might be Corless blocks the way north. Anto avoids him by scuttling behind a truck, wincing as his big arm catches on something and breaks it.

"What was that?" asks Ryan from inside the vehicle.

Anto freezes, terrified his breathing will give him away, but he's trained to wait, still and quiet as a rock, and this he does.

"What does it matter?" Karim slurs with the strong drink they gave her as an anesthetic. "Why, my dear, after today, you can't possibly imagine our pretty friends need to sneak up on us?" Anto strains to hear her through the wall of the vehicle. "They've taken the whole area around Sligo, captured at least a hundred thousand people. They can make as many monsters as they desire with no need for subtlety. Check if you like, but you'll just end up shooting another cat. Or—and here's a novel thought!—you could just save your bullets for the real job. Holding the line here, as we've been ordered."

Ryan doesn't like that one bit. "So we're just going to abandon the whole northwest? Sligo? Donegal? Roscommon?"

The news has Anto grinding his teeth, because of course Boyle and its survival college are on the wrong side of that line. But he can't give up now. Not when his goal lies mere miles away. He'll keep low and at the first sign of trouble, he'll—

"The boy is here," comes a gravelly voice from right behind him. "Outside your truck." Anto jumps. His giant's arm flexes around the backpack, crushing a jar of beans in the process.

"Oh, Ryan," says Karim. "Are those the sweet tones of our new visitor? Down from Dublin to play the tourist?" Her voice turns hard. "Such a shame you didn't shoot after all . . ."

Anto hears no more. A shadowy figure pulls him by the collar around the truck to where a bonfire waits, while Anto tries to keep beans and grenades from tumbling out of his stolen pack. He smells old leather and sweat.

Released from the grip, he falls before the fire and looks up. "Lawlor," says the stranger. This is no soldier, although he carries himself like a fighter, with a square jaw of the type often seen in comic books. He wears a trench coat too small for his heroic frame and a filthy, floppy hat. "Lawlor," he says again, focusing now on the arm the Sídhe transformed. His eyes are like blue laser beams from a movie and Anto fancies he can feel them burning him where they touch his skin. "You're no spy," the man says, almost with regret.

"Excellent," says Karim. "That's settled, then. Good-bye, Detective Cassidy. *Such* a pleasure."

She is standing on the steps at the back of the truck, one hand in a sling, the fire gleaming off the moisture on her face. Her other hand rests on a holster at her side.

"We gave you permission to question the little chap, not to throw him around like a sack of turnips. He's one of us now, after all. He is not to be harmed."

"I haven't finished," says the man, Cassidy.

"Oh, but you have, dear detective, you have. Look! Perhaps you fail to recognize this object? We call them guns, and my pointing it at your face is an invitation for you to toddle off back to Dublin."

The detective, if that's what he is, shows no fear at all. Not of the gun, nor of the men and women crawling out of tents to either side, forming fists or drawing knives. On the contrary, he takes several paces toward the truck.

"I have a mission. From the government."

"The government? The ones our grandparents voted for and who never left power? Do go on." Her limbs tremble. She will fall over at any moment-anyone can see that. Her gun points more at the ground now than at him.

"It is my job," Cassidy says, "to root out the traitors that are among us." He's a big man. A ball of tension, as though he has not once relaxed since his time in the Grey Land. Maybe he can't. Those fists of his could make a red smear of Karim along the road before she could raise her gun again or before any of the squad could intervene. He's probably crazy enough to do it too. Some survivors carry a death wish with them, but it seems that this Cassidy has yet to meet anybody capable of granting his. He's a strong man, yet his face is weather-beaten and aging. The time is not far off, surely, when he'll get his heart's desire.

"I'll answer!" Anto says. "I'll answer his questions. Sure what harm?"

Karim sits down suddenly, her face leaning against the metal frame of the truck. "Charming," she says, just as Ryan stops her from falling out onto the ground. "That's . . . that's settled, then."

Cassidy nods and, without even looking at Anto, strides away into the darkness. Beyond the camp he turns on a windup flashlight to light his way.

"You don't have to follow him, lad," says Ryan.

Anto smiles at him, but picks himself up to go after the stranger.

They travel across a field, frost crunching under boots, until they're a little above the muttering camp and standing by an old stone wall with tiny icicles glinting in the blue glow of the detective's flashlight.

"I see they grabbed you," Cassidy says. "The Sídhe."

Anto catches himself turning away to hide his left arm and has to force himself still.

They both look for a moment up toward the stars. Anto feels afraid. Not for himself, but for the Nation. He has been focused on Nessa these last few days, but now, hours after doing battle with a giant made of tortured human beings, it's finally coming home to him that the Sídhe are *here*. This world with its stars and glinting ice, with its green fields and his parents and younger siblings . . . it has been betrayed.

So many nights he has woken, thinking himself in the Grey Land again. Far from being a silly dream, it's starting to look like prophecy.

At last, Cassidy speaks. "What we must do for the Nation is hard," he says. "Our enemy will kill us all, down to the last baby. Our job is to make it tough for them. We will spit in their faces as we go down."

Anto shivers.

"There were traitors in your college, boy. Just up the road from here."

"Traitors, sir?" Anto sits up. "You mean . . . Conor?" Conor made himself king and was going to let the Sídhe come back to Ireland. Only his death prevented their return that time.

"I don't mean Conor. There were others too. Girls."

Of course. Girls. That terrible, terrible rumor.

"You seem nervous, Lawlor. Have you something to tell me?"

"No."

The eyes are like drills. The wind isn't helping either, and Anto realizes that the clothes he put on are nowhere near thick enough for the escape he's been planning. His teeth chatter. The cold invades his thoughts too.

Girls. Traitorous girls. Oh, not Nessa! Please, God, please don't let it be her.

"One of the girls confessed," Cassidy says. "The one called Melanie. Your fellow veteran."

"Oh." Anto shudders. "Oh."

"You know something." This is not a question.

"We had a conversation one time . . . Melanie said . . . I think she said the Cauldron was real. That the Sídhe could use its power to heal people. Something like that."

"She was sounding you out, son. I know that for a fact. The girl herself told me. She told me everything. And lucky for you, she convinced me you weren't involved. Indeed, lots of witnesses saw you in action. I commend you for what you did for the Nation that night. Bloody work. Good work."

Anto swallows, remembering it.

"But here's the thing. Your girlfriend, Vanessa Doherty, was involved too."

Anto can only stare. His eyes are stinging in the wind; his belly has gone all loose, as though he's eaten rotten food and is about to pay for it.

"You look shocked, son. But not surprised."

"What's that supposed to mean?" Anto cries. "Not surprised! Not surprised?! What are you even saying? You don't know Nessa."

"You're wrong there, son. I know her better than you do. Strong, she is. Stronger than you and me both."

"Exactly!"

"She held up under questioning, like nobody I've seen. And I left that room, in spite of my misgivings, thinking she was innocent. People get lucky in the Grey Land; we all know it. Maybe even she got lucky with those legs of hers. Legs that would have gotten her trimmed from the herd in a less forgiving society than our own great nation. And as I left her there, I even felt regret for the . . . manner of my questioning."

Anto tenses. "What did you do to her?"

"But it turns out I was wrong. As are you, son. I can read your mind. You're thinking how sweet she is, that pretty little thing. You're thinking she couldn't have sold us out to our enemies who are even now Calling our last few children away to be murdered. Not her, not Vanessa Doherty.

"But she did it, son. She sold us. The Sídhe recognized her strength. Knew it would be useful to them and added to it by making her even stronger. Ensuring her survival in our world as well as theirs. And just when we had caught her and put her in prison—"

"You put her in prison? Nessa?" Anto didn't think there were any prisons anymore. How can the State afford to feed criminals? But he knows from the movies what terrible places they are, and the thought of Nessa locked away after all she's been through terrifies him. "That's why I was made to join the infestation squad, isn't it?" He's trying not to shout—Nessa wouldn't want him to. But he's not as strong as she is and his spittle flies in the wind with every word he speaks. "They sent me here so I wouldn't find out she'd been taken away. Well, Detective, you're wrong about her. I don't care what you think you know. What that lying Crom-twisted Melanie told you. Nessa would never do anything to hurt us."

The detective's next words are almost too quiet to hear. "Then how can you explain the rescue attempt?"

Anto stares, uncomprehending.

"They came for her, her allies. They went to enormous effort to get into the prison. A dozen of them digging right into her cell. Putting their bodies between her and the bullets of the guards. Their leader was even overheard to say . . . well, I don't speak their filthy tongue like you youngsters! It's made all these betrayals possible, if you ask me . . . But in English, he said something like, 'We came here for you. To keep our promise. We will never harm you.'"

"No," says Anto. He's shaking his head. "*No.*"

"You need to speak to me," Cassidy says intently. "The fate of the Nation could hinge on what you know about her. Are there other spies? Did she associate with anybody strange? Did she give you names? I've come all the way up here. I need to know."

"Oh, Crom, please. Oh, Lugh."

Cassidy grabs him by the shoulders and hisses into his face, "Stop speaking that language and listen to me, boy! Listen! She's a traitorous little bitch and the sooner—"

"NO!"

The giant left arm has a life of its own. It throws the detective two yards across the frosty grass. Then it swings again to smash one of the rocks from the wall so that splinters fly everywhere, tearing Cassidy a new scar across his cheek.

"You're lying!" Anto screams it into the teeth of the cold wind. "It's all a lie!"

He runs, eyes streaming, his great big arm banging into everything and dragging on the ground, off into the darkness.

THE ESCAPE

After the visit of the Herald and the attack of the snake that bit Lena Peekya, there have been no further incidents at the school. But smoke rises from the town of Boyle. The countryside holds its breath and, for the first time that Aoife can remember, the hooded crows have fled the trees around the burnt-out skeleton of the dorms.

The last of the students and staff crowd into the gym. Alanna Breen stands by the climbing wall, her back straight, her face shiny with burn scars. Plump Mr. Hickey hovers by her side along with handsome Nabil and the scowling Taaft.

Aoife waits with the remaining twenty-eight students, rubbing at her neck where it was splashed by, well . . . by whatever was left of the girl running behind her. Her skin feels warm there, prickly, as though something is crawling and probing. But her fingers find nothing whenever they touch it.

As if reading her mind, Liz Sweeney mutters, "What a waste! At least Lena could run a bit. Not like you or that stupid Krishnan."

"Why can't you ever leave me alone, Liz Sweeney?"

"There's nobody else left in our year. We need to stick together."

"You call this sticking to—"

"Quiet!" says Liz Sweeney. "Can't you see the Turkey's about to speak?"

Indeed Alanna Breen, principal of a dead school, has opened her mouth, and everybody hushes to hear what wisdom her smoke-damaged voice will produce.

"My children," she tells them in her perfect Sídhe, "you are the heart of the Nation. If you don't live, it will be as though we adults never lived either, as though nothing we did mattered.

"So we need to get you out of here at once. Radio reports came in of . . . I won't hide it, of terrible attacks pushing into Donegal and Mayo and now down toward . . . toward Longford."

"By Crom!" mutters Liz Sweeney, stunned. Aoife can only stare, her heart fluttering in panic. What Ms. Breen is saying is that the enemy has gotten between them and Dublin. The students are trapped behind enemy lines.

"Miss?" Aoife is surprised to hear herself speak. So is Liz Sweeney, obviously, who hisses her disapproval.

"What is it, Aoife? We don't have much time for questions. We need to organize our escape now."

"That's just it, miss," Aoife says. "I was wondering . . . I . . ." She takes a deep breath, pushing against the impatience she sees on Ms. Breen's face and her own nerves. "I was wondering if some of us could take the . . . the pills."

A moment of silence follows her comments, with wide eyes staring at her, and yes . . . at least one of the Year 4s, Lada, dares to nod in agreement.

"I knew it!" says Liz Sweeney. "You dirty coward. You spear-licking mutton waste."

"Enough!" says Alanna Breen. "That's enough. No, Aoife. We need to think about the Nation. We need to live for it, and that's exactly what we're going to do. I know all of you. Your hidden strengths. Any one of you might grow up to become the savior of our people. Is that not so?"

Nabil nods. "And don't worry, Aoife, all right?" His eyes are the deepest brown she has ever seen. They hold hers long enough to remind her that this man will die before he will let anyone hurt her.

"All right," she whispers back. She is trembling all over. Somehow, speaking up in front of a crowd has scared her every bit as much as the Sídhe.

It all goes quickly after that. Everybody is made to eat, regardless of their nerves. Warm clothing is found, and Ms. Sheng comes in before dark with the news: "The road is clear. I hear mortars firing to the southeast. It probably has them distracted." She's a skinny, elderly woman with the longest neck Aoife has ever seen. But she's far from fragile and is said to have smashed several of the enemy with well-thrown rocks during the fighting before Christmas.

Taaft looks excited. "I didn't get my fill of killing 'em last time," she says. "I'm ready for another go, but listen up. The rest of you gotta run, OK? No talking. Nothing. Me and the French frog," by which she seems to mean Nabil, who scowls at her, "we do all the shooting and talking. You just have to obey orders and run where we tell you. We're going right down to the main road. Sheng will be in the front to make sure there's nothing waiting for us. Slow jog all the way."

She's not expecting questions, but she gets one from Mitch Cohen. He's twelve years old, but barely taller than Bronagh Glynn in Year 1. His parents spoke only Sídhe to him and he struggles with English a bit. "What if for us something is waiting?" he asks.

"We got to take our chances, kid, while they're distracted with the army. We'll win this. We're the ones with the guns, remember. You and I just got to get out of the way until the regulars arrive."

And out they go, running two by two in total silence, except for Alanna Breen and Mr. Hickey, who both have bicycles. Ms. Sheng has a bike too, and has gone on ahead.

It's one in the afternoon, but clouds are moving in over the watery sun. Aoife is running alongside Lada Bartoff, but Liz Sweeney muscles her way in, presumably so the two Year 5s can keep "sticking together."

This is madness, Aoife thinks. Her bare feet slap down on the rumpled, icy surface of the road. Trees loom to either side; they could contain any number of ambushes, any number of snake things like the one that got Lena. She shudders, missing a step, and only Liz Sweeney's sure fist saves her from a tumble.

"Idiot," mutters the other girl.

They don't see a single bird. No foxes or hares or anything else. Aoife is so sick with worry that the sandwich she ate earlier is a restless hot ball in her stomach.

In front of her, Lada Bartoff comes to a sudden halt and Aoife runs into the back of her. Everybody else stands stock-still, while Nabil, at the front of the column, raises a fist to keep them that way, his dark-handsome face straining to see what lies ahead.

Aoife should be looking down the road too, but she's distracted by a fluttering in the trees. The crows. The crows are here after all! And she feels such relief to see those dark little shapes settling onto the branches nearby. She alone seems to care enough to look up at them . . . and she convulses. She can't help it. Her jaw clenches, biting her own tongue bloody. Because, on the nearest branch, a face is staring back at her, that of a tiny old woman molded onto a birdlike body. But it's not a bird at all. It clutches its perch with full-sized human fingers that emerge from a skirt of black feathers. Even these have been made of human skin, each one individually crafted by loving, cruel hands. The creature grins, as do a dozen others that surround it.

Before Aoife can say a word, Ms. Sheng comes flying back toward them on her bike. Fifty-five years of life have made her as fit as a top athlete, and of all the staff, Aoife has always considered her the most mentally stable.

She leans low over the handlebars, threads of grey hair streaming out behind. Ms. Sheng is a woman who cycles every day and knows the potholes and bumps of this road like she knows her own face.

But even thirty years before, at her peak, when the roads of her Kilkenny home were as smooth as glass, she never moved so fast as she is doing now.

It's not going to be enough.

Other dark figures round the corner behind her. They come on horseback, all of them shouting who knows what. It doesn't matter because they're moving at a fierce gallop, weapons of some kind raised above their heads.

"Get off the road!" Nabil cries.

The first of the horsemen catches up with Ms. Sheng. A weapon swings, and even at this distance, her blood is the reddest thing Aoife has ever seen.

Then Taaft has Aoife by the shoulder and is shoving her toward the nearby trees. "Get off the road, moron! Off! You too, Krishnan, you long string of crap!"

Everybody else is already leaping into the undergrowth. Lada and Bronagh, Mitch Cohen and Bianconi. None of them wastes a second looking backward, but Aoife can't help herself.

"I'm so sorry!" a voice cries. It's one of the riders, Ms. Sheng's murderer, and she sees now that it is a man—or rather two. One has been twisted into a headless horse by the Sídhe. His face has been moved down to the chest. The eyes are mad, and the tortured mouth exhales clouds of mist with every breath. Another man—the "rider"—grows out of his back. This one has swords of sharpened bone instead of hands and the face of a kindly farmer. "I can't help myself!" he cries. "Run! Don't let us catch you!"

Aoife does. Finally. She's the last of the panicked students. A gun goes off—Nabil's probably. The shots are calm and steady, but already a number of the centaurs have left the road too, heedless of brambles, smashing through the skirts of giant rhododendrons.

"There's a girl here! A girl!"

Above Aoife's head is the tiny crow-woman she saw earlier.

"She's a slow one! Come and get her!"

"Leave me alone!" Aoife shouts.

"Not until I've fed on your tongue!"

Aoife runs in among trees. She cries out when something grabs her coat, but it's only a thorn and she tears herself free, plunging after the others as more shots come from the direction of the road and the crow-woman cackles above her head.

She stumbles into a clearing, to find Lada Bartoff picking Mitch Cohen up off the ground. Both look up in terror at Aoife's arrival, but they should have been looking the other way. A centaur bursts through the foliage.

"I don't mean it!" he wails, and his left sword hand cleaves into Lada's shoulder and down as far as her belly. "Oh, no! I've killed somebody else! Oh, no!" He tries to shake the body off his weapon, but he can't.

His "mount" prances about, as though panicked, and any moment now Mitch will get one of the clawed human feet that serve the creature as hooves in his neck.

Aoife plunges forward and drags him free. "Come on, come on." And together they push in under a huge spruce.

The forest is full of screams of students, the shouted apologies of centaurs, and tiny little voices that cry, "There's one here! Don't miss this one! Oh, what a feast!"

Aoife is stumbling through the woods. Branches slap her in the face. She has lost her hold on Mitch's skinny wrist and is no longer even sure where the road is. And then, as though parting curtains, she pushes aside the branches of a fir to see one of the woodland paths ahead of her.

"Oh, God!" says a voice. "I'm ever so sorry!"

One of the centaurs is out there, stalking somebody. The tortured lower mouth on the "horse's" chest drools. The upper man's torso gleams with sweat and the kindly face grimaces in genuine sadness. "They're making me do this, don't you see?"

Nevertheless, the sickles of sharpened bone that serve the creature as hands drip with gore.

Before him, a long branch in her hand, stands Liz Sweeney. The girl is breathing like somebody who has run a marathon, her mouth wide, gulping in the air. She doesn't look afraid though, not even slightly. With her back straight, her eyes narrowed, and her jaw set, she is the very image of Macha, goddess of battle.

"Oh," the centaur says, stepping closer. "It's good you defend yourself. I hope you win!"

One of his blades slices through the air and cuts her branch in half. The other whistles in toward the girl's neck. But she's gone, rolling away and back on her feet in an instant to strike the "horse's" back with the remains of the branch.

The lower mouth whines and spins around to follow Liz Sweeney. She whacks it again. "Oh, don't anger my mount! Don't be cruel! It can't help itself!"

The girl leaps back before the sweeping blades, but there's a stone waiting just behind her and down she goes. Clawed hooves dance forward. Liz Sweeney rolls, as the earth is stabbed behind her hard enough to send stones skipping. She fetches up against a rotting log with nowhere else to go.

Aoife has no memory of picking up the rock, but when she brings it down on the horse's spine, something snaps and the lower mouth screeches. The hind legs collapse onto the path.

"Oh, no!" cries the upper body. The blades reach back for Aoife, but she throws herself out of the way, as her fit young body suddenly remembers four years of training.

"Oh, dear," says the man's torso. The whole creature has rolled over on its side. "I'm so glad you're getting away. Honestly . . . but did you have to hurt my poor mount? Was that so necessary?" The blades of bone keep slashing in Aoife's direction, but they can't touch her.

"Come on, then," says Liz Sweeney, "you waste of space. Come on."

Come on where? A gap in the trees allows Aoife to see all the way back to the road. More centaurs, each one apologizing for what they're about to do, are gathering to take Nabil down. Lovely, kind Nabil.

They should have me instead.

She feels exhausted, her senses overwhelmed by the sounds of violence; by the scent of pine and the bulge of roots against the toughened soles of her feet. She is running in the wrong direction, following Liz Sweeney toward her death.

But then, a great *bang* drives both girls to their knees. A cloud of dust engulfs the monsters, and when it clears they have been replaced by a mass of dead and bleeding flesh.

"Was that . . . ?" Aoife's ears are ringing, her vision a blur. "Was that a . . . a bomb?"

Liz Sweeney grins and rises again, but at least three of the monsters remain alive.

"We have to get out of here!" cries Aoife. "Ms. Breen would want us to . . ."

And then she sees him: a boy standing right in the middle of the group of centaurs. He snarls like an animal, tall and dark-haired, his left arm a ridiculous lump of muscle. It's Anthony Lawlor! Anto! Where on earth did *he* come from?

It doesn't matter. The boy grabs one of the creatures by the hind leg—"I deserve it," it screams—and he swings it like a club until the remaining centaurs lie dead.

Then all is quiet. A few of the horrible bird-women look down from the branches, but even they keep the peace, shocked, perhaps, by what they have just witnessed.

It's carnage on the road. Bodies lie everywhere, friend and foe alike. Bianconi is unconscious. Mr. Hickey's legs peep out from beneath a butchered "horse" and Taaft just stands grinning at all of it. Finally the sergeant spots the two girls.

"What?" she shouts, although they haven't opened their mouths. "Can't hear a word you're saying. Kid had a grenade. Can you believe it?" Blood spatters the sergeant's face, none of it hers.

Anto trembles amid the bodies of those he has killed, but nobody approaches him, as if he's no different from any other creation of the Sídhe; as if he might strike at them. But finally he looks up, and it's Aoife's eye he catches.

"I came . . . I want . . . I want to speak to Ms. Breen."

"I'm sorry," says Nabil, putting down his weapon. "She has been injured. She may not have much time left."

DEATH OF A SCHOLAR

Alanna Breen can't move her legs. In the branches up beyond Anto's head, she can see one of the crow-women peeking from behind an abandoned nest. It licks its lips, slowly, deliberately. One wing rubs at where its belly must be.

Alanna doesn't care. She's resting on the boy's lap. She knows her remaining hours can be counted on one hand. She remembers another boy long ago, his face twisted in spite. "You'll never be a mother! Look at you! The squashed, ugly head on ya!"

But he was wrong, whatever he called himself. She's been mother to hundreds. She molded them more than any biological parent and shepherded them through the most terrifying days of their lives.

She knows them all by name, never forgets them. Rarely feels anything less than love, and even the monsters like Conor, she pities rather than hates.

Her breath hitches. Oh, lord, it hurts! A bubble forms at the side of her mouth. Blood, maybe. She wouldn't look, even if she could.

When Anto came and lifted her up, she saw the state of her bike and knows her poor body won't be any better.

She wants to moan with the pain, but she's not going to do that. Her job is to be strong for the children, and she'll keep working right up until the very last beat of her heart.

Poor Anto, she thinks. He's in pain too, this child of hers. She sees how his eyes avoid the carnage he created. He's a vegetarian, isn't he? He was the one who wouldn't even kill the animals on Pig Day. How much worse to have murdered—as he probably sees it—the intelligent, suffering centaurs. The victims of the Sídhe.

"It's all right," she tells him. She wants to pat his hand, but her own won't move. She knows why he's here. It distresses her that her last moments on God's green earth must be spent hurting him further, but the truth will serve him better in the long run.

"I'm looking for Nessa," he says. "I . . . I know she's not here but . . ." His face twists, trying to hide the hope he feels, but you can't keep such a feeling from your own mother, can you? Your real mother.

Alanna Breen, known to her students as "the Turkey" or "Gobbler" or a hundred other terms of abuse, wants nothing more now than to slip away. She has worked so hard! But she summons the will, as she has always done, to do the right thing.

"She's gone, boy. I'm sorry . . . Accused of betrayal. Out . . . out in a boat . . ."

———

Anto feels the old woman die. It's early afternoon in winter. He crouches on a freezing road covered in the bodies of dead children and the monsters shot by Nabil and Taaft, along with the ones he blew to bits himself. He could have killed one of his own side with his carelessness. But, just as happened the first time he used a grenade, his giant arm did exactly the right thing. Maybe he can't miss now. Or maybe it's beginner's luck and the next time it will go off in his hands.

His new limb doesn't care. Unlike Anto himself, it comes from the Grey Land and it likes to kill. That's what it seems like to him.

"Give her over, kid," says Taaft, her English harsh after the formal elegance of Ms. Breen's Sídhe. The principal's voice will never be heard again. He should mourn for her, the famous scholar. The shepherd who brought so many through hell.

"'Give her over,' I said."

Taaft takes the body away and a darker pair of hands helps Anto to his feet. Nabil.

"You all right, my friend?"

He's not. He's not all right. It's not because of the death he's just witnessed, or the giant made entirely of human beings that he helped to destroy yesterday. Anto has seen the Grey Land, after all. His imagination has no more unexplored dark corners.

Except for one.

Nessa is gone. Not dead! Dead is easy, as any student of a survival college can tell you. The bells ring. You weep, yet you make damn sure you get up again afterward. The problem is that Nessa will live on, her name on everybody's lips as a traitor. It's a bitter, terrible thing.

And she may live on in another way too: as a centaur sent to kill; as one of the nasty whispering crows in the trees above. His knees tremble under the enormous weight of his arm. His throat feels thick, his stomach a rock.

"But she didn't even do it!" he cries.

"I know, my friend," says Nabil quietly.

"She isn't a traitor. They don't know her like I do. The guards didn't even ask me! They just put me out of the way in case I'd cause trouble." He's shuddering now, his whole body an engine of sobs and snot. "She couldn't have betrayed us! She didn't!"

But in his soul a voice whispers, *She would do anything to survive. Conor for all his strength couldn't resist the Sídhe. Nor Melanie. Nobody could.* And how can Anto explain what Cassidy said to him? That thing the prison guards overheard, about how the Sídhe sacrificed themselves to protect Nessa?

He shakes his head, angry now, furious. He jerks himself free of Nabil's kind hands. "I can get her!" he cries. "I'll take a boat. I'll find her in the Grey Land and bring her back!"

"Anto," Nabil says. "Anto. I'm sure you're right. You knew her best. But if she was sent to the Grey Land . . . it's already too late. You know that, my friend. They will have transformed her. It's not like a Call where you have to resist for only a day. Or what feels like a day. I'm so sorry."

Anto knows Nabil needs him to pull himself together. That's what instructors always want from you: Don't stay down. It's just that this time he doesn't know how to get up.

"They're here!" a soft voice calls. An answer comes from another direction: "They're here!" A flock of birds takes to the sky, all of them dressed in black, unnatural feathers, all with the wizened faces of old men and women. "They're here, they're here, they're here!"

"We need to go," Taaft says. Her arm rests on Nabil's as though it belongs there. Most people think the two instructors despise each other, but Anto has seen them together and knows it's a lot more complicated than that. "Gather them up, Froggy. Don't want to be hanging around when the reinforcements arrive!"

Nabil and Taaft call together as many of the survivors as they can find. In a way they are lucky, for their strange battle with the centaurs has produced no wounded at all. Students are either alive or dead. Others may have wandered off into the forest, but a cold-hearted decision is made not to go looking.

Nor will they bury the casualties.

Krishnan pulls a weeping Mitch Cohen away from a red smear nobody else can recognize. Bianconi the Boar gets a spare pistol he claims he can use. Then it's off again, in under the trees while the crow-women swoop down to the road.

"They're going to feast on our dead," Liz Sweeney tells Aoife. "In case you were wondering."

"Leave her alone," Anto says. His voice is hoarse from crying. He's not sure if he'd prefer to be here or lying dead back on the road.

"What's it to you?" says Liz Sweeney.

She's always been a strange girl: as tall as he is, her eyes slate grey, her cheekbones sharp enough to gouge stone. She might have been a model in the old world, but here and now she reminds Anto more of a mercenary from the movies. Or one of those assassin girls in the tattered books on his grandmother's shelf.

"I won't have you touching me," Liz Sweeney says.

Anto stares, but the girl is talking to Aoife, not him. "I know you're in love with me, and I won't have it."

"What?" Aoife is shocked. "How, by all the gods, could you think that?"

"You risked your own life to save mine. Don't think I didn't notice. A coward like you! By the Morrigan, you must want me bad!"

Aoife's eyes all but fall out of her head, so widely is she staring.

The whole group is moving down a path that runs parallel to the main road leading into town. Little Bronagh Glynn walks ahead of the three Year 5s, as though asleep. Some Year 3s follow on after, two boys and a girl, with Taaft bringing up the rear. Anto can't see past the lanky Krishnan to the front of the column. He's not even sure how many are still alive.

"That's wrong, Liz Sweeney," Aoife is saying. "I don't love you. I couldn't love anybody except Emma."

"Oh, yes, Squeaky Emma!"

"Don't call her that!"

"But she's dead now, so—"

"Don't!"

"—so now you want somebody else, and I'm the obvious candidate. Well, I'm not that type, and even if I was . . ."

Aoife staggers away off toward the front, pushing past Krishnan, uncaring of the branches that slap her on the way.

Liz Sweeney shakes her head. "She's wasting energy doing that. Can you believe it?"

"You should leave her alone," Anto mutters again, but he hasn't the heart for an argument. All he can think of is Nessa, who fought so very hard to live. More than anybody else he knows. And then, the horrible irony of finding herself in a boat bound for the Grey Land. The terror of it. The fury. The unfairness. What must be happening to her now?

He shudders. He told Nabil he wanted to get in a boat himself to go back for her, even though he would inevitably arrive too late. He's so relieved he doesn't have to go, and so ashamed by his own relief. He is empty. Worthless.

"I don't know why she's obsessed with me," says Liz Sweeney. "But who are we to talk, eh, Anto? We were both in love with traitors. Me with Conor, the Crom-twisted king himself! And you with that ragged sow, Nessa."

He stops breathing altogether. Every thought is like a needle in his brain. Liz Sweeney has no idea what she's just done. "Oh, yeah," she continues. "I heard what the Turkey said to you before she closed those bulging eyes of hers."

He clenches his giant fist. His muscles bunch. He'll kill Liz Sweeney. He, the vegetarian, will kill her dead with a single punch. "Come on," she says, hurrying forward. "We're holding up the line." And Liz Sweeney lives another day.

VENGEANCE

Nessa is still alive, but not alone.

She clings to a lonely rock clustered with foul-smelling barnacles. A few hundred yards from where she hides is the shoreline of the Grey Land, and there a group of half a dozen Sídhe have formed a chain and are wading out toward her.

"We felt your arrival, thief!" cries one of them.

She's tired enough that she slips a little, cutting her good hand on one of the razor-sharp shells that cling feebly to the rock. She still has her sopping, half-burnt prison uniform. How strange to be here with clothing!

"What will you become?" shouts another of the Sídhe. "A horse? I need one for the war! Or a mouse to feed our hawks?"

They seem to think she lies closer to shore than she actually does, and this might have something to do with the way she upended her boat. Perhaps it would have deposited her right in their laps if she hadn't altered its course. But they keep moving out from their initial position and will find her soon enough.

"The thief is not dead," one says, a man's gorgeous baritone. "I can feel that much, and . . . and there's something else." He raises his chin as though sniffing the air. "Something beautiful."

"Oh, yes!" a woman replies, her hair glimmering with bits of glass and metal. "I can taste it even from here!"

Nessa's breath quickens. She has nowhere to go. Nobody she can call on for help. She could swim directly away from the shore until she drowns. But what if one of them is a better swimmer than she is with her two broken fingers? They'll catch her easily and turn her into something terrible. And the pain of it! An agony, a horror she will feel forever, because it's not like this is a Call that ends after a single day.

They're still coming forward, arms outspread, smiles huge.

Behind them, the land gently rises away from the sea. Over there it is raining ash. Farther left, a volcano spits angrily, blasting burning rock down onto the world, and Nessa realizes that she was wrong to think there was no safe place for her in the Grey Land, because she alone of all humanity can claim fire as a friend. If only she could get there!

"She can't breathe water," says the male Sídhe on the end of the line. "Not yet, anyway. She must be behind that rock. Yes! Yes! She is the beating heart of a promise. Can't you feel it? The sweetness of it on the air." No further word is spoken, yet all at once the six of them are surging forward, four women, two men. They split after a few steps so that three of them can come from either side of the rock. They shout with joy while still several yards away. One man takes

166

a hunting horn from around his neck and blows loud enough to raise the dead.

A lesser girl would have panicked at this stage and set off swimming, but although the rhythm of Nessa's heart is urgently requesting flight, she has a lifetime's experience in overruling it. She would have been dead long ago otherwise, sharing the cold ground with a legion of those other girls.

The Sídhe slow now as the water rises to waist height on them, chattering excitedly about all the changes they will wreak upon her body.

"I would like a monkey," says one woman, her face like something out of a Disney cartoon. "But I want its head facing backward and oozing boils on its neck that sparkle in the glittering sky! Oh, how I will make her dance for me!"

The two groups surge around the rock to left and right, but Nessa, waiting for this, throws herself forward instead, over the top of her hiding place and straight into the sea behind them. She doesn't make the mistake of closing her eyes. Even under this oily water, even in the poor light of the spirals, she perceives the shadow of legs. During her patient wait she has pried a razor shell from the rock. She uses it now to hamstring the man with the hunting horn, his blood unfurling like a flag. She abandons her weapon and before the others can turn around she's already swimming through the water, powerful arms working like an engine, her injured fingers begging her to stop.

She gains a lead of twenty paces, as they wade awkwardly after her.

But they're laughing of course. How they always laugh! And with good reason, because they have an eternity to hunt her down, while she, friendless, with nothing to eat, can only grow weaker.

Closer to shore, her hands begin to tip the bottom, but she won't stand just yet. Nessa knows she can't rely on her legs to get her out of trouble, so instead she drags herself along until even her knees are scraping on rock.

The enemy gain on her again as they reach the shallows, although they laugh less now, saving their breath for the chase.

Nessa scrambles upright, gathering up stones along the way. Now she fires them off. She hits one woman in the face, hard enough to send her back into the water.

Four remain uninjured, grinning, delighted, *close.*

They stumble to a halt no more than five paces away.

"Why do you not run?" asks the remaining man. He looks innocent and sweet, with dimples marking his flawless skin. His voice is as soft as a boy's.

"And why do you smile, thief?" says the princess who wants Nessa for a monkey.

Fear, is the answer to that question, with a good dollop of adrenaline stirred in too. Nessa has thrown all her stones. Used up all of her advantages. Any of her classmates in this position could simply turn now and run. They are trained for it, trained to go for hours if necessary. They can fight too, so much better than she can, for although she outmatches most of them in the strength of her arms and shoulders, her legs will betray her at the slightest nudge.

She forces her grin wider, wide enough to match theirs.

"I have been changed," she says, filling her voice with a confidence she doesn't feel. "Changed by Dagda himself. Look! See my skin?"

They *can* see it, somehow in this light, the faint, porcelain-like quality it has borne ever since her Call.

The monkey princess shrugs. It makes her seem human, despite those large eyes and her clothing of spider silk and glittering scraps of metal. "And why should we not change you again? Killing you is forbidden of course—we can see the beauty of the promise on you. And great power will come with its fulfillment. But Lord Dagda would not deny us the simple pleasure a monkey brings."

"He will want to see me himself," says Nessa, hoping against hope her words will have some kind of effect on them. But all that happens is they laugh and the woman says, "We will show you to Lord Dagda when we have made you lovely!"

"Dagda wouldn't want that!" Nessa pushes back against the rock behind her, as though she could disappear into it. "You *must* believe me!"

"Who can believe a thief that took our lands from us with iron swords?"

The monkey woman, Lassair, reaches out and rests her hand on Nessa's shoulder. She licks her lips. All she needs to do is to squeeze and the girl's arm will elongate or shrink, or fall off altogether. Or grow fur. Nessa's bladder actually gives way in the absolute terror of the moment, but with all the water around them, with the stench of the air and the oily sea, her enemies fail to notice it. All they hear is her steady, steady voice, which, unlike her legs, can bear the weight of entire continents. In this alone she is not like any other human they have ever seen before. Begging is what they have come to expect. The word spoken most often by human lips in their presence is "please," usually followed by "don't!" By screams and tears or pathetic defiance.

Calmness is not part of their experience.

"Dagda will want to see me," Nessa asserts again, "*exactly* as I am."

"This is an attempt to fool us. To escape." Lassair's graceful fingers tighten ever so slightly.

Nessa looks the woman right in the eye. "No. That's where I'm going. To see Dagda. I mean it. I promise it."

The acrid, half-poisonous air of the Grey Land seems to shiver around them, or is that just Nessa's imagination? She suddenly feels light-headed, her legs even weaker than before. It is only with the greatest of effort that she keeps them from buckling and driving her into the water.

The Sídhe woman releases her hold as though scalded. All of them bow their heads, hands together like the most fervent of believers in church. "Thank you, thief. Thank you. We will accompany you to see Lord Dagda at the Cauldron."

Nessa manages a nod in return. Lassair walks her gently to the shore, even lending an arm for support. "Do you mind," she asks, all courtesy now, "if we wait a moment to retrieve our comrades that you wounded?"

"Uh . . . not at all." Nessa's head is spinning. *What just happened there? They thanked me. They actually thanked me. But for what?*

Nessa's two victims are helped to shore and neither bears her any ill will. One of them grins from a mouth of smashed teeth; the other has horrific new wounds on his ruined leg that could not have been caused by the shell she slashed him with.

"Scavengers," the man says happily. "While I lay in the water."

"Doesn't . . . doesn't it hurt?" asks Nessa.

"Oh, yes! You must be proud, thief, very proud! The Cauldron would take a thousand heartbeats to heal me at this distance! But I have the honor of accompanying you there and will recover more quickly as we approach."

The Cauldron is real, Nessa already knew that much. Dagda himself told her so during her Call. In legend it brought warriors back even from death, but this creature seems to think it will heal him anywhere in the Grey Land. He winks at her. The other man slaps her on the back like an old comrade.

All of a sudden it seems that her captors have come to trust her and she still can't figure out why.

It doesn't matter, she thinks. It's perfect. For she intends to murder them all. Maybe even try a little experiment. Let's see how quickly the Crom-twisted Cauldron brings them back to life when she rips the heads off their corpses and feeds them to the next monster she encounters.

She looks at them, at their heart-stoppingly beautiful faces. She feels only hatred, her whole body thrumming with spite. Of its own accord, her fake grin widens.

Anto. Anto would be horrified. Sometimes she thinks the slightest glimpse into her thoughts would kill the love he has for her stone dead. Megan, on the other hand—her memory perches like a little red-haired devil on Nessa's left shoulder and nods approvingly. Her imaginary suggestions are as foul as they are brutal: *I know where you can stick their heads! Right, Ness?*

After what feels like a few more minutes, they set off across a beach that burps noxious gases. They climb a steep path up the side of a cliff. Nessa has to use her arms a lot. She struggles to maintain even a gentle pace and her captors see how her left hand makes her wince and sweat.

Breathing easily, they begin to speculate among themselves as to how best her body might be altered to work better.

"My monkey idea was the best one," asserts Lassair.

But the now-lame Hornblower interjects. "More of a baboon though, don't you think? We could make the thief's arms longer and put suckers on them like that boy from before, do you remember? I made a trellis of him and kissed you to the music of his tears."

"But I *want* a monkey. Imagine pursuing it through the clinging forest? How long before it would be consumed?" And the fairy princess's laugh is so beautiful and so infectious that Nessa has to fight to keep the hatred from her face.

At the top of the cliff lies a plain of mud. Ash starts to fall then, sticking to everyone in the party and obscuring a stand of finger trees nearby.

"I'm slowing you up," she tells the Sídhe. "You go on ahead if you wish."

"Come now!" says Hornblower. His skin is so smooth the drifting flecks of ash fall away from it at once. His jaw alone would win him any election on earth, while his eyes are all a-sparkle with sweet innocence.

"Did you not hear us before? Let us give you better legs. I could bend those back for you. Make you fleet as a faun!"

"No. I am as Dagda made me and I will stay that way until I see him. But . . . but if you escort me to those finger trees, I could make myself some crutches. And for you too until you are healed."

"Crutches!" he cries in delight. "How many lives since I heard that word! Yes, yes, a fine game indeed. Let us have crutches, you and I! Come!"

Astonishingly, the others let the two of them go alone into the trees. It is darker here, away from the silver light, with angry hissing from among the roots. Something altogether larger growls deep enough to be felt through the packed earth between the trees. "Away with you!" Hornblower shouts. "Eat one of your own! This thief is not for you!"

Another growl and the trees shake.

"You wish to be shaped again? Shall I make of you a prey animal?"

His words induce a panic. Branches—whole trunks maybe—shatter as the monster lumbers away.

"This is exciting," Hornblower confides. "I think . . . My memory has been broken so many times, but I think I might have had crutches when still we lived in the Many-Colored Land. As a . . . as a boy? Yes, I was a boy, I think. I followed animals. I cannot remember which type now. I think we ate them, or perhaps it was they who ate us. And there were dogs, but none we could talk to like the ones we have now."

Nessa is searching among the branches. She is an expert at this, but her damaged left hand can't cope.

"Oh," says Hornblower, "let me!"

Before she can move, he takes her hand and squeezes. The pain! Oh, she had forgotten the pain! Nothing Cassidy did can compare to this! It's like hammers pounding her bones to powder. Like needles of fire and acid ripping into each individual pore. She screams, all her precious illusion of calm ripped away in an instant. "Get away! You're not to touch me!"

"Oh," he mutters, abashed. "I forgot. I just wanted to fix your fingers."

Nessa totters, barely able to see through eyes full of tears, her breathing hoarse as an old man with TB. Hornblower touched her for only an instant, but she'll have a whole day of such agony the moment they realize she's lying about Dagda.

Quickly she takes control of herself. All he did was heal her, that's all. *And we'll make him pay for that*, Megan whispers. Nessa can only agree. She can't fathom the strange trust the enemy are putting in her, but she knows she needs to take advantage of it.

Crutches are the one thing she understands better than anybody. Even in this alien wood where black sap spurts like blood, she quickly fashions a pair perfectly suited to her height and weight.

"Can I try them?" asks the innocent monster by her side.

"You're too tall for these. Too heavy. Here. Hold them, while I prepare yours."

He's as eager as a child, standing proud and straight as she sizes him up. He nods wisely when she picks out an appropriate branch for him, and she thinks, *By Crom! He's pretending he understands what I'm doing. No different from a real man.*

She's especially careful with the way she breaks this new branch off.

"Now," Nessa says, "I need you to open your mouth."

"Why?" he asks, just as she shoves the sharpened stake right down his throat.

She leaves him there, drowning on his own blood. This is her second killing, counting Conor as the first. She barely remembers that one and still isn't quite sure how she went ahead with it. Her memories are vague in the extreme.

But now, as her crutches carry her out of the far side of the wood, faster than most humans can run, her eyes fill with tears and her half-empty stomach threatens to spew what little nourishment remains to her out onto the ground.

"He's not even human!" she tells herself. "He's a monster! They're all monsters! They will torture me for an eternity if I let them!"

None of that seems to matter. She needs to watch where she's going, skidding down a pebbly path while spider bushes reach for her crutches. One tumble, one broken bone, and she's done for. But all she can see is Hornblower's blood. The surprise on his face.

"I'll do it again!" she cries. "I'll do it all again!"

Exactly! crows Megan's ghost. *We'll kill the lot of them! We'll make this place a graveyard of the Sídhe!*

THE PROMISE

Nessa is fast now, faster than her enemies could ever be, hurtling down the slope toward a vast coastal plain. But she can't keep this up for long. Already the sweat is blinding her, her breath rasping like sandpaper in air that itches and burns as it goes down.

Don't think about it, don't think, push! Push!

Giving up is not how survivor Testimonies get written. The way it works, the way it always works, is that you stay alive, for one more minute, or a second even! In that time your pursuers may trip. A smother tree might wrap them in its bark . . . And maybe, just maybe, you'll add enough stolen seconds together for the Call to end and send you home.

But this isn't a Call, is it? Nessa's not going home, unless her home is here, where even the air hates her.

She skips through a field of knee-high trees, scattering whole tribes of tiny men. In the distance a larger "animal" roars and a herd of naked human antelope scatters in terror.

Nessa doesn't stop to look. Ten minutes, fifteen, maybe even twenty she keeps it up. Longer than ever before! And then, like a horse ridden until its heart has burst, she is simply lying in the freezing muck.

And what has she achieved? The enemy can't be more than a few hundred yards behind her and she has left a trail of blood and snot and broken twigs that nobody could ignore.

And yet the horn never sounds. No cries of delight issue from the top of the hill where she left them. Why are they not coming for her?

They're in no rush, Nessa thinks. They said they could feel the promise written by Dagda into her flesh. The one that said only Conor could kill her. They think they can find her anywhere. But they're wrong about that. Nessa hasn't forgotten the volcano she saw earlier.

Hours away, in the direction of her flight, the mountains begin. As she watches, the clouds of ash clear just enough for her to see the violent glow of lava. *They won't be able to touch me there.* She'll rest a few minutes first and then be on her way.

———

Nessa wakes with a start. How long . . . ? How? The silver spirals spin as they always have. Her stomach heaves with hunger.

She has a little cry, although Crom knows she's not entitled to one. She never pitied the weepers in the dorms at school. *Just get on with it!* she used to think. *What good will it do?* The answer then was the same one she has today. None. It's all just a waste of water. But there's nowhere she needs to be right now and the tears won't stop, so she just lies there weeping quietly.

If Anto were here—she would hate for him to be here! To see her sobbing like a baby! But not even the Grey Land could destroy her happiness then, she thinks. She lets herself sink into the fantasy for a while. The two of them here together. His great strength allied to her will. They would conquer all before them. His smile. The smell of his skin . . .

But slowly, slowly, something intrudes.

Singing.

She freezes, straining her ears. She doesn't recognize the music, but it's the same angelic sound you would get from a children's choir at Christmas. Sweet, high voices, innocent and sacred at once. She scrambles to her feet because beauty almost always signals danger here. Where? Where is it coming from? She looks up, almost falling again in surprise.

Massive black shadows fill the sky, a dozen maybe, each with a body the size of a car and wingspan of four yards or more. The song drifts to a close, as one by one the figures peel away from the flock and come screaming out of the sky. They seem to be moving away from Nessa, off toward the mountains, but when they hit the horizon they wheel around, one after another. Tiny, tiny dots, growing fast as they shoot toward her, barely a yard above the surface of the plain.

And the song begins again, glorious harmony that would once have filled every opera house in the world and thrown Puccini and

Bizet into despair. But the creatures themselves are far from beautiful. They are human flesh, of course, stretched over a batwing-shaped frame of bones, their sagging bellies trailing jellyfish fronds along the ground. Only the faces remain human, although they have two of these each, both singing. And on their backs, these eagles or bats or whatever they are, each carries a Sídhe warrior.

Nessa has spent too long staring. The first is now upon her. She lurches to one side, swings a crutch, only to have it yanked away by the trailing fronds. The force of it spins her around, throws her helplessly into the path of another.

Instantly, dozens of sticky tentacles, none thicker than a finger, wrap her tight.

Great wings power them up into the air, leaving Nessa's stomach behind on the ground.

The girl has no idea where they plan on taking her, but, by Crom, she knows she won't be going quietly. The wrapping fronds have pinned her arms together with the one remaining crutch, while the world shoots away a long drop beneath her feet. Even *her* strength won't free her here. Nessa is left with only one appalling option.

She doesn't hesitate. She bites right through the nearest fleshy ropes until she is gagging on human blood and bits of . . . "Meat," she tells herself. "It's just meat." But the monster howls and shudders. It lurches in the sky, and one of the heads cries, "Oh, such pain! By the Buddha! The pain!"

The other voice is just weeping, although now and again it utters words in what might be French. *Show no mercy!* Megan's ghost whispers. What choice does Nessa have, unless she wishes to become a monster herself?

Only two of the strands are gone, out of maybe forty that grip her. The mountains have grown large since she last looked at them, their tips gleaming white except where ash stains them from a great belching mouth of fire near the sea. She bites again. *I'm already a monster*, she thinks.

By the time she has freed her right arm, both mouths are screaming in their childlike voices and her own face is a mass of gore.

And then, with the air flying past her, she hears another voice.

It is the Sídhe rider, leaning precariously over his mount's side, his hair gleaming like a ribbon in the wind.

He nods appreciatively at the wreckage she has made, uncaring that he hangs above the abyss or that the bat-creature's flying has grown dangerously lopsided due to his weight. Nessa ignores him, for what can he do to hurt her?

"Stop it!" he shouts above the wind. "I am trying to help you." He sees her astonishment and nods. "You were right to leave the others. The way across the mountains is the quickest route to Dagda, but it is not so easy to cross the heights on foot unless you know the way. So when my squadron learned what you were trying to do, we followed along to get you there on time. We only wish to help."

"No! It's my death you want."

"But your death is promised to another."

"To Conor, you mean? He's in the grave himself!"

"Yes." The Sídhe smiles. Behind him the mountains grow ever larger, their sides forested with twisted, twisting trees. "He *is* dead. We have already found another king to replace him. And yet, it is Conor who will kill you. But first you have a promise of your own to keep. You must see Dagda."

Nessa twirls high above the ground. A promise? She made a promise? And it all becomes clear to her. This is the reason the first group of Sídhe refrained from hurting her. And she laughs. What idiots they are! Just because they are obsessed with keeping promises doesn't mean she has to be. She could have sworn to do anything, it seems, anything at all, and they'd have bowed and scraped to her for it. She laughs. She can't help it. Are they really so easy to fool as all that?

But whatever the reason, Nessa has no interest in rushing toward Dagda just so she can be murdered by some type of zombie Conor.

She bites and bites again, while the beautiful man urges her to stop "for her own good." It's all just encouragement for Nessa, until suddenly her host swings down from the flier's back and grabs hold of some of the unbroken fronds nearest him.

"This is wonderful!" he shouts. "You fill my heart with joy."

Nessa takes this as an invitation to punch him with her now free right fist. All he does is laugh and spit a tooth in her direction. It misses, falling away into the void below. Then he reaches up into the belly of the creature above him, his hand sinking deep into its flesh. If the two voices screamed before when Nessa attacked them, they are now as loud in their agony as air-raid sirens. Nothing is more painful than the molding touch of the Sídhe! The wings cease to beat entirely. Nessa is spun around and the surface of the Grey Land comes corkscrewing up toward her.

"Steady!" shouts her enemy. "Steady there, my sweet one!"

Desperate flaps of the wings follow—just in time—for suddenly they are skipping over the canopy of a forest like a stone over a pond, scattering leaves and spreading panic among a tribe of hideous crawling apes.

Nessa must have been holding her breath. By the time she has released it and looked up again, the Sídhe is holding what looks like a viper in his hand. He has fashioned it from the flesh of his mount and it is still attached to the flier's belly. The serpent has a fanged, questing mouth and hideous, dribbling nostrils that expand and contract where they sense her presence.

"Only the weakest of poisons," the Sídhe assures her. "I need you asleep rather than dead."

The viper comes at her, the head snapping, the jaws dripping. She fends it off with a handful of fronds and it sinks its teeth into them: once, twice, and again a third time.

"You have poisoned my mount," says the Sídhe. "That was *not* clever of you."

"Why not?" she asks.

"You will regret it, dear one. You will suffer now."

The great wingbeats slow. The Sídhe releases the "snake." He shoves both hands deep into the belly above him. Not this time to

183

reshape it, but because they are now spinning out of control and he needs something to hold on to.

All of a sudden the twin voices stop singing and the fronds holding Nessa in place slacken. The second crutch tumbles down into the trees, and she herself has to grab on for dear life to keep herself from falling after it.

They hurtle through a pall of smoke and . . . there! Right beneath her lies a river of lava such as she dreamed she would find. *Now,* she thinks. *Now I'll let go.* But the river is gone again, it's gone, as their failing mount veers to the right.

"Remember I tried to help you," the Sídhe says. "You will have to walk to find Dagda."

"I will kill myself first!" she snarls.

He laughs and laughs, but stops as she releases her hold, falling down and away.

AN ARMY

The remaining students and instructors of Boyle Survival College huddle in an abandoned house in Longford town, while snow drifts down the fogged-up windows.

It's been a week since the invasion of Ireland began. In that time, they have traveled no more than forty miles. They've stolen supplies from hastily abandoned defenses. They've heard reports over a dying radio that Galway is under siege from a thousand different horrors, and every captured village gives the enemy more innocents to turn into monsters.

Yet all of the reports agree on one thing: The Sídhe themselves, famous for how little they care for their own lives, are rarely seen. They hang back from the fighting. They send their "heralds" ahead to demand surrender, and keep waves of monsters between themselves and the human army.

But the group wastes little time on this puzzle. They just want to get back to safety.

As night falls, they block out the windows so they can have a fire. Aoife, it turns out, knows how to cook. "Polish stuff, mostly," she explains. "From Granny. The owners of this place even had spices. Can you believe it?"

"The smell will get us caught," Liz Sweeney says. However, Longford town lies completely empty, leaving them their pick of houses to hide in.

Shadows dance on the walls. Anto's stomach rumbles. He's drooling like a cartoon character, and he sits drowsily with the others in the front room, content as a dog before the flames. How can he be enjoying this when Nessa is gone? When she is dead, or much, much worse?

The students of Boyle have only now reached the front lines, but they've had a dozen horrible encounters along the way. One of the Year 3s was Called, returning as a completely exsanguinated corpse. Bronagh Glynn was carried away by something that gibbered and laughed as it ran off on spindly legs, and Liz Sweeney had to take over Bianconi's pistol after his right hand got too close to a pair of centaurs.

Aoife emerges at last with Mitch Cohen as her helper.

"Taaft and Nabil are having theirs in the kitchen," she says.

Some of the food she serves in mugs. "Tastes amaaaazing!" Krishnan says, his Adam's apple bobbing in appreciation. But his look turns to outright jealousy when Aoife comes into the room again bearing two portions far larger than his. "Yours has no meat," she whispers to Anto. Even with so much death and horror around, she always remembers he needs extra calories and goes to great efforts to look after him.

"Thanks," he replies. For some reason he has a lump in his throat.

But Liz Sweeney's helping is even larger: a mountain of mashed potatoes, along with winter stores of meat and vegetables from jars.

The bigger girl shakes her head. "Don't think you can win me over, Aoife." For some reason her eyes slide over to Anto when she speaks. "I'm not into that. I'm not like that tiny little sneak you used to hang around with."

"Don't eat it if you don't want it," Aoife replies, quiet as a mouse. She's staring at the taller girl, not with hatred, exactly, and certainly not with the lust Liz Sweeney mocks her for.

"Oh, no! It's mine now and I'll eat every bit." Liz Sweeney digs an enormous nugget of mash out with her spoon. "Every. Last. Crumb. I intend to live, even if you don't." She squashes the food into her mouth, chewing, swallowing, while her greedy spoon has already dived in for a refill.

Then it pauses. Liz Sweeney wheezes like an old smoker. She blinks and her eyes are brimming with tears.

"Every last bit?" asks Aoife. "I don't think you're able for it."

Liz Sweeney growls and takes the next bite. Sweat beads on her forehead. Her skin has turned red enough to light the whole room. Every few seconds she has to pause to cough, but still, she won't give up or back down, and the spoon dips again into the bowl. Her hand is trembling now, reluctant to cooperate. With only two spoonfuls remaining, the food tumbles from her grasp and she is bent double, tears streaming from her eyes, gasping, wheezing. Anto and the five other remaining students have all been staring, their own food untouched.

At last, Aoife kneels down next to Liz Sweeney. "You told me I'm a waste of space. You're right about that. You're right, and I don't care if you say it or anything else you want about me. But next time you insult Emma, it'll be broken glass in your food instead of chili powder."

She retreats to the opposite corner of the room with a small bowl of food of her own.

Finally they all settle down to sleep.

After days of walking, after witnessing so many horrors, Anto welcomes the escape, hoping only for oblivion.

However, he does dream.

For once it's lovely, because Nessa is there with him. He smells her clean skin. He basks in the smile that she saves for him alone, listening as she draws for him a picture of the future. Everybody used to think she was so reserved, but with him, at the end, it was very different. "You want a dog, don't you, Anto?"

"Um . . ."

"I knew it. But up there"—she means in Donegal—"we'll need more than one. For company. I like collies best. What do you think of collies? Good."

He is lying with his face on her belly, totally relaxed, more happy than he's ever been. But then, from nowhere, a calloused hand covers his mouth. His eyes fly open to the dark, cooling room in the abandoned house in Longford. Taaft is right there in front of him and she whispers, "Shut up. Keep schtum." Then she's gone, to wake somebody else in the same way.

Anto realizes he's lying on somebody's belly after all, his normal arm around her waist. Liz Sweeney of all people. She meets his eyes. The sun is just starting to creep in through a crack in the curtains, making a perfect crescent moon of her left cheekbone. She shrugs. Looks away.

He should apologize, but then the street outside fills with sudden noise: the shouts of a troop of centaurs, dozens of them all together. "Please don't make me hurt somebody! Please!"

Anto looks around the room. Nabil and Taaft are back in the kitchen. The others huddle together: Mitch and Andrea, a Year 3, holding each other tight; Krishnan, curled into a ball, but still taller than Seán beside him; and that girl with the birthmark, Niamh. Only Aoife sits alone, arms around her knees, eyes tightly closed.

He crawls up to the window, peering around the edge of the curtain, while Liz Sweeney does the same on the far side of it. He gasps, but dangerous as that is, he can't help himself, for the whole world beyond the glass is a churn of monsters.

Furry beasts run close to the ground emitting wordless, screeching cries. So tightly do they crowd together they seem to form a living carpet.

This is why Taaft woke them.

Meanwhile, "crows" have come to roost on the chimney. How they squabble just above the heads of the cowering students! "I'll find them and eat their faces!" "No! No! I will!"

And in the sky with great batlike wings, trailing a nest of tentacles behind them, three creatures soar, singing so incredibly beautifully that Niamh Fegan starts to weep. She has to bite down on her own hand to keep herself quiet.

Trapped, Anto thinks. *We're trapped*. He's not sure he cares. But the parade of monsters outside the window goes on and on and he can't help remembering that each and every one of them has been twisted out of a living human being. *We made the Sídhe into monsters, now they make monsters of us*. It's the human thing to do, isn't it? It always has been. We bomb and impoverish others. We starve their children and gape in outraged surprise when they turn our cruelty back on us. *But why Nessa? What did she ever do to the Sídhe?* She could be out there right now, her lovely mouth full of fangs. Her eyes on stalks, her elegant hands sharpened to points and dripping with poison.

Something flashes in the distance. A moment later, the house shakes, and suddenly, across the street, an entire building explodes. Shrapnel tears holes in the living carpet of monsters. They screech and wail, but more explosions flower everywhere at once.

Taaft pokes her head around the door. "Stay put," she yells over the sound of the bombardment. "We're as safe here as anywhere. We'll just have to take our chances." She returns to the kitchen, presumably to consult with Nabil.

The students know a bomb from their own army could hit them at any moment. Or a swarm of beasts could barge through the door in search of shelter from the battle. But none do. The creations of the Sídhe obey whatever orders they've been given. Many of those outside, though injured by shrapnel or falling buildings, though they be burning alive, crawl onward, regardless, never once deviating from the path. Doubtless large numbers of them will make it through to the human defenders, wherever they are. The retreat of the army will go on and on. All the way back to Dublin.

And once there . . .

Anto imagines the people living in the city. His parents. The twins. His cheeky little sister. He feels nauseous. His great fist clenches, wanting to smash the traitor who allowed the Sídhe back in, the new king of Sligo. Whoever he is. Wherever he is.

They've got to get out of here, he thinks. They've got to get back home.

⁂

He staggers off in search of Nabil, finding him in the kitchen. Taaft has her arm around him, smiling lazily.

"I hate you," she says to the Frenchman. "But you'll do."

"Well," he replies sadly, "I don't hate you, Sergeant."

"It's only been ten years, Froggy. I'll get you there."

Anto taps the wall to get their attention. They step apart, although it's not the first time he's seen these two together. At least they're wearing clothes now.

"Surely we can't stay here," he says. "There are so many of them. If . . . if they get ahead of us we'll never make it home."

Taaft snorts. "Are you planning to carry us over the lines with that big arm of yours, kid?"

"No need to speak with him like that," Nabil says. "What the sergeant is saying, Anto, is—"

And that's when Liz Sweeney comes rushing in, her face red, her breath fast. "Giants! They have giants in the street. They're breaking the doors of all the houses and searching them. They'll be here in ten minutes."

That gets their attention.

"Ah," says Taaft, suddenly all business. "Then we'd better get out of here after all. We'll make a run out the back. The Arab can go first and find us another hideout. Me and Liz Sweeney to cover. You got any of those grenades left, kid?" Anto nods. "Keep them ready."

In no time at all they've gathered the others into the kitchen.

It's still early enough that the land outside is lost in shadow. But they scouted it well and they know that a vast overgrown garden lies out the back, with plenty of cover from the sky, even at this time of year. A vegetable patch lies between here and there though. A good ten yards to cross, with nothing to hide them other than the distraction of the bombing.

"Time to go," Nabil whispers. "Me first." He doesn't need to say who goes next. The instructors have been training them all week. They have a specific marching order, and every child right down to the youngest has been shown the rudiments of loading and firing the automatic weapons. "In case," Nabil said delicately, "either myself or Sergeant Taaft should fall while doing our duty."

"You might, Froggy," Taaft replied. "But I'm made of sterner stuff."

And now it's time to leave. The sky still flashes with bombs, while in the distance a whole street appears to be burning, sending a black pall of smoke into the freezing blue sky.

Nabil runs just like the soldiers out of the movies, his rifle ready for anything nasty that might be hiding in the first of the bushes. He disappears in among the frosty branches of a rhododendron.

"Wait!" Taaft warns Mitch, who's next in line. A whole minute passes before the Frenchman reappears and waves. "Now. Run, kid, and keep it quiet." Niamh goes next, followed by Krishnan, who breaks the rules by looking up over his shoulder.

"I swear," Taaft says, "one of these days I'll kill that boy." She curses again as he trips over his own feet, but already Andrea is out the door with a backpack of food bouncing on her shoulders.

"Anto! Get a move on."

Anto's face chills in the air immediately. His back hurts in all the usual places. It was never designed to carry an arm such as his. He has balanced it out a little by hanging a bag of supplies and grenades over his right shoulder, but it's far from ideal.

All this effort to survive, he thinks. And for what? Nessa is gone. The Sídhe are winning. Pushing into the heart of a country with no manufacturing capacity for new weapons. Every person they capture only adds to their strength while weakening the defenders.

"I'm moving on," Nabil tells him. "You're in charge now until Taaft comes over." He doesn't wait for acknowledgment, but disappears farther back into the garden.

Aoife appears at the back door. Her cheeks are red and her hair finger-length. She lowers her head and runs. Anto remembers how she saved his life once, forcing him through a window at the burning school. And then, later, fighting with him outside against the shrinking Sídhe. She's not the coward that Liz Sweeney takes her for. It's just that her heart has been torn out. That's all. Like his.

"I've found them!" a voice shouts suddenly. "I've caught them!"

It's one of the crow-women. It has swept down from the chimney of a nearby house and flaps frantically above the running girl's head. Its voice is too small surely to attract attention above the sound of the bombing, but Aoife stumbles to a halt, staring up at the creature in horror.

Anto jumps up from cover. "Come on, Aoife! Run!"

More crows are coming, all of them taking up the cry of alarm, flying in formation.

Aoife looks across the remaining five yards of the vegetable garden toward Anto. Her face screws up in sudden puzzlement.

And then she's gone. Her warm winter coat settles neatly on top of her tracksuit. It will never fit her again.

AMBROSIO

Nessa plunges down into a stand of greedy trees. They cushion her fall and she crawls away even as they begin fighting over her. "Crom twist you for saving my life!" she cries. But it doesn't stop her rolling downhill and pulling herself over a rock until she's lying in a shivering heap behind it.

Above her the spirals turn, indifferent to her plight. Some are small enough to be mere dots, others she couldn't cover with her fist. *Are they stars?* she wonders. *Could they be worlds in their own right?*

It's the sort of thing Mr. Hickey back at school would have loved. She can imagine the excitement in his voice; see him leaning forward, shooting ideas into the class like a gun. "What if the Grey Land's like a bus, calling from town to town? It's close to our world now, isn't it? Isn't that what has allowed the Sídhe to work their horrors on the children of Ireland? But when their world drifts away again, it must go somewhere, right? Somewhere *else*. Oh, the places the Sídhe could visit if their spite didn't poison them!"

They don't want other places though. They want Ireland. And according to the one she just escaped, they have already found a new king to revoke the treaty and let them back in.

Nessa pulls her gaze back to ground level. The flying beasts have gone and she sees no other life on the rocky slopes to threaten her. At this rate, it's hunger that will have the last laugh, and that's not such a bad way to go.

She stands, shaking all over, and begins trudging in the direction of the volcano. She'll find herself a cave too hot for the Sídhe. Then she can close her eyes for the last time. She'll dream of Christmas—not the one she's just had at home, but the one that hasn't happened yet, that will never happen, where Anto's parents are there too, and everybody's grinning and saying, "This is great! It's wonderful! But . . . but aren't you too young to be getting married?" And the happy couple will laugh. "Things are different now, you know? We're veterans. That makes us adults."

More than adults really.

They could apprentice themselves out to one of the thousands of elderly farmers without surviving children. He'd have a grumpy plow horse, but Nessa, Nessa would charm the fetlocks off him with wizened winter apples. She would press her face against his warm hide . . .

No! No! She clenches her fists. She *will* have all of those things still. She needs a place of safety, yes. Access to fire. But not so she can lie down and die. Nessa will plan. That's what she'll do. She will live, even if she has to eat rocks, or the Sídhe themselves.

Something flies at Nessa's forehead just as she's struggling across a flat stretch of cold mud. She ducks and feels a stinging line run across her scalp.

Here it comes again! A flittering thing, barely visible in the pale silver light. She swats at it, but misses as it darts to one side and finally hovers just out of reach.

It's a little man, she sees, with wings on his back that flutter too fast for the eye to follow and with a toothpick-sized spear in his hand.

"I don't want to crush you," she says wearily. "Go away."

"Such violence, my child!" he replies, although his voice is almost below her threshold of hearing. "I am a man of the Church. Father Ambrosio. Allow me to bless you! Any blessing you desire, and all I'll have in exchange is a single eyeball."

He bobs about in the air, seeming to take Nessa's lack of reply as a desire for more talk. "I can understand your reluctance, my child. Perhaps you think charity is for others only?" His voice is scolding now. But then, suddenly, it turns sad. "Or perhaps you despise me, holy beggar that I am. You refuse to put yourself in my rags, to imagine what it is like to be twisted by our pagan overlords so that you must eat eyeballs or suffer again the pain of your making." Father Ambrosio shudders. "Eyeballs are all I can think about. Oh, the taste of them! The fine juices, so expressive of sorrow. It's been too long already, I fear . . . You, lovely child, you are my last hope." He hovers a little closer, but still not close enough. "Why won't you speak? I am not a cruel man. Not at all! I will pray for you—entire decades of the rosary! Although God cannot hear us in hell. Or is this just purgatory, do you think? With somewhere even worse waiting for us?"

"You're not getting my eyeball," Nessa tells him.

He grins triumphantly. "I am. I will. I will have them both, and at my leisure! That mud you are standing on has trapped you, bless it! When your hands stop working, then, my child, I will do as I must. Unless that shameful thief Brother Peter gets to you first! But he's not here, is he? He's not! He's not! And it's all mine!"

Father Ambrosio has been talking for quite some time and now Nessa realizes why. For her legs, weak on the best of days, have grown positively numb. As though anesthetized. The lack of feeling has traveled as far as her knees already and creeps higher with every beat of her heart. No plants grow anywhere around her, and what she had taken to be twigs earlier are in fact the parched bones of other creatures.

The little man flutters a little closer.

"Exactly," he says with a grin, and follows the Sídhe word with a few phrases in Latin that are no doubt both witty and wise. "You cannot get away from it, my child! Not by yourself. But, if you're quick—if you let me take an eye now—I'll tell you how to escape the mud. But believe me, the moment you fall to the ground it will be too late for you and I'll have to be blessed careful not to get caught myself, do you see? An eye," he says. "Just one of them, and I'll tell you the trick of getting out."

"Do you promise?" she asks him.

The priest shudders, raising his hand in front of his face. "How dare you!" his little voice cries. "How dare you doubt me, a man of God!"

"It's just a promise," she says. "Promise you'll show me the way out."

"Very well then, I will give you my word. Is that what you want to hear? Look!" He cuts the palm of his hand with the tip of his spear. It's impossible to see, but he must be bleeding. "By my very blood, I will tell you the way. By the blood of Our Savior even!"

"Why won't you just promise it?"

"Curse you!" The priest is almost in tears. "Curse you! There *is* no way out, all right? I will have to risk myself now when you fail to escape. Can't you see how unjust that is? When it costs you nothing anyway? You are doomed, so why sully your soul with one more unnecessary cruelty? An eye! An eye! It's all that keeps the pain away!"

Nessa's legs shake. Lucky for her she has learned over many years to keep them locked in position, but how long will that keep her off the ground?

Five feet away, a hand-high ridge of stone shows her where the energy-sapping mud ends.

All right then.

She swings her arms as hard as she can, like twin pendulums.

"What are you doing, foolish child?" asks the priest. "Why won't you help me?"

At the third swing, she tries to kick forward with her legs. They fail to cooperate, but that too she is used to. The ground smacks into her belly and chest. Her fingers scrabble at the stone shelf.

By Crom and Lugh, it's cold! By Dagda! By Danú herself! Nessa's muscles spasm. The whole front of her torso goes numb.

"It's too late, you villain! Now you can't breathe!"

She doesn't need the little man to tell her that. Black motes swim before her eyes. New spasms ripple through her back so that it arches up, loosening her grip on the ridge, but she catches it again on the way down, and her arms, growing colder, but still working, jerk her body forward until she can get her head and neck out of the danger zone.

Yet the air won't come, for the mud still holds her chest, a dead weight, a nothing. Her heart begins to slow and her movements grow weaker.

Now the little spearman flies in for his attack, a barely visible fluttering in the darkening tunnel of her vision. Nessa's right hand swipes at him out of instinct. Then, with her biceps trembling like a dying bird, she heaves one last time, scraping herself bloody on the rock, collapsing on the far side of it.

Air! By the gods, air! Why won't it come? Instead there are stabbing pains all over her body and she knows the flying man has attacked again, and that she is gone.

The first surprise is that she wakes at all.

Nessa is a mass of bloody scratches on breasts and belly and legs. Random pains stab at her calves, but now she realizes this is just a sign of the numbness wearing off. At least she can breathe again, and even the rotten bleach-like air of the Grey Land comes as a welcome relief.

"Ah . . . You devil . . ."

Gingerly, she rises. The little priest is trapped between two rocks. He must have fallen there when she struck at him, and now, clear as day, one of his wings twitches uselessly.

"You . . . you have murdered me," he says.

There is an obvious reply to that, but Nessa can't be bothered making it. Megan's ghost, on the other hand, is full of suggestions. *Harvest those wings of his, Ness. They'll make great toilet paper.*

In spite of everything, Nessa can't help grinning. Megan would say something just like that if she were here. Or worse. Probably a lot worse. But Nessa should get moving now. The safety of the fire is calling her.

Just lie down . . .

But she can't, she can't. Nessa isn't capable of giving up even if the only home left to her is hell itself.

"At least kill me!"

She turns. The monk or priest or whatever he once was looks up from the two rocks that have trapped him.

"I'm nothing but food," Father Ambrosio says. "I would forgive you if you ate me. I mean . . . after. If you were . . . quick."

Earlier, she considered cannibalizing the Sídhe, but now the thought revolts her. Nor can she contemplate leaving the little creature to a lonely death. He cannot help what the Sídhe have made him, can he?

She frees him easily, pulling him up. He is naked apart from a little loincloth he must have made for himself. His body without the wings is no larger than her two hands and he weighs less than a robin would at home. He groans when his broken wing falls askew, tiny eyelids fluttering, body trembling.

"How long have you been in this form?" she asks him.

"Who can know such a thing in this place? A long time. Before that, I was a horse. But what does it matter, my child? Just do it. It is a kindness that God will forgive."

She could snap him in two. It would be the easiest thing in the world for hands like hers, but her stomach isn't up to the task and she has to fight against the nausea even as she grips him . . .

"Wait!" he cries. "I . . . I can't do it, my child. I . . . I've changed my mind. Leave me. Just leave me here."

Relief washes through her and her stomach unclenches. "If you insist," she whispers. Nessa is looking for a good place to put him down when she spots something. A tiny stick—his toothpick spear, with a point on it made of who knows what?

Doesn't matter. It makes an excellent splint that she ties on with a stray thread from the rags of her uniform. She hums as she works, a song of her mother's about the stubble fields of autumn. Then she rips yet another piece of her shirt away to make a sling for him.

"You're taking me with you?" Father Ambrosio asks, stupefied. "Why?"

"I don't know yet," she says. But it's a lie. Already the loneliness of this place is wearing her down. It's worse than the hunger, she thinks, not having anybody. Even one of the Sídhe's monsters seems like a gift from God right now.

Soon enough, she's heading back up the slope, her little enemy in the crook of one arm. She stumbles often in this rough terrain with no crutches and no obvious materials to make them from.

After a while the little man says, "Prolonging my life is a cruelty."

"You asked for it!"

"I asked to be left alone!" He waves a tiny hand. "Well then, let me repay your cruelty with cruelty of my own." She cocks an eyebrow at him. He's no stronger than a butterfly and his body is sheened with sweat.

"You can eat here," he says.

"What?" She stops walking. "Eat your miserable corpse, you mean?"

"That too, yes. But I meant you could do as our masters do and eat roots."

Out of nowhere, her mouth fills with enough saliva to drown in. Her head spins and she has to lean her weight against a rock. How right he is! This is cruelty indeed!

Seeing his arrow strike home, Father Ambrosio nods, smugly. "You know the way some of the trees bleed when you cut them?"

"That's edible?"

"By all the saints, of course not! That, my child, is the devil's vomit! But any plant that doesn't bleed has roots that will keep the likes of you alive."

"Impossible," she says. "We would know this. We have years and years of Testimonies . . ."

"Really, child? Your people come here to this land of horror—of *poisons*—and randomly eat things?"

"Oh," she says, feeling foolish, "I suppose not. Nobody would take the risk. We only ever stay here for a day." Her eyes travel over to a stand of spike bushes, harmless to all but the most foolish of travelers.

"What about . . . ?"

"Yes, my child," he says. "Those ones are edible. There'll even be water under there. And, yes, I need some too. Bless you and curse you."

Nessa is tired enough that she cuts herself a little when pulling the first bush out of the ground. As promised, a grey root comes up with it, and the center is soft enough to chew down easily. The girl expects it to taste as bitter as everything else in this place. To burn or to poison her, to drug her or turn her guts to water. Perhaps this is the little man's vengeance on her.

None of these things happens. Instead a mild, fruity sweetness fills her mouth and every tissue of her body quivers with relief. *Am I the first*, she wonders, *to find food in the Grey Land?* Nobody else who returned from a Call was ever here long enough for nourishment to be necessary, and who would want to risk it?

Father Ambrosio takes sips at the water the plant was hoarding but refuses the food. Nessa is too greedy to care.

It will be some days before the consequences of what she has done become apparent to her, and by then it will be too late.

In fact, it is already too late. The food has begun to change her.

She limps off in the direction of the lava she saw, bearing the little priest in a sling, keeping him well away from her eyes.

AOIFE

A oife waits all alone, bathed in sweat. Is it supposed to be so warm here? Maybe she's back in her stepfather's kitchen, asleep before the range as he tinkers with the old clocks he used to fix on the side.

But no, her nose wouldn't be streaming in his house. It wouldn't be stinging as the air attacks her mucous membranes. Her eyes are squeezed shut, but she forces them open.

In the distance, a beak-shaped mountain stabs through the horizon from below. She's standing on dry-packed earth in the midst of shattered rocks, while plumes of steam come belching through cracks. Is it poisonous? Maybe if she stays here, if she just lies down for a bit, the gas will finish her off. Maybe—

A horn blares. It's halfway between a screech and the sound of nails on a blackboard. It stands the hairs up on her head. It tells her time is up, that she really should have taken the pill when she had the chance, because her hosts are on their way, happier to see her than any mere human could be. Aoife freezes, but then her training takes charge.

Run! Run! Never stand still!

It's all slopes here. She skids down them, falls and cuts a knee. She climbs over a leg bone as large as she is, then dodges around webbed-over rocks where a small man-faced creature struggles and cries, "I didn't mean it!" over and over again.

She runs and runs. Eyes follow her every step. She can feel them. It's like an itch. Like needles.

And here comes the horn again! A hundred yards behind maybe. And, oh, Crom! There's another horn off out to the left. Two parties! Two groups that know she's here, that will race each other for the privilege of causing her more pain than any human can endure. And the sooner they catch her, the more time they'll have to do their work.

The slope is steep here. Would she break her neck if she dived forward? But what if she failed? They're bound to catch her then!

She skids between two boulders, yelps as a spike plant stabs her shin. The air now smells of rotting meat, of death and misery.

"I heard her!" cries a happy voice. "The thief is close."

"No!" calls another. "Drive her toward the Promise Holder! Think of the fun! Why else was she pulled *here*?"

"Oh, yes! Oh, yes!"

The Sídhe are just yards downslope of her, running parallel to her course behind a line of rocks.

Was Emma this afraid during her last moments? Did they drive her too toward a promise holder—whatever or whoever that is? Did they taunt her? Oh, how they defiled that body! The only one Aoife has ever loved. How they poisoned that skin, twisting its creamy surface into pus-filled cracks and scales! They murdered her. They murdered Emma and actually found it funny! Laughing like they're laughing now!

And Aoife screams. She has never made such a sound before, never felt such fury rippling through her sinews and bones. She surges left and, heedless of consequences, leaps. Speed, gravity, and hatred lift her over the rocks, a human cannonball that smashes into a group of Sídhe on the far side.

Bones snap—but not hers. She goes rolling and skidding away. She's still screaming though. She grabs at a branch on her way past, ripping it from a tree. Then she's back on her feet again, surging up *toward* the Sídhe.

There were only two of them, it seems. The one she landed on may be dead. The other applauds even as she charges toward him, and he's still laughing when she batters him to death with the branch and his own hunting horn. "Emma!" she cries. "Emma!"

Every muscle in Aoife's body is trembling. Blood covers her hands and two broken bodies lie before her, their huge eyes staring, their glittering skin bruised and torn where she struck at it. She is too tired for emotions. She wants only to lie down and sleep in the hopes of forgetting all of this.

"Ooh," says a lovely, lovely voice. "A feisty one!"

She drops the hunting horn. Standing on the rocks that she herself jumped over only moments before is a party of eight Sídhe. Two carry spears made of bone, although why they need weapons in this home of theirs, Aoife has no idea. Another grips a bow.

"Put an arrow in the thief's leg," one suggests. It's a man, his heroic arms bare but for an eyeless snake with human lips that twines around his left bicep. "We will have such a long time to play with it then."

One of the women tosses her head. "No! It's my turn and I want to see the look on its face when it meets the Promise Holder."

"I still say the arrow!" insists the man. The bow wielder lazily takes aim.

Aoife, her rage spent, doesn't so much as move until the arrow grazes her face. Then, out of nowhere, she has energy again, and enough terror to fill a stadium. She never even wonders how the archer could miss such an easy shot. All she knows is that there are too many to fight and they have all day to do whatever they want.

Their joyful shouts follow her. Their feet patter so lightly on the rocks behind her. It sounds like a summer shower.

Over to her right, soil shifts and Aoife hears a noise such as a sack would make when dragged over sand, but larger than that—a thousand times larger.

Her breath is turning ragged. She is wasting far too much energy on panic. She leaps between stones, spins away from the grasp of slimy, smoking weeds . . .

And then the dragging sound turns into something more like the ripping of a house-sized sheet of paper. The soil in front of her explodes. Lumps of dirt smack her in the face. Dust clogs the air, and rising before her is something like the body of a worm or a snake. Moist blinking eyes form a line along the top of it, while a hundred mouths make up the belly, each one snapping and cursing, licking at the air with human tongues, drooling, babbling. And the stench of their carnivore breath! The stench! A pair of lips cries, "Over here, girl!" Another cackles. A third pleads starvation in a foreign tongue.

The great body sways, ready to fall upon Aoife, who has nowhere to go except back toward the Sídhe. It has something resembling tentacles, but with fur. The tentacles snake across the ground toward her, twitching with anticipation, and she sees with revulsion that instead of suckers, the insides are lined with yet more clacking, drooling, hungry mouths. It will wrap her up, and rip her flesh away, all at once.

She freezes in terror, but then . . . the monster bursts into flame. One minute it's there, and the next its many mouths unite in a terrible scream. Another jet of fire shoots out from behind a boulder and ends its pain.

The silence that follows is complete. Even the vents pause in their belching of steam.

"It's all right," a voice says gently.

Aoife forces herself to turn, although she knows this is the end. The Sídhe drove her here, right to this spot, as surely as the farmer's dogs chase sheep toward the shears.

It's a woman this time. Just one by herself. And Aoife gasps when she sees who it is.

"Ness? Nessa?"

The relief fills Aoife's eyes with tears and sends her to her knees. Of course, she thinks, of course. She heard Nessa was exiled here. But instead of dying, she has been using her control of fire to stay alive.

"Nessa," she says again. "You saved my life."

The girl doesn't reply. She looks as though she can't, as though her jaw is locked in place. Her eyes seem so large in the dull silvery light, glistening with tears of their own.

Aoife rises, takes a step toward her. This is the bravest girl she has ever met. A familiar, friendly face to drive away the horror all around.

Then a tiny little man with wings lands on a boulder off to the side.

"She has nice eyes," he says, smiling.

"Ignore him," Nessa tells Aoife, as if the creature is a friend of hers, as familiar as Aoife herself. "You'll be safe with me. I don't know how you got here, Aoife. Maybe they're taunting me. Or you, for that matter. I don't know. But I have a cave where you can wait out the Call. And I hope . . . I hope you'll take a message back for me."

She holds out her hand. Aoife reaches to take it. It's the most natural thing in the world, after all. Even in this world. But with bare inches separating their fingertips, she hesitates. She looks up, meeting Nessa's large, puzzled eyes. There's something wrong with her friend. Something deeply, deeply wrong. And finally she sees what it is and her whole body goes cold with horror.

"Oh, Crom."

Then Aoife turns and begins to run, harder than she's ever run in her life.

She sees . . . some terrible things over the next few hours, or however long it really is. But none of them is as upsetting as her meeting with Nessa Doherty, the Promise Holder.

THE TRAP

The moment Aoife disappears and the crows start raising the alarm, Taaft and Liz Sweeney come running from the house. There's no point in keeping quiet now, is there?

"Follow Nabil!" Taaft cries. She means this command for Anto and the other students still crouching on the far side of the vegetable garden. Speed is of the essence now.

"They're here! They're here!" shout the crow-women. Liz Sweeney and Taaft barge into the bushes beside him.

"Move! Move!"

A fist the size of a child's head crashes through the side gate into the garden, and Anto knows there are giants on the other side. The next blow will knock it from its hinges and then the monsters will come trampling through Aoife's lost clothing.

"We can't leave her," he says.

Taaft punches him in the side of the head. She gets him by the collar and pushes him back into the bushes even as the gate splinters. Fronds whip at his face, spraying icy droplets down his collar, with Taaft, relentless Taaft, urging him deeper into the overgrown garden.

"No!" He tears himself free and turns back toward Aoife's empty clothing.

"Don't waste your breath," Liz Sweeney protests. "She'll come back dead anyway. You know her."

He does. And what he also knows is that Aoife's braver than they give her credit for. She deserves even the tiny chance at life the Grey Land affords them all.

"Run," he calls over his shoulder. "I'll slow them down for you."

"Thanks, kid," Taaft says. She's not the type to waste breath on a lost cause. "Let's go, Liz Sweeney."

Three giants have broken into the garden and they're standing in a circle around Aoife's clothing. Others can be heard tearing the house to pieces.

Anto has never seen them this close before. They have tiny heads—half the size of his own, with the features all scrunched one atop the other. Thick slabs of bone armor their upper bodies and each of them has a crow-woman clinging to their shoulders, whispering in their ears.

The whisper turns to a shout when the first grenade lands right at their feet.

"Run!" screeches a crow to her giant. "Run, you clod!"

It doesn't save them. The bang knocks Anto over and leaves his ears ringing. One of the giants crawls away, weeping exactly as a small child would: a hiccuping, pitiful sound that tears at Anto's heart. *That could have been me.* He was supposed to be one of them, after all.

The others are down and three crow-women are flapping around them in a circle. "Oh, no! My boy! My precious boy!"

A roar comes from the house. Two more giants burst free of the back door; one of them has the entire metal frame stuck around his shoulders, but he doesn't care, and the pair of them come charging across the garden, through the wreckage of their comrades and the burning rags that are all that remain of Aoife's clothes. Anto staggers to his feet as the first massive fist flies at his face. He ducks behind a tree.

"After him!" cries a crow's voice. "Circle left!"

The second giant is waiting for the boy on the far side. Anto parries a punch with his massive left arm, but his human legs buckle. Were it not for the fact that his enemy is still wearing the rusting door frame, he would die now. The frame catches among the springy branches. The boy dives free while the creature scrabbles at the foliage, whining in obvious distress.

Anto doesn't want to hurt it—the gods know he doesn't. But the evil left arm the Sídhe gave him has no such qualms. It strikes the monster, hard enough to crack bone.

"Ouch!" cries the giant. "I have an ouch!" Oh, Crom! Anto recoils at what he's done. The whole left side of its body is a crumpled, bleeding pulp of flesh.

And the crow-woman screams at him, "How dare you! You brute! You nasty brute!"

She dives at his eyes while Anto swats her away, queasy from the stench of blood and the harm he has inflicted.

And now the first giant, the one without the door frame, wraps him with two arms that might as well be bands of steel.

"Crush?" it asks.

Something lands on Anto's shoulder. He can't move. Even his left arm has finally met its match.

The crow-woman's "feet" are human hands, and the feeling of her perching there is exactly that of his own mother squeezing his shoulder in encouragement.

"Good boy, Malcolm," says the crow-woman. "Good boy. Yes. Crush his heart, but if you damage his face, whatever will I have for my supper?"

It will be quick, Anto thinks. *Good-bye, Nessa. Good-bye, my love. I know you weren't a traitor.*

The creature's muscles begin to flex. Not even a second remains before it brings its strength to bear, but that splinter of time is the boy's entire world. The giant's sharp sweat overwhelms his nose; the heat of its body is like a hearth at his back, and its breath wheezes slightly, and bubbles too as it prepares to obey the loving commands of the crow-woman.

But then a shot goes off and Anto is spattered with warm gore. The crow is gone, the grip loosened so that he tumbles to the icy earth. Another shot. Crow-women wail in terror and despair. "My boy! You hurt my boy!"

And suddenly Liz Sweeney's angry face is right above Anto's. It is one of the most welcome sights he has ever seen.

"I need you to help me with Aoife," she says, spitting the words at him. "Stupid cow is alive."

"You . . . you came back for me?"

"Well, *you* came back for *her*. What is it about that sterile heifer? You fancy her? You know she's not into boys, right? Oh, come on. Be quick about it."

Aoife lies trembling on a pile of her own smoldering clothing. They pick her up between them, while crows fly overhead, some weeping for their "lost boys," some still calling the alarm. But the swarm of monsters that earlier filled the road beyond has petered out.

They leave the crows behind, pushing through bushes and trees while Aoife shivers violently between them.

"Wait," says Anto. "This is far enough. Nobody's following. Let me give her my coat."

"Don't be an idiot. It's too big. And where will you loot another to fit around your arm? She can have mine. The little twist already made me waste the last two bullets in the gun, and now this! Bah! By Crom, it's cold."

But she's gentle in wrapping the coat around Aoife, and she winds the girl's feet in bandages to keep them warm. "Of all the people to survive the Grey Land," she mutters. Then her heroic brow creases. Perhaps Liz Sweeney is realizing that she's the last Year 5 who has yet to be Called. It could take her any second now. Or it might drag the tension out over another two years. "Bah," she says again. "But at least we can be sure Aoife's no traitor."

"We can?" asks Anto.

Liz Sweeney looks at him scornfully. She has such a proud face. Strong too. Free of doubt. "The Sídhe don't need anyone else. They've already won, haven't they? The king has let them in."

"If they've won, how come I've only seen one of them since the invasion? They should be . . . I don't know . . . enjoying this. Taking a bigger part in it. Instead they send monsters to do all their work for them."

She sneers. "Scared, I'd say."

Anto can't agree. "They're never scared. Only happy."

As though she is listening, Aoife shudders. But her eyes are screwed tightly shut and she mutters prayers to herself. Who knows what she's seen?

"We need to keep moving," Liz Sweeney says. "The others will have gone on, thinking we're dead."

But at that very moment Nabil appears right beside them. "No more talking," he whispers, but his brown eyes are shining. Then he shocks Anto by hugging them both. "You are heroes," he says. He throws Aoife over his shoulder as though she weighs nothing and leads them off to where the others are waiting two fields away.

Taaft has scowls for both Anto and Liz Sweeney. "You got lucky" is the most she can manage, and Liz Sweeney hangs her head as though deeply ashamed. Clothing is volunteered by the students to replace what Aoife has lost. The wind is rising and all seven of the children are shivering, although they have squeezed together like penguins with Aoife right in the center.

Behind them, the shelling has come to an end. To the west, fires spread through the center of town. Nabil suggests they return to a shop that they looted on the way in. "We need to get Aoife at the shelter," he says.

"*In* the shelter," Taaft mutters. "Can't you ever learn English?"

"Can't you learn Sídhe?"

"The enemy's tongue?"

"The *children's* tongue."

"Ha! It's more an advantage to the Sídhe we speak their garbage language than to us. Always has been. They'd never have gotten a king without it!"

"They would," says Liz Sweeney, although it's not like her to contradict her hero, Taaft. "They'd make another envoy like the one with three heads at the school . . ."

Everybody knows the smart thing is to stay put and wait for darkness. But they'll lose Aoife and possibly some of the others to cold if they do that. Instead they cross open fields to a nearby farm. And here they find the first signs that the evacuation of Longford wasn't as smooth or as easy as it first appeared. A dozen giants lie broken on the ground, along with great numbers of sniffers, centaurs, and other monsters the group has yet to encounter. *How,* Anto thinks, *did that thing with the hooves even walk?*

Inside the barn, dead soldiers lie scattered about among bales of hay.

Andrea stares, fascinated. "Why do all of them have gunshots to the head?"

"You must be stupid," Liz Sweeney tells her. "They shot themselves. Any who didn't will be a monster by now."

"They were brave," says Nabil. "And they left us their guns. You can have one each."

Taaft can't believe it. She laughs and shakes her head. "Oh, you messed-up frog. I don't care that you showed the kids how to shoot, but you gotta know they're more likely to blow off their own feet than to hit a Sídhe, right?"

"They deserve a chance" is his only reply. "Here, my friend," he says to Anto. He hands the boy a pistol. "Better for your arm than a rifle."

"Thanks."

Anto turns to find that Aoife is awake and that she's staring right at him. She's not fully herself, he can see that. She gapes at him, a look of utter sadness on her face. And when she speaks her voice is far too loud, as though she is unaware the enemy is hunting them.

"I'm sorry," she says. "I'm sorry, Anto. I saw . . . I saw Nessa. I think I was meant to. I think they . . . wanted me to. I saw her!"

He can only stare back, his heart lodged in his throat. But this is far, far too important and he forces himself to speak.

"Is she . . . is she alive?"

Aoife tries to answer him, but she's sobbing too much. The best she can manage is a nod. Yet he can tell that this is not good news.

"Have . . ." His arm aches with the pain of its making. Blood pounds in his ears. "Have they turned her into . . . ?" He waves outside to where the dead monsters lie.

"It's worse." Aoife is hoarse now after her earlier outburst. "She almost had me. I saw. I mean, it *was* her. Definitely her. The way she walked was the same, but . . ."

"What?" Tears run down his face.

"The whole thing was a trick. She was pretending to save me. But then I saw her skin. At the last minute. Her eyes are bigger than they were before. And her skin . . . Anto, her skin *glitters*." Her voice rises to a screech. "It glitters!"

THE LOWEST EBB

Anto has been particularly stupid. He ran when Aoife told him what she'd seen. He had to get away from it. And so here he is, outside, alone. Exposed to every danger.

Far overhead, beautiful voices sing in harmony. Angels, Niamh calls them, although the creatures making the music are hideous to behold, with their batlike wings and a trailing skirt of tentacles. They could so easily swoop on the foolish boy. But these two already carry prisoners, trussed up like presents for their Sídhe masters.

Anto doesn't care anyway.

He stumbles in between vast rusting sheds, his back aching from the weight of his arm. He doesn't want to think about her, about Nessa. He can't. Anything but that.

Behind a window are twenty-five-year-old election posters for the crisis government. Nobody has voted since. Ministers die in office, to be replaced by somebody almost as old as they are. They sign orders. They decide who gets medicine and who does not. They apportion guilt without courts, and sometimes . . . sometimes they get it right.

But there's a new ruler now. At least in Sligo there is. The lowest of the low. Worse than any minister with a red pen denying medicine and food to the old and the sick. Worse than the Sídhe themselves . . .

The posters blur in his vision and a great, racking sob tears through his chest. There's no escaping Aoife's terrible news. He can't deny it anymore. The king, it seems, was not the only one to betray Ireland. "Nessa," he whispers. He pushes at the sides of his head, as though he needs to protect the world from the madness within. His gut churns, nausea creeps up his throat. "My . . . my Nessa. My heart." And his lips grimace and twist like tortured worms until, eventually, they spit out a new word for her, for the only love of his life. "Traitor. My girl is a traitor."

But then he jumps, because a voice answers him from the shadows. "Yes, a traitor! I bet she slept with all the boys."

One of the little crows hops onto the creaking roof of the nearest shed. This one has a man's face, no bigger than his right fist, wearing a scraggly beard. "You are right to weep for her," it says. "Tears. Bitter, bitter tears."

"I don't know how I can feel this way," Anto says, "after the . . . the terrible things I have seen. Friends killed. The whole country dying and . . . and no way home."

It cocks its head, the human eyes blinking rapidly. "That's good." It has such a kind voice. So understanding. "That's very good. It means the end is near."

"I know." Inside, behind Anto's grief, lies a yawning emptiness.

"There's really no point," the bird-man continues. "You should kill yourself."

Why not? Anto thinks. He has nothing. No future, certainly, and no past he wants to revisit. Nessa has poisoned all that. And what of the present? In his mind's eye, he sees the soldiers back at the barn where the others are. Each one dead with a single shot. They were smart. He should be smart too.

He draws the pistol at his belt, studying it in the grey light. It will be quick. His hand won't even shake, he's sure of that, for he feels nothing, is nothing.

The bird waits. It must know there's a movie reel of horrors playing in Anto's skull, doing its work for it. But the poor creature just can't leave well enough alone and it whispers, "You think you're at your lowest ebb, my boy, but you're not. It's going to get worse, a *lot* worse."

Anto looks up. "How?" But he knows the answer.

He's a freak: a boy with a mouse's heart, who would prefer to trip over rather than crush an ant. And seeing this in him, as one of their jokes, the Sídhe pumped his arm full of spite. He's no better than a weapon now. Only good for violence and pain.

And suddenly, impossibly, Anto laughs. "You are a funny little thing, aren't you?"

"I . . . I'm just doing my job."

The boy stands, and it seems that all his sorrow and guilt slide off his shoulders to smash themselves on the rubble below. He flexes a massive fist. He has seen it break walls and doors. It has shattered bones like eggshells, with neither feeling nor conscience. And all the while, poor, pitiful Anto, the "nice guy," the vegetarian, the pacifist, has fought to contain its evil.

He laughs again; he can't help it. How simple it all is. It is time to give in. To accept the gift of the Sídhe and embrace the pleasures of destruction rather than hiding from them.

No more mercy! No more holding back! The Nation needs warriors, not whiners.

"Thank you," he tells the bird. Then his unnatural left arm wrenches free a piece of the drainpipe and, before the crow-man can flee, he has smashed the creature to a pulp. He's breathing hard, grinning. He's alive again. Alive.

When finally he turns to leave, he finds Liz Sweeney standing right behind him. He has no idea how long she's been there.

"How much did you hear?" he asks. Not that it matters.

The girl looks at him with her head cocked to one side. Her fine, athletic frame displays caution, but no fear. No need for that when she carries her new rifle as though she was born with it. Liz Sweeney, he realizes, is a warrior too, worthy of respect.

"I heard enough," she says at last.

"Enough for what?"

"It's good you got over that traitorous sow."

Anto's vision turns dark for a moment—his giant fist clenches. But he forces it to relax. She's right, isn't she? How can there be more tears? Even now? Angrily he blinks them away. He is a new man. He will make himself a terror for the Sídhe.

"Did Nabil send you for me?" he asks.

Her face reddens. "No."

That's when they hear the gunshots.

For a moment Anto freezes, thinking he has abandoned his friends only for them to suffer a terrible attack. But the action is more distant than that. He sees a flash on the horizon and realizes somebody is fighting there. An advance, he thinks. The army is pushing the Sídhe back. Which means . . . which means if he and his friends can get there, they might find a way over to their own lines!

If nothing else, it's a chance for the new Anto, the weapon, to be unleashed.

———

They run back to the barn together, excited to share the news. Nabil has already heard the shooting, however. He shakes his head sadly when Anto suggests it's an advance by the Irish army.

"No, my friend. It's just another little group like ours." He points to the dead soldiers whose pockets are still being looted by the students. "Or like these. Left behind by the retreat. Well, the enemy has found them now."

"Let's help them, then!" says Taaft.

"Sarah"—he touches her arm and lowers his voice, but Anto is close enough to hear everything—"our duty is to keep them alive. All the children."

"It's war now, you idiot. Don't you see that? And here comes a gift, dropping right into our laps. Allies! Professionals. And with most of the fighting off east, the enemy will have their backs to us and their trousers down."

The others are all enthusiastic, waving guns that are too big and too dangerous for them. Apart from Aoife, who's sleeping like the dead. Anto's glad of that. The weak part of him—the pathetic lover boy who won't give up on the dream of Nessa—is still hoping to make a comeback. All this old Anto needs is a word of hope from Aoife. Maybe she'll say she imagined it all. Or lied for some reason.

But Aoife keeps her eyes closed and the new Anto clenches his massive fist, ready for battle.

Nabil stands blocking the door. "We can take them," Taaft says. Anto growls. Liz Sweeney grins beside him, gripping the boy's normal arm in her excitement.

"It is madness," Nabil insists. "All this hiding is hard, yes. But we have our duty, Sarah, our duty."

"It's Sergeant Taaft to you, Froggy. Ma'am, if you prefer. Now step aside."

"Wait for dark. We won't be seen from the air."

He won't move, so she punches him hard, once, in the stomach. He shows nothing. "We're going," Taaft says. "Not you, Mitch. Stay with Aoife. Shoot her in the head if we don't make it back."

"I can't stop you," Nabil says at last. He hangs his head, as though deeply ashamed. "I'll back you up."

"I know you will." Taaft shocks them all by kissing him on the lips, as though they were alone together with only God watching. Then she leads them outside.

A DOZEN STEPS

A mountain dominates the horizon, its shape as cruel as a crow's beak, its summit a magnet for lightning, for spinning tornadoes and flocks of piranha bats in constant wheeling motion. Nessa wants nothing to do with the place. The Sídhe, however, have different ideas.

She crouches next to a fire she has made, her bones already full of its heat, while her enemies giggle somewhere out of sight.

"If they think they can drive me toward Dagda," she tells Father Ambrosio, "they have another thing coming!" She has burned several of the enemy in the past few "days." The rest have learned caution, but not fear.

The sound of their laughter merely heightens her loneliness.

Oh, Aoife, she thinks. *Why did you run from me?*

Nessa has slept three times since her old classmate appeared on her Call. If she had just waited! Another human. An actual human to talk to. Her arms flex. Nessa is not the hugging type. Far from it. But if she had Aoife here now, she would squeeze her half to death.

Instead she has to swallow the sobs that would only delight her enemies.

Father Ambrosio clears his throat.

"She ran because of your skin, child."

The girl refuses to look at her own hands, but she knows they glitter in the firelight. Her eyes too see deeper into the shadows than ought to be possible. They're too large, belonging more to a cartoon character than a human.

"The roots are changing you. You shouldn't have consumed them."

"You told me to!"

"I told you it was possible. And now I'll tell you this, which you ought to have known. Nobody who eats the food of fairyland can ever return home."

"You're wrong!" She must have shouted, because the laughter of the enemy increases whenever she does that. The last time was when she woke from a doze to find the priest licking his lips and sneaking toward her face.

"You're wrong," she repeats, more quietly. "I'll go back to normal when I get out of the Grey Land."

He shakes his head, filling her with so much anger that flame dribbles from the tips of her fingers.

"I'll find a way home, priest. You'll see. I'll head back to the beach where I came in. People arrive by sea all the time. I bet there's a way out there too."

He sighs a tiny sigh. "If that's your plan, why don't we start walking toward the coast?"

"That's exactly what I've been doing. Haven't you noticed? I just need to keep that mountain at my back."

"And yet," he says, "it grows no smaller."

She swallows, feeling the grit in her throat that never leaves her here. "That . . . that must be an illusion. We've been walking and walking . . ."

"Oh, dear child . . ." His splinted wing flutters. "God does not listen to us in hell. He never heard my prayers when the devils first caught me and turned me into a horse for their sport. Or again, later, when they transformed me into this pitiful wretch you see before you. The pain, my child! The pain! That was the only answer I got. But . . . but I tell you this: I pray every day that my wing heals before we pass beyond that mountain, because . . . because . . ."

He starts to weep. At least she thinks that's what he's doing; it's hard to hear.

"You don't need to worry," she tells him gently. "We're not going there. I'll never bring you anywhere near there."

"Ah, you foolish girl!" he cries, all bitterness now. "You . . . have . . . promised. To see Dagda. Don't you understand anything? There is no getting out of it. You will see him."

"I would kill myself first!"

"No. You won't. You can die, of course, if a boulder falls on you, or a whipper catches you just right . . . But you can't choose death for yourself until your obligations are completed. You can't kill yourself any more than I can."

"Why not?"

"It is part of our making, we creatures of hell, that we must always seek to preserve this wretched existence for as long as we can. It's why I begged you to kill me and then begged you to stop. Do you remember? I don't have it the worst. God help me, I know that. You should see the dogs! Some of our masters' clothing is even alive. Forever! Oh, the pain! The pain!"

He is breathing dangerously fast. "You," he says, "will travel to see Dagda."

"I won't," she whispers.

"You will. And he will turn you into something beyond terrible. Because he's the most evil of them all. He is Lucifer himself. He designs his creations especially to suffer. To hunger for the agony of others."

Don't listen to him! Megan hisses. *He's not worth wiping your arse on!*

Nessa staggers away from him. She looks toward the crow's beak mountain. Is it true? Is it pulling her closer with every step? She experiments, turning first one way and then the other. She feels no attraction whatsoever. Nothing. The relief of it! Her heart steadies; her breathing slows.

"You scared me, Father Ambrosio," she says, finding her first smile in this place. She lifts him up into the crook of her arm. "But we're going to be OK. Come on."

She turns her back to the mountain and strides forward, fire at the ready in case her tormentors should show themselves. She waves away flecks of ash that fall in her eyes, wheezing only a little in the burning air. It's easy! Along the way she fills her belly with roots, before setting off again.

"Is it night or day?" she asks her passenger.

He shrugs, as if to say, *I've done my talking.*

"I just thought you might know." Again a shrug. "We'll sleep here," she decides. "We can hide among those boulders and continue when we wake."

She looks back toward the crow's beak, to reassure herself that it still lies behind her, that she hasn't been going the wrong way these last few hours. She smiles to see that all is as it should be. "I'm sorry," she tells Father Ambrosio. "I'm going to have to put you between a pair of rocks so I can get some sleep. I like my eyeballs just where they are."

He shakes his tiny head, and then, with a voice full of genuine pity, he says, "You do realize, you poor girl, that you have walked no more than a dozen steps?"

It can't be true. It can't. But there, just behind her, lies the blackened shape of the last fire she made.

"No," she whispers. "No." Her weak left leg gives way, leaving her on her knees, her face in her hands.

And now the laughter increases. It comes from behind bushes and rocks; from dips in the ground hidden by puffs of steam drifting out of volcanic vents. The enemy have seen her abject failure to escape her fate.

One by one, they rise from their hiding places. Only four, it seems: three women in glittering costumes of spider silk and metal; one prince, too lovely to exist even in a movie.

"You have learned," he says. "How wonderful! You will keep your promise. Our only wish is to have the joy of escorting you. To see—"

He halts, mouth hanging open, as Nessa raises her gaze to his. He must have expected despair. Instead the human girl is laughing at him, laughing at all of them. He cocks his head. Pleased, but puzzled.

She sets a bush alight with a wave of her hand, before touching it again and absorbing its heat.

"I am grateful to you," she tells the prince. "I was running from my promise."

The four Sídhe exchange smiles with each other.

"That was stupid of me," Nessa says, "because the answer was obvious all along."

"What answer?" he asks.

"Your invasion of the Many-Colored Land has already begun, has it not?"

They nod, delighted, eager.

"Well"—she smiles back at them—"that means you must have opened a door. A door that will take me home."

The prince shakes his head. They all do. "There is no escape, sweet thief. For you will have to see Dagda first. And then Conor will—"

She need only point to set him on fire, and that's what she does. She burns the prince. She burns all of them.

"Not the heads!" screams Father Ambrosio. "Curse you! I don't like them cooked!"

And later, when they're walking again, this time directly toward that terrible mountain, with all its lightning and other horrors, the priest says, "Those devils were right, you know? When Dagda sees you—"

"He won't."

"But your—"

"The Sídhe gave me the answer, the fools. I'll just do what they did. I'll spy on him from a distance. I'll see Dagda all right. But he won't see me. And I'm making another promise, a new one—"

"Don't!" he says. "My child! Don't be foolish!"

"I am, Father, but it's a promise to myself, and to God or the gods or whoever's listening. I have decided to win. I'm promising that I will beat this place and that I will see Anto. Do you hear me? I, Nessa Doherty, promise that I'm going home!"

There's no shiver in the air such as accompanied her first promise, but she feels one inside her chest that is every bit as powerful.

MORRIS

For all of Taaft's eagerness, she won't let them move faster than a steady jog.

"Whoever the defenders are," she says, "they'll hold out a few more minutes. We've got to be smart in helping them."

Anto is struggling to keep up. His back burns with agony, his breath puffs in front of his face, and all he can hear is the crunch of everybody's boots in the snow. Determination pushes him on. That, and the fairy limb, throbbing with the urge to pound and smash.

You'll get your chance, he tells it.

Liz Sweeney stalks at his side like the pale goddess of war. Andrea holds her rifle away from her body as though she's more afraid of it than of the enemy. And probably she should be.

Ahead of them, the siege is heating up. An angel swoops out of the clouds overhead, smoke and light pouring from whatever it grips in its tendrils.

The monster drops out of sight behind some nearby trees. Gunfire follows. The creature struggles back into the air, and then falls to earth over the far side of the road. But in its wake it has left behind . . . fire!

"Never seen them bomb things before," breathes Liz Sweeney.

And now they hear the sudden roaring of sniffers. The shouts of giants and the noise of a dozen guns all firing at once, even as the flames seem to increase. Somebody is shouting in English. "Fight, curse ye! Fight!"

"Let's go!" Taaft calls, and everybody surges forward at once, toward danger and death. Even Nabil seems to have forgotten he's there to protect the children. The gentleness of his scarred face has fallen away to reveal whatever it was that drove him to Ireland in the first place. The thing he was and never wanted to be again.

They've had a week of hiding. Of running away while their country and their families fought against the horror on their behalf. And now—for once!—they can do something good. Something right. They'll rescue a few of their own or die in the attempt.

Beyond a rotting fence lies a cluster of farmhouses. One whole wing burns while sniffers—a cross between a lion and an elephant with a blade for a trunk—stand silhouetted in front of it.

"No farther!" roars Taaft. "Only a fool wants to get shot by their own side! Kneel and fire. Like you were taught. Take your time. Don't waste your bullets." They spread out, pluming the cold air with their panting breath, rifles raised. Other than Liz Sweeney, none of the kids has fired a real bullet before. But they want this and they have Nabil and Taaft to stiffen the line. Neither of the instructors knows how to miss at this range.

Anto still has a few grenades. He launches the first just as the others open up. In half a minute a dozen monsters fall. More go down before the enemy even realize that the bullets are coming from behind rather than from the trapped defenders.

There's a roaring inside one of the buildings. A giant emerges on fire, his scream high-pitched and pitiful, but even as he falls to his knees he manages to point out into the fields and that's enough. Two of his fellows who have been tearing lumps off a wall with their bare hands turn now and come lumbering toward their new human attackers, each with a crow-woman flying overhead and urging it on.

"The knees!" shouts Nabil. "Go for the knees!"

Thick plates of bone make the head a bad target, and more slabs of it cover the torso. A giant falls, weeping from the pain, so that everybody is raining fire on the remaining one, while its crow-woman guide shouts, "My boy! They're murdering my boy!"

"Look out!" cries Krishnan. The first giant hasn't given up. He has found a lump of rubble. Krishnan turns his gun on the beast, but he's forgotten how to reload and now it's too late. There's a warm splash of blood and Andrea is simply gone.

"Keep firing!" shouts Taaft. The second giant goes down, but suddenly the sniffers are here. Their sinuous, feline bodies seem to squirt out of the glare of the flames.

A sniffer's trunk whips toward Anto's face. Its sharpened edge shears through the hot barrel of the boy's pistol, but then he catches it with his great fist. Oh, it feels good! No regrets! Power and more power. He hits again and again, shouting he knows not what.

To his right, Liz Sweeney growls, half panicked, half furious, "Crom take you all!" But her gun goes off.

It's mostly quiet after that. The whimpering of a giant. The crackle of flames. To Anto's left, Niamh lies broken, empty eyes staring up as the moon emerges from the clouds. He wanted a fight, didn't he? He needed it. They lost two of their own, but so what? This is the world now. As it is. As it always was.

Taaft is grinning. The years have fallen away from her, her shoulders straighter than ever, and Nabil . . . Nabil can't look at her, such is his anger. He never wanted to come. Not at the risk of the students' lives.

Taaft pays him no heed. "We need to check for survivors inside."

"I'll go," says Liz Sweeney. Her smooth skin glistens with perspiration. "Come on, Anto. You're coming with me."

He feels giddy. Like he's clinging high up on the outside of a building, buffeted by winds, but knowing he's strong enough to hold on. Cautiously they creep forward until a single shot brings them to a halt. "We're human!" Anto calls, careful to speak in English.

"How do I know that?" The speaker follows up his words with a fit of coughing.

"It's all right," says Liz Sweeney. She rarely talks English. It makes her sound childish, or innocent somehow. "Come on out. What choice do you have anyway? You want to burn?"

"Better than getting twisted! Oh, to hell with it. I'm coming. Relax the cacks."

A tall young man ducks out through the smoke, his eyes streaming, his body like that of a Greek statue. An earlier age would have made him a movie star, or a model at the very least.

"Any others?" asks Anto.

"I don't understand." His voice is resonant, despite the smoke, his grin confident.

"It's a simple enough question," Anto says, but Liz Sweeney has caught on quicker than Anto. She repeats the demand, but in English this time.

"Ah! Well, I'm all on my lonesome, I'm afraid. The others preferred a bullet when they thought there was no way out." He grins. "You should have come an hour ago; you might have found them still in one piece."

"Don't you . . . don't you speak Sídhe?"

"Not a word. My parents didn't believe in survival colleges."

"And yet you . . . you lived through the Call?"

"Ooh! Hashtag stating the obvious! Doh!"

There's something about him that puzzles Anto. It's not that he got out of the Grey Land despite missing out on a college. Such things have happened before. Indeed, in the beginning, the tiny number of survivors had no other choice.

Perhaps it's just jealousy, he thinks, for the contrast between the man's physical perfection and his own Sídhe-twisted arm. But he'll have to think about that later. For now, even Liz Sweeney is too tired to probe for information. And Taaft will want them to get as far from this fire as possible, before something worse than the sniffers comes to check it out.

But first they feed Niamh and Andrea to the flames. Nabil insists on it. He closes their eyes, more tender than any parent, hissing at anyone who treats the bodies roughly.

"It's not like they're going to wake up!" Liz Sweeney mutters. All she gets for her trouble are scowls.

And then the group, along with the man they rescued, run back the way they came.

The stranger keeps up effortlessly. He seems to be in his early twenties, athletic and handsome. "Call me Morris!" he says. Morris's eyes gleam with enthusiasm as though everything he looks at belongs to him and meets his approval.

"You're cheerful," Anto growls. "Didn't you lose friends today too?" He trips over the English. It's just not the right language to use with somebody so close to him in age. And the response he gets in return is so full of bizarre words it barely makes any sense at all.

"An absolute crap-tastrophe," Morris says. His grin is the whitest thing in the universe. "But I'm no snowflake. I've seen some real shitshows in my time."

Anto gives up trying to understand him, putting his head down until they get back to the shed and the others.

———

It's dark by then. Everyone is wrung out. Not just from the fighting but from half a night spent crouching in terror as shells rained down and an army of monsters marched past. Everyone wants to throw themselves down to sleep, but Nabil drags them out again to find a proper house to hide in. Two more hours pass until he's satisfied.

They stumble inside, racking the cupboards for food, finding nothing.

"I'll get supplies," Nabil tells them. He's still angry with Taaft, Anto thinks, and probably just wants to get away for a while. But she has other ideas. "Good. I'm with you, Froggy. Somebody, set a watch. You know what to do by now." And with that, the two instructors are gone.

Liz Sweeney is already snoring on the only sofa, her gun perched dangerously against her face. Seán, Mitch, and Krishnan all huddle together for warmth, their breathing beginning to slow.

Anto feels the pull of sleep himself. He's been half swallowed by the most comfortable armchair he's ever sat in, so that for the first time in weeks his back feels perfectly normal. And his arm . . . he senses that it too is *satisfied*. He has set it free, fed it on savagery, so that now all it needs is rest.

But somebody is staring at him from the corner of the room. Aoife, her eyes glistening in the dark.

"You must hate me," she whispers.

It's not Aoife's fault she saw what she saw, but all he can manage to reassure her with is a clearing of the throat.

"Listen," she says. "I know how . . . how you feel. I do, because I was the same when Emma died. I just wanted to sleep and never have to face it and . . . and I begged Ms. Breen back at school, I . . . I begged her for the pill."

Anto nods. He knows the pill she means and why she wanted it.

"I was wrong, asking to die," Aoife says. "I didn't know that until I was *there*. I didn't understand the point of the whole thing."

"There is no point." Anto's voice is a hideous growl that has Mitch whimpering in his sleep. "The Sídhe will win. You escaped the Grey Land, we both did, and it followed us home. You should have taken your pill." His arm flexes restlessly.

"Sure," Aoife says. "The darkness wins in the end; I know that. But here's the thing I realized: Emma died. My stepdad died. Babunia too. But not before they made *me* happy. For a while. For a bit. It wasn't permanent, but sometimes it was *so* sweet. Gods, those kisses I had! Cakes too. And stories when I woke after a nightmare."

What is she even talking about? Anto just wants to sleep; that's all he wants.

"I'm going to live now, Anto. Not so that we can win, but to . . . to, you know . . ." He doesn't. "So that *I* can make some difference to somebody else. To anybody. If I'd taken the pill I'd never have had the chance. But I do now. Do you see?"

Perhaps Aoife thinks his sleep-heavy head nods, because she nods back and finally—finally!—she closes her eyes and he can rest. Oh, gods, how he needs it.

But then he suddenly remembers the young man they rescued from the farm. Morris. He must still be in the cold kitchen alone.

Anto forces himself into wakefulness. Why should it matter? Why should anything matter? But the thought of being vulnerable before this stranger makes him deeply uncomfortable.

"Oh, relax the cacks," Morris whispers when the boy comes in. "I'm happy to take first watch. I imagine I'm more rested than you lot. We Sligo men are tougher than we look."

"You're from Sligo?"

"*Was* from Sligo! Past tense. Hashtag OMG. Whole place is taken over. They have a king now. That's all the Sídhe needed. Somebody to revoke the treaty that banned them from coming back to Ireland." He grins as though the whole thing is a joke. Then he stretches like a cat, perfectly at home.

"Well," says Anto, "I'm sorry, Morris, but I'm going to have to tie you up for the night."

The stranger's eyes narrow. The two of them are as good as alone now, for a bomb wouldn't wake the others. Morris holds a rifle. He is at the very peak of physical fitness and looks as relaxed as a man climbing out of a warm bath.

"I see your arm there, lad," he says. "How do I know you're not one of *their* creations?"

"We just pulled you out of a trap."

"Too right. You just rescued me. From the Sídhe. That's why you should trust me."

Anto is too tired to argue.

The stranger grins. "A point for me!" he says.

His face is so . . . *clean*. There's no other word for it. He reminds Anto of a pop star from one of Granny's boy bands, his teeth straight enough that a master builder might have placed each of them by hand. He seems to swim in Anto's vision, so tired is he. His knees are trembling.

"All right, then," Anto says, nodding.

Morris nods back, and that's when Anto hits him—right hand only, but hard enough to distract so that his long and irresistible left arm can wrap around the man and pin him to the ground.

"What . . . WTF! Don't you know who I am?"

"No," says Anto, flipping him over onto his stomach. "That's the point."

Anto puts his knee in the small of Morris's back to hold him down. There's something hard there, but he ignores it. He stuffs a dusty rag into the man's mouth and ties his hands with his own belt. Then, to sounds of muffled outrage and the bucking of his prisoner, he finds a bit of rope from one of the packs and ties Morris's wrists to his ankles.

Then, and only then, can he sleep.

THE HURT

U p! Wake up!"

Sergeant Taaft can rock entire buildings when she shouts. They've all been asleep, huddled together in a pile for warmth. Aoife stares around herself as if she has no idea who any of them are. Liz Sweeney curses the rifle she must have been sleeping on the whole night.

"Up!" says Taaft again.

Nabil is at her shoulder, his scarred face serene. "We're not under attack," he says, "but you must explain why this man has been tied up."

It's Morris of course. Groaning and shaking in the corner. The room smells of his urine, and from the quality of the light through the crack in the curtains, Anto realizes they must have slept through to late afternoon, with Morris unable to get out to relieve himself, lying alone in the freezing cold.

"Well?" says Taaft, looking around.

"I'm . . . I . . ." Anto scrambles to his feet. "I'll let him go now, Sergeant."

"Oh," she says, her face hard as marble. "You bet your ass you will!"

Anto has no idea how he managed to make such fine knots last night, but the huge fingers of his left hand are far too clumsy to untie them now, so he cuts them open with his knife instead.

Morris is gibbering, unable to get even a sob out through his chattering teeth. Anto tries to help him stand—*what was I thinking?*— but the man pushes him violently away before falling over due to a lack of circulation. Everyone can see the stain on the front of his fine trousers.

"You've lost it, kid," says Taaft to Anto. But there's no heat in her words. His sin is minor in the scheme of things. She's about to say something else, but the moment she opens her mouth she is drowned out by the singing.

They've all heard angels before. Their beautiful voices are a promise of attacks, but now it's like a huge choir has come to life right above them. A thousand throats opening up, and every one in perfect harmony with its fellows, male and female, piping children, baritones, sopranos, bass.

The room shakes with sound, so that everybody reaches for something to hold on to. Mitch weeps. Aoife's round face is stretched toward the ceiling as though she wishes she could fly up through it to join the singers.

And then it fades.

"Listen," says Nabil, "my friends. There is some news." They can tell from his face what kind of news it is already. The only kind of news there ever is. "We caught one of the talking snakes last night. It . . . it was boasting. Galway has fallen. Limerick too maybe."

"And Dublin?" Anto asks. He hasn't thought of his family in days. How could he be so selfish?

"It's under siege. Or it soon will be. While you slept we saw three behemoths made of at least a hundred people each heading down the Dublin road. Some of the victims . . . I am so sorry, my friends. Some of them were wearing army uniforms."

By now Morris has found his feet again. He throws a look of pure hatred at Anto.

"Well, lad," he growls, "you can go shag yourself, so you can." Anto should feel guilty, but there's something about the phrasing the man has chosen that he can't quite put his finger on. For a second he wonders if Morris is one of those Sídhe that have taken over a human's body. Like Frank O'Leary back at school.

Anyway, why should Anto feel suspicious of somebody the Sídhe were working so hard to kill?

"I'm out of here," says Morris.

"No," says Nabil. "You heard the angels, my friend. You could be seen from the air."

"Well, I doubt they'd treat me worse than you assholes did. I'm going, and you can't stop me." He shoves his way past Krishnan and out the front door.

Taaft rolls her eyes. "Oh, let him go, Froggy. What do we care?"

Nabil turns to her, working every muscle in his body to hide his fury. "You wanted to rescue him, Sarah." Anybody else would have added that they lost two comrades as a result, but Nabil is too polite for that. "I will talk to him some sense."

Anto moves as if to follow, but Liz Sweeney grabs him by his giant arm. Oh! It comes *so* close to ripping itself free! He needs all his control just to keep the evil in check. Perhaps she realizes it too, because she releases him at once. "It's none of our business, Anto," she says.

"This is my fault. Maybe if I apologize, he'll come back. I won't be long." And off he goes.

The two others are out of sight behind the hedge, but he can hear Nabil well enough when he says, "Listen, my friend, we did not mean disrespect, we—" The Frenchman stops for some reason and Morris's next words sound like they're coming through a smirk.

"Is this a pistol I have in my pocket, *my friend*? Or am I just glad to see you?"

A pistol! Anto had tied Morris up, yet never even thought to search him!

A shot rings out. Anto breaks into a run, catching himself on the hedge, ripping free, slipping on frosty ground, before wrenching open the gate.

And it's too late! It's too late! Nabil is on his knees, hands pressed tightly to his throat. His eyes bulge in astonishment, terror, shock. And Morris, like a character in one of those Western movies who has just made an impossible shot, mimes the blowing of smoke from the barrel. Blood pours between the dam of Nabil's fingers. Then he falls, right onto his face, smacking against the cracked, frosty footpath.

Morris grins and points his gun again.

"I want you to know, you big-armed freak, you had the king of Sligo in your hands and you blew it." He grins, enjoying himself too much to pull the trigger just yet.

Anto feels no fear. "You're a traitor. You're mad. The likes of you have destroyed the whole country."

Morris frowns, as though surprised. "OMG, really? Destroyed this dying little bog hole? The country that fired me from every job? Humiliated by all those thick-ankled cows who wouldn't give a lad the time of day? Well"—he spits, making sure it lands on Nabil's corpse—"they're not laughing at me now. I've hunted enough of them down, and just as soon as I get back to my kingdom and gather another gang of beasts, why, I'll come right back here for those friends of yours in the house there. It's not like they're going far anyway."

He stretches out his hand, weaving little circles with the barrel. What is he waiting for? Pleading? Anto doesn't have it in him anymore, but he should feel something, shouldn't he? The man lying dead at his feet is one of the finest human beings he has ever met. Strong, but gentle. Eternally polite and protective of the students. But he might as well be a stranger now.

Nessa's betrayal has ripped everything human away, every normal emotion. Only the arm feels anything now. And it wants what it always wants: to break something.

"You killed Nabil," Anto says. His voice sounds like it belongs to a machine.

"And you're next, bucko," says Morris with a cheeky grin.

The front door opens and Anto knows Taaft and the others must have heard the gunshot, but they're being cautious, not charging into the street. This gives Morris all the time he needs to pull the trigger once more.

Nothing happens but a dry click.

"Ah" is all Morris can say. He flings the gun at Anto's head and runs off down the street.

It's getting dark again. There are probably monsters in the area. Anto doesn't care. He charges after the young man, who, although unburdened by a giant's arm, lacks the fury that drives the boy.

Morris squeezes past the wooden back gate of a garden. Anto knocks it right off its hinges with a single punch and batters his way through the trees behind it and out onto the road where Morris is already tiring. The man is cursing under his breath. He calls on saints; on Jesus; on Mary and Joseph. The boy is almost close enough. Almost. He reaches out with his longer left arm just as Morris leaps—

There's a body lying in the street. Anto trips over it, topples, rolling down the hill to land in a heap.

The king of Sligo laughs, full of joy and relief. He can't resist a final taunt. "Good luck in getting back to Dublin!"

Anto doesn't even try getting up. He's had a vision, just a flash really, of a lovely, lovely face, and he thinks, *Is Nessa really a creature like Morris?* Could she ever be so callous? And yet, she must be even worse than him if she now looks like a Sídhe. What other explanation can there be?

"Hang on . . . ," he calls. "Wait . . ."

Morris keeps his distance, ready to run, but he cocks an eyebrow in the fading light.

"What did they give you? What did the Sídhe promise you in return for revoking the treaty?"

Morris laughs, still a little out of breath. But he spreads his arms wide, as if to say, *Behold the man*. And he replies, "This! Youth! Handsomeness! My new life is awesome!"

And off he goes before Anto can recover his feet.

Youth. Of course. Anto realizes now what has puzzled him about Morris all along. Despite his appearance, he speaks like an old man. Words like "WTF" and "awesome" belong to his granny's generation.

———

Back at the house, he is confronted with Nabil's corpse all over again. Taaft is acting nothing like herself. She has turned the body around and is frantically trying to clean away blood with what looks like a curtain. All she has done is spread it around. But Nabil doesn't object. Even in death, he seems embarrassed by the fuss, all the more so when Taaft kisses him. She sobs. Taaft of all people! Taaft whose voice dripped with contempt whenever she spoke to the Frenchman.

"Ah, Walid . . . ," she sobs. Was that his first name? Walid?

Anto's stomach is in a knot. His muscles too. The arm still wants to hurt somebody, but who? He can't stand to watch anymore.

How, he wonders, how can the world still be here without Nabil around to steady it? Without Nessa? With armies of monsters marching right now toward Dublin, ready to perform unspeakable acts on his mam and da? He goes to open the front door with the wrong arm and almost wrenches it from its hinges.

Inside, Liz Sweeney is waiting for him.

She takes his human hand and leads him up to the box bedroom. The curtains are closed and the last of the day has fled. Her lips are hot against his, but she senses his hesitation.

He shouldn't be doing this, whispers his old self. He should be happily married in Donegal. Planting, laughing. Growing a beard and climbing mountains or whatever twisted thing they do up there.

"She's dead," Liz Sweeney growls, and Anto knows exactly who she's talking about. "By Crom, I'm here. I'm still alive. For a while. Alive."

Oh, Danú, she is! Her body, her skin. The smell of her! Her breath fast, her hands inside his clothing . . . And he can't stop it then. A hundred Sídhe at the door couldn't stop it. He literally tears her clothes away and then his own. Who knows who last slept in this bed, smelling of must? Who knows how he got here or why he hasn't had the decency to die yet?

That'll teach you! he thinks. *That'll teach you!*

But who is he talking to? Nessa? Or the part of himself that's too Crom-twisted stupid to break free of her? She's another king of Sligo. That's all there is to it. A traitor who, should he ever see her again, he will kill with his own two hands.

Later Liz Sweeney falls asleep, though the whole bed shakes with his sobs as, drip by drip, the last of his love seeps away, and he is free.

THE IMMORTALS

Who knows how many days have passed, or if time has moved at all?

A storm forces Nessa and Ambrosio into a cave for shelter. It scours the earth with great spiraling fingers of dust and vegetation. Mighty trees are ripped up by the roots and sent screaming into the sides of mountains.

Yes, they actually scream.

At first the cave seems less intimidating. A monster lived here once, but an intelligent one, and Nessa makes a torch of her finger so she can study the designs daubed on the walls.

"Is it writing, do you think?" she asks.

And Father Ambrosio snorts. "Greeks," he sneers. "Schismatics. No wonder they were damned here. And no, I can't read it. The only word I know is 'fish' and I don't see that. The drawings should be easier."

"Drawings?"

"Above your head, my child."

Five little stick figures. Two adults, two children. A baby. A flat-roofed home.

She might not be able to read Greek, but the artist's loneliness reminds her of her own. She has to turn away then, before the sadness can smother her.

"Oh, by Our Savior's wounds!" cries the priest. "Save your pity. Whoever it was, *what*ever it was, it drew those pictures in blood. Yes!" He grins at the look on her face. "Did you think our creators provided us with paints now? And who do you think filled this cave with so many bones?"

"Well, it wasn't the poor creature who drew these pictures," she says.

"Of course it was, child! Who else?"

"I mean that the blame lies with the Sídhe for making it the way it was. They are the real monsters."

"And who made the Sídhe the way they are?"

"Not me," Nessa whispers. "It wasn't me. It wasn't anybody I know. The ones responsible are dead a long time ago."

"Ah, the famous Milesians," he says. "Your ancestors, no? They were the ones who forced the Sídhe to suffer such horror for all eternity! Your only crime, child, was to profit from it. To live in their homes while they continued to suffer."

"That's not fair."

He flutters up onto her shoulder, his wings so much stronger now.

"Don't even think about it," she tells him.

"I always think about it, child. But I won't. I'm not even hungry."

The two of them watch the storm. Already its force is fading here as it moves off in the direction that she too must follow if she is to keep her promises and escape. And suddenly it strikes her that if she is trapped by her own words, what must it be like for the enemy.

"All those promises the Sídhe make, Father. Are they fools?"

"Not at all, child. Strange, yes. Cruel, capricious. Joyful and playful and sometimes as innocent as babes. What they are not, however, is stupid. At least not where promises are concerned. They word them ever so carefully!"

"But . . . but they can't keep them all, Father."

"You are right. It's like . . . it's like a gamble they take, my child. The two worlds drift slowly about each other on a great ocean, theirs and yours, each too tiny for the other to see."

"That . . . that doesn't make any sense, Father."

"But it makes perfect sense, child! God and Lucifer each see each other as the devil, do they not? Between humans and Sídhe, it is the same. Ack!" He pounds a tiny fist onto the skin of her shoulder. And then the momentary energy leaves him again. "But what do I care about sense? I, who sent both astronomers and astrologers to the stake? It is simply the way of it. The worlds attract or repel one another over lifetimes, and the rules are complex beyond my understanding. But look at it this way: We humans are the treasure ship and they the filthy pirates. We need to keep them away, for in those times that they are close enough to board they steal away the likes of me to share their hell with them. They work all kinds of wickedness!

But then the currents pull us apart once more, spinning us away for generations, maybe whole centuries . . ."

"They've been stealing people away every single day for the last twenty-five years! Surely we should have drifted apart by now."

"I have already given you the answer, child. Promises. The power of binding, remember? Each promise kept between them and us is a lash that ties the worlds together."

"And a broken promise can push them apart again?"

"Exactly, child, exactly! But worse. A broken promise is like a whole barrel of powder going off! Or so it seems to me, because it is the only thing they fear."

Nessa shakes her head. "I will teach them to fear me too. You'll see. Come on, Father," she says. "The storm is gone and I want to test these new crutches."

———

They work perfectly. Nessa all but flies down the slope and springs halfway up the face of the next with the ease of a young gazelle. She feels as strong as she ever has. Every step takes her closer to danger, but if she can escape Dagda's attention, that also means she's nearer to home and to Anto's welcoming arms. He needs her. She knows that, and already she can imagine the delight on his face when they meet again.

She sleeps where she can as the "days" pass. She hides from house-sized predators. They're not interested in her. Eagerly they hunt down swearing and sobbing beasts that are larger than elephants.

Above her head flies Father Ambrosio. His wing has healed and his belly bulges from all the creatures Nessa has burned from their path. "Water!" he'll cry when he sees any. Or "Monsters!" or "Sídhe!"

Although there are never as many of the latter as she expected. As though they have all gone elsewhere.

"You look more and more like one of them," the priest tells her.

"Good. It's keeping me safe." And it is. Twice, seeing her in the distance, the enemy has waved at her. And then there was that monster, with fangs as long as her arm, the one that referred to her as "master" and backed away, trembling all over.

"Good," she says again.

She carries kindling in Father Ambrosio's old sling. At sleep time she uses the last of the heat in her bones to make a fire. She buries her hands in it, glorying in the sensation of filling herself up to the very brim.

It is not a human that stalks toward Dagda and his Cauldron. It is a weapon.

If only Anto were here, she thinks. *We'd be unstoppable.* He with his mighty fist and she with her fire. She imagines the Sídhe bowing to them both. And then . . . why, if the enemy could just forget their hatred, their madness, if they could put it aside and use all their tremendous magic for good, a true paradise could be fashioned from the hell that is the Grey Land.

"A fantasy," Father Ambrosio tells her one evening. "You think to defeat the Sídhe with powers that they themselves gave you?"

"I made them give me my power," she tells him. "I took it."

"Dagda made you, child, whatever you think. He knows everything about you."

"Then I'll keep out of his way. You know the plan! I'll see him from a distance, and then . . . I'm gone. Disguised as one of them if I have to."

Father Ambrosio says nothing. He's been here so long he can't remember what hope smells like, let alone the taste of it.

Crow's Beak Mountain has grown so enormous now that its own foothills hide it from her. But Father Ambrosio scouts out a pass between it and one of its lesser brethren. And it is at the top of this, having climbed it for what felt like two days, that Dagda's domain is finally revealed to her.

Fires burn down there. So many that she feels a sense of vertigo, as though she is looking down at the stars of home. But these are just bonfires. They twinkle on the plain below her, surrounding a town-sized crater, a perfect circle filled with a glowing liquid that could be mercury or molten silver. Even as she watches, bubbles form that must be as large as whales.

"The Cauldron," says Father Ambrosio.

"That's . . . ? But . . . but I thought . . ."

She goggles at it in amazement, but not for long. That's not what the promise wants, is it? So already she is moving down the hill, faster than necessary.

On a gentle slope like this, with good crutches, Nessa could almost fly if she wanted to. Stopping, however, is not so easy, and so it proves, because when she sees a pair of Sídhe on the path ahead of her, she hasn't a hope of altering her course before they turn and spot her.

She decides instead to accelerate. The fetid air whips past her face, stones scatter, and spider bushes move all too slowly to pull her down. The figures are too surprised to react.

She smashes into the pair of them like an artillery shell, flinging them aside and using their bodies to soak up her speed, so that a mere ten steps farther on, she finally skids to a halt.

Then she has to turn back upslope to finish them off, fighting gravity and the reluctance of the promise. It'll be a temporary death at best she can grant them, what with the Cauldron so near. It will have to do. She can't have anyone tattling to Dagda!

She reaches the first of them: a woman with tangled hair, lying stunned where she fell.

"Oh, bless you, child!" calls Father Ambrosio from above. She can practically hear him salivating.

Nessa studies her victim. It's a woman with scarred arms. Tattoos decorate her neck: a rose, a sailing ship. Nessa stretches out a hand, ready to unleash fire, but then she pauses, her eyes catching again on the scars.

They're old.

Shouldn't the Cauldron have healed this woman? Shouldn't it have perfected her?

"Finish her!" cries Father Ambrosio. "Please!"

Yes! says Megan's ghost.

But the other enemy, only now recovering himself, shouts, "We're human!" And then, driving a swooping Father Ambrosio away with a wave of his arm, he cries, "Gah! I hate those things!" Nessa sees with a shock that, despite the glittering of his skin and the large eyes, actual wrinkles line his forehead and pinch the corners of his mouth. "Arra, look now," he says, more in bewilderment than anger, "you've broken my arm. And poor Veronica's legs too, by the looks of them."

"Good," Nessa growls. She's shaking from the fight, adrenaline draining from her body, leaving nothing but confusion in its wake. "You're traitors. The Sídhe would have twisted you otherwise." She needs these people dead. She needs it or her plan lies in ruins. Yet, when she looks at the unconscious woman at her feet . . . sees that tattoo: so personal, so human, the fire seems to recoil from her fingertips.

The man nods at her predicament. "We're no different from you, girl. We made deals in order to live. Some better than others, but what choice was there? And if it was just the likes of me and poor Veronica, you could say there was something wrong with us. But it isn't, is it? You'll see when you get down to the bottom how normal it is. A thousand of us honest to God human beings living in the shadow of the Cauldron. Our aging stopped in its tracks. Free of disease. And when it's all over, when the conquest is complete, we go home again. It's been promised."

"And what did you have to do in exchange for all of that? For them?"

A look of terrible pain crosses the man's craggy old face. Then, angrily, he shakes his head like a horse driving away a fly. "What does it matter, girl? Sure, aren't they all dead centuries ago anyway? I'm here now. I have no . . ." Is it the pain of his arm that makes him hesitate? "I have no family. And no regrets neither. I will be young again, and soon! Oh, yes, even one as lowly as me hears how well the invasion is going!"

She stares, unable to take in his last sentence. It means her friends and family are already under attack. Yet it also means a door is open. A door home.

The fire boils in her. Time to end this.

But then the man bows. "Anyway," he says, "you are Nessa. Am I right?"

"How . . . ? How do . . . ?"

"Sure we're here for you, aren't we? Me and Veronica both. To greet you on Lord Dagda's behalf. He felt your approach and thought you might be more inclined to trust your own kind."

"I trust none of you!" she says.

He laughs. "Sure how're you any different from us? You who will strengthen my lords when your promises are kept? Better for Ireland if you had died during your Call, but no! No! You just had to live, didn't you? You had to!"

He grins, an old man's grin. "Lord Dagda didn't need you to trust us, in any case. We're just here to take your mind off things."

"What things?"

Then she hears applause. Laughter follows, delighted and sweet. And from behind the rocks all around a dozen more people appear.

Sídhe this time: There's no mistaking those huge, unnatural smiles for human.

Something shoots out of the air—Father Ambrosio!—and smacks the man right in the face. How he screams! But Nessa is already turning. Time to make a run for it. Nobody can catch her on a slope. But the woman with the broken legs is not as unconscious as she appeared. She knocks one crutch away and Nessa goes tumbling to the ground in a puff of dust.

She rolls, makes it up onto one knee. The first of the Sídhe are here. A beautiful, beautiful woman whose smile could melt the most calcified human heart. But Nessa points and she's the one who melts instead. Now Nessa's up again! Three more of the fair folk block her path. Didn't anybody warn them about her? She cooks them where they stand. A man grabs her shoulder. Another has an arm around her neck, chuckling happily in her ear, until they too burn away. And still the Sídhe are unafraid. More and more of them coming, until, with her fire all gone, they bear her to the ground, laughing like a giddy heap of children until she lies still.

THE PARK

Anto comes downstairs in the morning. Everyone is there. Aoife avoids looking at him altogether. Krishnan and Mitch are holding hands. They are badly matched—one so gangly he might have been created by a particularly unimaginative Sídhe; the other tiny enough to be eight instead of twelve years old. They stare defiantly around the room. Who, by Crom, do they imagine cares? Do they think the Nation needs *their* children all of a sudden?

But when Anto turns, Liz Sweeney has appeared behind him, her whole manner that of the cat who got the cream. His heart misses a beat, but not in a good way. It's not from love, because he knows what that feels like and he knows what it feels like to betray it too. *We're both traitors now*, he thinks, *me and Nessa.*

Anto wanders into the back garden, where he finds a pathetic little grave waiting for him. Nabil, of course. Taaft lies unconscious beside it, a large empty bottle of something foul clutched in one hand.

He plops himself down, feeling the freezing damp soak through his old tracksuit.

Like a scholar, wandering the ruins of a once-mighty city, he looks inside himself. Is there anything worth saving? The arm is still there of course. Ready to fight again. To pound, to smash. The rest of him serves no purpose. Maybe he should try something heroic. He could fight his way down to Dublin to save his family. But he'd never get there in time, not with a whole army in the way.

He is empty. Numb. A withered pile of ash. Yet, if he looks carefully, deep down, a single ember burns, and as he pokes at it, it flares, suddenly white hot.

Hope. Anto hasn't tasted it in so long that several heartbeats pass before he recognizes it. Aoife got it right, he realizes. Because even a ragtag group such as theirs might have a chance to make a difference.

He runs into the house. "Get up!" he shouts.

The others look at him, totally startled.

Liz Sweeney says, "We'll never make it through to Dublin now."

"We're not going to Dublin," Anto replies. "The Sídhe aren't going to Dublin either, are they? We've hardly seen a single one." Then he surprises himself, and the others too, by grinning hard enough to hurt. "Don't you get it? We never see them because they're all too scared to die in the fighting, now that they've found their promised land. I like that they're afraid. I love it. And here we are, behind their lines with a load of modern guns and ammunition."

The students are all nodding, slow, vicious smiles spreading across their faces. Even Aoife looks frightening. Of all people!

"But that's not even the best part," Anto tells them. "That guy we had here last night. That Crom-twisted, backstabbing murderer was the king of Sligo. The king the Sídhe made who let them through the gate up there. Well, we had a king over in Boyle too. Remember that? They were trying to open a gate, but when Nessa"—he catches himself, swallows, and manages to carry on—"when the king of Boyle *died*, the gate shut in their faces and their invasion failed."

"By Crom," says Krishnan, his Adam's apple bobbing. "If we'd known. If we'd killed him!"

"Oh, we'll kill him, all right," says Anto. "He boasted he was heading home so he can have more monsters to command. He enjoyed that. Enjoyed wiping out the people trapped in that farmhouse. And then he pretended to be one of them!"

"I'm in!" cries Krishnan.

A shadow has appeared at the door, stinking of cheap alcohol.

It's Taaft. Her eyes are so puffy it's a miracle that she can see anything. "We're killing that man," Liz Sweeney tells her. "Morris."

"He's mine," Taaft says simply.

Anto nods. There'll be plenty of blood for everybody, he thinks.

———

Among the wreckage of the town are enough bikes to mount an army. Liz Sweeney knows how to fix them up, and Krishnan is no fool either when he's not showing off for Mitch. So, while only bald tires are available, they gather several of these and other spare parts, before taking the road back toward Carrick-on-Shannon.

The students travel by day—utter foolishness of course. Except that's what Morris will be doing, and the thought of losing him in the dark is too much for any of them to bear. Still though, that first afternoon a fine covering of twenty-year-old trees hides them from the air. It's cold, but sunny. Wind rushes past their faces, and animals of every kind can be seen in the bogs and hedges and fields.

Oh, it's fun! Anto thinks. How can anything be fun? And yet it is. Krishnan races madly after birds, skidding dramatically along the rims of potholes that could swallow him. There's no bike large enough for his lanky frame. He's like a clown in a tiny car. Mitch laughs, and even Aoife finds an uncertain smile when a downhill stretch makes them all feel like they're flying through flashes of sunlight.

At one point they skid to a stop in a panic as something monstrous crashes through a nearby field. But it's just a poor horse with too many legs, the sort of thing the infestation squads used to hunt. It doesn't even see them as it blunders by.

Soon enough though, their road takes them right to the edge of an empty town with a dozen overgrown housing estates to either side of them.

"He could be anywhere," Liz Sweeney whispers. "Remember when we passed through here before? There must be a hundred houses, right?"

"We know where he's going," Anto insists. "Back to his kingdom."

Minutes later they reach a park along the edge of the river, and here they're rewarded with the sight of a single Sídhe. It's the first Anto has seen since the one he killed with a grenade when he was with the infestation squad. The glittering man doesn't even notice them. He's staring at a tree. One hand reaches out to it, trembling, his face awed.

"So beautiful!" he cries. "Oh! Oh!"

Afraid to move, they watch him fall to his knees. Softly he weeps, pressing his face to the trunk. "I only ever wanted to come home. Oh, my home!"

He doesn't hear a sound as they ease bikes to the earth and pad across the grass. Their attack is like the frenzy of sharks. They rip him to pieces in utter silence, and when there's nothing left they just stand there, wordless, dripping with blood that's no different from their own.

I am a beast, Anto thinks. He tries the thought again, like probing at a sore tooth with his tongue. But he feels no regret.

A sudden *squeak* makes them jump. Another Sídhe is there, watching them from a bush, her perfect mouth stretched open in horror. She freezes as they advance on her. "I . . . No!" she says. "I can't die here. Not yet! I can't feel the Cauldron. Please!"

Her golden skin has shining freckles. Her cheeks curve sweetly enough to break hearts. But who has room for one of those? Guns, yes. And knives too, which are far more satisfying.

"You're on a Call," Liz Sweeney whispers. "This is what it's like, you filthy twist! This is what it feels like to be us!"

The woman runs then, or tries to. They give chase, their faces contorted into grins. All the grace of her people has deserted her and the first rock she comes to trips her up, a weeping, sprawling heap.

"Wait!" It's Aoife who calls a halt to the gory blades. Tears drip down her face. "We can question her, can't we?"

Anto shudders. Is that . . . is that *relief* he feels? "Yes." His voice is hoarse. "We have a mission now. A mission. We need to know where Morris is."

Krishnan covers the woman's dangerous hands with cloth and secures them behind her back, while Liz Sweeney goes through the pouches at her belt. "By Crom," she says. She has found a white pulp and is sniffing at it. "Kind of sweet."

The Sídhe, still weeping, snaps at her. "Thieving my food? You think if you look like us we will spare you after the conquest? No! We can see beyond the skin to your hearts. We will know our own, we—"

Liz Sweeney kicks her hard, twice, and is going in for more when Aoife drags her back.

"Get your hands off me, Aoife! I told you I'm not interested! I have a boyfriend now."

Aoife hisses, her look so severe that even Liz Sweeney falls silent. "I'm going to question her. That's all there is to it."

But the Sídhe woman won't say another word.

They spend a night shivering in a house, not daring to light fires, huddling together except for whoever's on watch.

By morning, the Sídhe is dead and Taaft is cleaning a large hunting knife. "Had to be done. I caught her looking at me."

Aoife hangs her head as though ashamed, but nobody says a word.

THE CAGE

A hundred deadly hands reach for Nessa, brushing her skin, while musical voices praise the power of the promise within her. She's on the ground, trying to writhe away. Crying out for fear they will make a beast of her; a living cloak; a work of "art."

But no, they're saving this prize for somebody else. For the worst and most imaginative of them all: Lord Dagda himself.

A few of the Sídhe remain outside the pile. They heal the humans—the eyeless man with the broken arm, the crippled woman. Both scream with the pain of it, a pain Nessa remembers from her own transformation. Another Sídhe gathers the bones of those Nessa has killed. For the Cauldron no doubt.

Of Father Ambrosio there is no sign.

Then the enemy pick her up. A dozen of them carry her above their heads, like the corpse of a deer, shown off to the rest of the tribe, although there is nobody here to see it. Down the slope they bring her, through rains of ash, laughing and excited. Chatting. "We are returning to the Many-Colored Land," one tells her. There is no malice in his face, merely an excitement that he longs to share with a dear friend. "I myself will go forth after Conor has killed you and our promise to him is fulfilled."

"Conor's dead," Nessa cries. "He burned in my arms!"

"Yes! Oh, yes!"

"Will you . . . will you bring him back to life in the Cauldron?"

"He did not bathe in the Cauldron at his coming of age. It does not know him, cannot remember him. Nor will it remember you when Conor has finally killed you. Your fate is to die, sweet one. And it will be glorious!"

It makes little sense to Nessa. The only important part is that they intend to kill her and that she intends to spite them by living and then finding her way home. She squeezes her eyes shut. She breathes and breathes again, fighting the terror that wants to lock her muscles rigid.

I'll bide my time. Nessa is thinking of all the bonfires she saw down by the Cauldron, each one a source of power. And what of the Cauldron itself? What if she swam in its silvery waters? Would it prevent her from dying here? Or would it make her one of them?

A village of filthy huts lies at the bottom of the hill. A great crowd of humans shouts as she passes. Many point. Some are as young and beautiful as the Sídhe themselves. Others, perhaps less careful in what they asked for at the time of their promise, are ragged and old.

A few have even been twisted into forms the Sídhe find amusing, and these sad ones scuttle from shadow to shadow, or shamble miserably about on elephant legs—if they can move at all.

Nobody is smiling here. They look like they've forgotten how, although the day of their triumphant return must be very close indeed.

Beyond the human village lies another, of a sort. It consists of hills with holes in them from which more Sídhe come sliding like worms. Nessa fears she is to be taken down there, into the damp dark of the earth. She struggles at this thought. Pointlessly, for they have a firm grip on her, until at last she sees where she is to be put.

It is a cage. Thick columns of bone form the bars, supporting a roof of dense greasy hair. And when they fling her inside, she finds herself on a warm floor of leathery skin, the veins pulsing gently beneath her.

"You won't be here long," her captors tell her.

They seal her in by molding two of the bones together so that the entire cage bucks and screams in terror and pain.

They laugh and pat it gently. Then they whistle up a pair of "dogs," one originally a human man and one a woman, their tongues lolling, their eyes eager.

"Our pets will mind you until Dagda comes," the Sídhe tell her.

"When, uh . . . when will that be?"

"When he needs the power the most."

They leave her there, some holding hands, some singing or laughing. One of them even skips . . .

"Twist you all!" she cries after them. She'll kill them. She'll kill every one of them if she can. But first she has to get out of here.

So she explores her prison, looking for weaknesses. She can't give in. Not to the loneliness that hangs over every breath she's taken since the day that Cassidy arrested her off the bus. Not to the despair, nor the odds.

The cage trembles around her. "It's all right," she says. She talks to it, in Sídhe and English and Irish. Can it be killed? Is she cold enough to do that after the way it screamed when the Sídhe twisted it closed? And even if she gets out, she'll still have to beat the "dogs" somehow. And then what?

As if they can hear her thoughts, the two "animals" start growling, "Dooooonnn't liiiiike! Doooonnnn't liiiiike!"

But what's bothering them is Father Ambrosio, hovering outside the cage in a blur of wings.

"There you are, my child."

"Father! You came back."

"Not the wisest course of action I have ever taken, sweet child. *Why should I help her?* I asked myself. I am damned, after all . . . God doesn't care what I do."

"So why?"

"Because I want to. For you of course—the only friend I've had in many, many lifetimes. And because I hate the Sídhe and will spite them if I can."

"Will you get me out of here?"

"That is beyond my gift, child." She strains to hear him over the fury and yowling of the "dogs." "No, there is only one thing you can do." He hovers above her and spreads his arms dramatically. "Challenge Dagda to a duel."

"A what?"

"Duels are his joy. Watching them, for the most part. Building creatures to fight others. Healing them and making them fight again. But he loves taking part himself too, and when he wins, it is always through guile. He has tricked a thousand opponents out of their heads, so that only the Cauldron can save them. He has lured humans by the score into death or wishing for it."

"Does he ever lose?"

"Not that I've heard. Not since the days of Nuada, or so my masters taught me when I bore them on my back as a horse. Which is why he will offer you anything you ask if you win. Because he thinks you won't."

"And you think I will?"

"Oh, you will have an excellent chance, my child! Excellent! Because, you, you have a trick of your very own."

"The fire?"

"Oh, right, the fire. Well, two tricks then."

"What's the second trick?"

"Me!"

"You? You will help me, Father? You'll risk them remaking you into something worse?" She's touched, because this has always been his greatest fear. And here he is, hovering just in front of her: nodding, smiling. Licking his lips . . .

"All I ask is an eyeball," he whispers. "You won't need two for the fight. I'll make it painless for you. I can do that. I'm sorry to ask. I wouldn't, only I—"

"Go away!" she shouts at him. "Go! Go!" She punches at him through the bars of the cage. He tumbles backward so that one of the "dogs" almost has him, its jaws snapping on empty air.

"You need me more than that eye," he cries. "I could fly around his face. I could distract him. Why, you can barely stand without your crutches! A puff of wind would knock you over. You fool! Nobody beats him! Nobody can even touch him!"

She turns her back on him, and soon he is gone.

"Good riddance," she mutters, already wishing he would come back. She fights and fights against the tears, although there is nobody but the "dogs" here to see them.

She should have let him have the eye. Both of them even! It would be worth it not to face this alone. And if nothing else, it would cause her promise to be broken, for how could she see Dagda then?

Nessa laughs at her own stupidity, setting the monsters outside her cage to growling. The enemy would make new eyes for her of course. They could twist them out of any other part of her flesh. No, she thinks. It's better that the ungrateful priest has fled. She will face this danger, as she always does, alone, with her back straight and a snarl on her lips.

"Easy now, my dears," says a sweet voice, and the growling of the "dogs" turns to whines. A woman is outside, scratching both of the "animals" on their unkempt heads of hair. She pulls gently on the male "dog's" beard. Tears of joy roll down the wrinkles of his face.

"Loooove you," he whines.

"No, me! No, me!" says the female.

The Sídhe beauty comes over to stroke the cage too and Nessa wonders whether she should make a grab for her hand, before remembering that their hands are the last thing any human should be touching. Instead she clears her throat.

"I want to make a challenge," she says. "To Dagda. A . . ." By Crom it sounds so stupid! So childish! "I want to fight a duel."

The woman's grin widens. "Yes. He said you would say that, and that I was to agree."

"He . . . he did?"

"And you are to have your walking sticks back. He aches to see them used in combat."

As if from nowhere the woman passes some roots into the cage along with a human bladder filled with water. "Eat slowly," she says. "It is not much, but you will be dead before ever you feel hungry again."

THE DUEL

Two strong Sídhe drag Nessa from the cage. She hears cheering. Word of the fight must have spread quickly, as men and women come slithering out of their burrows in the earth, to appear as beautiful and happy as angels.

Her Sídhe guards parade her among them. Today they will see not one but two promises fulfilled. Their grip on the Many-Colored Land will strengthen and they will send more and more of their monsters through the door until it is a safe place for them to live.

How they cry out with joy, their sweet voices echoing from the walls of the Cauldron. With deadly hands they reach out to touch the thief—she who has challenged Dagda himself—and they watch her fighting not to flinch, as though they would harm her! The very thought!

Fires burn everywhere. The flames rise tall as a house, feeding on bones and bleeding wood, on leathery old leaves and feebly struggling spider bushes. Twice the girl makes a dive for one of them, but the enemy are ready for her, with one woman even throwing herself laughing into the flames to prevent Nessa from reaching them.

"Oh, what spirit she has!" they cry. "Dagda will be pleased with this one!"

Nessa sees humans among the crowd too—she knows how to recognize them now, to see through the glittering skin to the rotten soul beneath. They stare at her hungrily, as though jealous of her impending death.

Farther on she goes, carried up into the hills. Small batlike creatures fly everywhere, croaking and calling out, wheeling in little flocks. One of them, no larger than her forearm, hops close enough to whisper, "Give up! Give up! What's the point?" It flaps away in terror when one of the Sídhe waves at it.

The hills of the enemy village turn out to have a natural arena at their center: a flat space, marred by the odd boulder, surrounded by a perfect ring of mounds. It's already crowded. Fair folk and their human allies jostle for space on the slopes.

Beyond the spectators, on the crown of each mound, lie more bonfires. But that is not what Nessa notices when at last her guards guide her right into the center of the open space and hand back her crutches.

She gasps, the eyes popping out of her head. There are *doors* up there. Not real doors, but the ghostly outlines of them, and each bears a familiar shape. She saw the like during her Call, didn't she? And before that too, the day Liz Sweeney chased her up the side of a Fairy Fort, only that one was made of stone.

A woman approaches Nessa. Glittering spider silk clings to her body, highlighted here and there by scraps of what might be bronze or gold. Even stretched into a smile, her lips remain full, her cheeks softly round beneath twinkling eyes large enough to feed Father Ambrosio for a lifetime.

A shoulder-high monster with the face of a human crocodile slides along beside her on a carpet of slimy tentacles. Its breath comes in painful whistles through its long mouth. Its eyes weep continuously.

"I am Lassair," she says, her voice as sweet as her name. "Do you remember me?"

It's no easy task to tell one of the Sídhe from another. Their perfection leaves little to stick in the memory. But the clothing rings a bell in Nessa's mind. "I met you the first day here. You . . . you wanted to turn me into a monkey."

Lassair beams. "Yes! We had such fun together!"

"I killed one of your friends."

"Indeed!" The woman claps her hands. "That was well done! A stake through his opened mouth. But now I must thank you, for it is the power of your death that will bring me home."

Megan's ghost chooses that moment to whisper, *Tell her to eat shit!*

But taunting isn't Nessa's way. She ignores the Sídhe woman, looking up at the bonfires on the tops of the hills. How can she get to them through such a thick crowd? How can she open one of those ghostly doors and go home?

The woman waits, stroking her weeping pet.

"What if I don't die?" Nessa asks.

Lassair laughs. "Of course you will die! A promise kept is powerful, but a promise broken can shake the very worlds in their orbits!" For a moment she loses her smile. "When Conor failed to kill you the first time, the consequences . . ." She shudders. "Luckily we found a way. We found a . . . a certainty this time. Your bones will stay here and I will ride the power of your death to my proper place in the Many-Colored Land. Now," she says, "our lord bids me tell you to choose a weapon."

Nessa snaps to attention. "A . . . a weapon?"

"Of course! You think him unfair? But no, he is like you, Nessa."

He is nothing like me!

"Your people took everything from us. Or tried to! They stole away all beauty, and yet"—Lassair indicates the tortured crocodile person at her side—"we made beauty of our own! They snatched away happiness and forced unjust treaties on us that only a human king can renounce. Yet, foolishly, they abandoned their kings, allowing us to make our own. And through all of it, through our struggles, Dagda's will has been firm and he sees this same strength in you, for all you are is a thief." She pauses, frowning at her pet. With delicate fingers she smooths away a lump from its back, while the crocodile's jaws open and it moans in what can only be terror.

"Please," says Nessa, "don't—"

"Of course," says Lassair, "my lord will cheat you. It is in his nature. He will watch you die, as shall we all. But you deserve a chance to fight. You deserve a weapon."

"Fire," Nessa says, taking a deep breath. They'll never let her have it. "I want fire."

"Fire?"

"Let me stick my hand in the flames for the count of a hundred. That's all the weapon I need."

"And that, thief, is your final choice?"

"It is."

"You do not wish for a blade? For a sling? You could have a spear."

"I want the fire."

And Lassair throws her head back and laughs enough to startle her tentacled crocodile. "Ah!" she cries. "It is just as my lord Dagda predicted you would say. 'Fire,' he said. The girl will ask for the flames!"

And Nessa feels a chill run through her bones.

They escort Nessa to the nearest bonfire at the top of the hill.

"I hope you will not waste your flames on me," Lassair tells her, without fear. "You will need them for Dagda."

Nessa has, of course, considered murdering this woman and making a run for it. But other obstacles await. A group of Sídhe have placed themselves between her and the way out. She would have to cook them all where they stand. And what then? Her promise will pull her back here very shortly; she knows that because already she aches to return to the arena and see Dagda, to get it all over with . . .

Stop it! she tells herself. *Stop it!*

She has to force herself to stay put and bathe her hands in the flames while the sleeves of her ruined prison shirt char away to ash.

"Perhaps it would be fitting after all if you burned me," Lassair murmurs. She holds Nessa's crutches. "I am named for the fire, you know?"

There is another way out. Less than twenty yards away stands a door. It's just a shadow, a ghostly outline for now, glowing a faint green that seems so out of place in this colorless world.

Please open, Nessa begs it. *Please, please open.*

And Lassair must know what she's thinking, because she laughs again and calls out over the sound of the crackling fire: "They only open one at a time, and only with great expense of power!"

"From . . . from promises?"

"From promises *kept*. Look!"

Nessa squints to follow Lassair's pointing finger. Exactly opposite her current position, on another hill, a hundred Sídhe have lined up in front of a door just like this one, banners flying in the ash-filled breeze. She can't see their faces, but something about the set of their bodies signals eagerness and joy. They're going home. To Ireland. Nessa's home. They will take it for themselves. They will kill her family and friends, or exile them here for an eternity of horror and madness.

"That door is next," Lassair says unnecessarily. "To finish the attack on Eblana!"

And Nessa shudders, for that is an old, old name for Dublin, the biggest remaining city with enough people to flood the country with monsters. It will be the end of Ireland, and Nessa's foolish promise, her hunger to live, has only brought it closer.

Of their own accord, her muscles turn her to face the arena. She made a promise after all, and it won't be denied, not here, not when it's this close to fulfillment.

Lassair approaches, the monster sliding along at her side, groaning and wheezing.

Kill the pointy-nosed little whore, Megan urges. *Just kill her for me.* And Nessa wants to, she really does. And what about that poor beast? Nessa could—*must!*—put it out of its misery.

The woman smiles, nods encouragingly, and it's all Nessa can do to resist. She needs the fire. Or does she?

"Tell me," she says, hiding all her roiling emotions. "Has Dagda made himself . . . like me? Proof against fire?"

The question seems to disturb Lassair, so that her magical smile turns to disgust. "How would the Cauldron recognize us if we altered ourselves?"

Nessa breathes a sigh of relief.

Lassair escorts her right to the center of the arena. The ground is not as even as it should be. Little hummocks pop up here and there. Rocks, even the occasional boulder. But nothing has been allowed to grow. At least Nessa won't have to worry about the Grey Land's lethal flora when she's fighting for her life.

Now Lassair turns to Nessa and bows. "My thanks to you, thief. I leave you to your fate. When Conor kills you, I will return to the Many-Colored Land."

"Dagda is not Conor."

"Of course not!"

And now Nessa finds herself alone in the midst of an area the size of the gym hall back in Boyle, with the crowd growing restless, especially up on the far hill where Sídhe wait for the door that must soon open.

Then silence falls. A man strides out to meet her, heroically proportioned, beardless; his glorious eyes shine beneath prominent brows. She has seen him before. Of course she has! Dagda, a living deity—even his name means "Good god!" His arms can tear an oak tree in half. His chin looks hard enough to shatter mountains, and his clothing—a living creature in its own right—molds itself to the contours of a body such as only a comic-book artist could believe in.

He is granite. He is the wrath of a tormented people made real, and his target is a lame, half-starved teenager.

She had meant to look away, she really had. But now he stands before her. Right before her, and Nessa *sees* him.

The air shivers. The door opens.

It comes like a flash that awes the watching thousands even more than the sight of a god, because sunlight pours through. Into the Grey Land. It dazzles in its golden beauty. And the blue behind it! "Oh!" Nessa cries, because in her time here she has forgotten the sky, the power of it like an endless pool of glory. And there's green too, but not the sickly hue of the ghostly doorways. This is the green of a joyful, fecund nature.

"Thank you," Dagda whispers. For all he is a god, he seems to be feeling more awe than anybody else. *That's good*, Nessa thinks. And she wonders, *Is there a referee for this fight? Are there rules?* She doesn't wait to find out.

As Dagda watches his troops file joyfully through the door, Nessa holds out a hand and unleashes the flame.

Nessa doesn't hold back the fire. She releases a good half of it. A gout of red fury that would melt, she thinks, a house.

When the flames die away, Dagda stands there, a little singed in the eyebrows and no more. "You forget, thief," he says, "I know you." He shrugs something from his back, something almost as large as she is. A slab of some kind. A board? A weapon? "I know your range and I stood just beyond it."

Nessa wastes no time thanking him for this valuable information. Instead she swings forward on her crutches and, before even hitting the ground, she spits a little fire in his face—just enough to blind him, she thinks. But the thing he removed from his back turns out to be a shield and he swings it between them just in time.

It screams when the flames hit. The horrible sound drives her staggering back.

"I am proud of this work," he says. "Do you like it?"

Tell him to shove it up his hole! Megan says, but Nessa can only stare.

Dagda made the shield from the body of a man. It looks like something out of a cartoon: a naked human steamrollered flat. The hands are splayed out in front, as though he is pressing against the entire weight of the world. And she sees too that her attack has set his hair on fire and blackened the teeth in his pitiful flat face.

And Dagda laughs. "Did you think you were the only one I could protect from the flames, thief?" He steps closer, keeping the "shield" up. "You have used all your fire now?"

"I have plenty left." But Nessa swings back, using the crutches to lengthen her stride, to move away faster. She needs to get behind that shield somehow, because, in spite of what she's just said, Nessa has only a few more shots left in her and then, well, then she's dead.

On the hill behind Dagda, the small army has almost passed through the door. Another large group waits on a nearby hill for their chance to leave. Lassair must be among them, Nessa thinks. Needing only Nessa's death for the chance to return home.

Don't get distracted!

She returns her attention to her opponent. He has not yet tried to hurt her, but now, from his belt, he removes a weapon, and the crowd on the slopes applauds, some even jumping up and down with excitement. Which is strange, for while Dagda himself looks like something that might have stepped from the frame of a Jim Fitzpatrick illustration, the weapon is the most primitive of spears.

Nessa expected a gleaming sword as long as her own body. Or some horror like the shield that would spit poison at her.

But all she sees is a little stick topped with blackened charcoal.

Dagda misunderstands her look. "Don't worry, thief," he says. "It is sharp enough. I am too impatient today to make you suffer long."

And then he leaps. It's an incredible feat of strength. From a standing start, carrying the weight of an adult human body in the form of a shield, he covers three yards and lands right in front of her. The rotten stick in his hand sweeps forward. Nessa stumbles away. The pain! A slash across her face, stinging, brutal, her own blood on her chin and a wisp of fire released by mistake, boiling free into the air.

Another stab comes for her belly; a third, her arm. The crutches swing her away just in time and a bubble of flame spat toward his eyes forces him to cover up. He laughs and laughs while Nessa scrambles off to the far side of the arena, breathing hard, bleeding, her already exhausted arms vibrating like the strings of a guitar.

His grinning face follows her. He's not even slightly out of breath. This has been nothing for him, nothing at all. She leans for support on what she takes to be a boulder at the edge of the arena. It turns out, however, to be a giant skull, its eye sockets disturbingly human.

"Well, she won't last long," says a voice. "But sure, what did you expect? She's what? A crippled little girl, am I right? And he's what? A hero out of legend."

Nessa realizes that between the giant's skull and the crowd she has backed herself into a corner, and already Dagda is walking calmly in her direction.

"But," says another voice, "she's fast, isn't she? I mean. It's a lifetime since I've seen one survive his first attack like that. Sure, sure, she had fire to push him back a bit. But still. She's a snake, that one."

These aren't Sídhe. At least, they don't speak like Sídhe.

The first voice says now, "Those crutches move her right out of the way. But look at the sweat on her! She won't survive another—"

Dagda's weapon sweeps toward her. She moves her head just enough so that the long blackened tip passes before her eyes. It is not charcoal, as she first thought. Nor is it wood or metal.

Before it can strike her again, she has fled behind the skull and away. The Sídhe applaud her, oohing and aahing when she springs over a rock like a mountain goat; when she uses the crutches to swing clear of a swipe from the spear, vaulting from boulder to hummock to boulder as Dagda pursues her, lacing her body with tiny cuts that leak precious fire as well as blood.

How long has it been since the start of the fight? A minute? Two?

Nessa feels light-headed. Her arms shudder with sweat and she thinks, *Oh, Mam! Oh, Dad! Anto!* And she remembers this same shattering exhaustion from her Call, when she clung to the walls of a monstrous stomach that wished only to knock her into a pool of acid.

On the hills above, the first door has now closed, taking all beauty away with it. The next door quivers, ready to open, and the Sídhe are impatient to return to the home that is also Nessa's. When she dies, they will see it and she will not.

She's fading fast. She knows it and the crowd does too, although they enthusiastically applaud her efforts. Across the arena she sees the giant skull, sightlessly staring back at her, and remembers the conversation she overheard there. Something about it is nagging at her. Something that—

And the second door opens.

Nobody is expecting that she's still alive. Even Dagda pauses and turns to look back and up. Light comes through again: weaker than before, as though so much time has passed that it is already later in the day.

And then the hillside above them explodes.

THE PLAN

Over the next two days Anto sees five more Sídhe lose their lives to him and his fellow savages. One of the enemy holds out against the initial assault, barricading herself into the upstairs of a house near Collooney.

Like the man they killed in the park, she cries, "I can't die here!" Their return to the longed-for Many-Colored Land has turned the enemy into cowards.

When Liz Sweeney and Krishnan drag her out, Anto places massive fingers around her shapely, bloody neck. "The king!" he cries. "Where is the king of Sligo? I will have his head."

Her fear falls away at once and she laughs at him, that famous Sídhe grin stretched wide. "What good do you think that will do, thief? Our promise to him has already been fulfilled!" She is all too happy to betray Morris. She even tells them where the gate is, and it's nowhere near any of the famous archaeological sites of Sligo. "We have three gates now," she boasts. She's smiling, because she honestly thinks that humans will keep their word and spare her.

Of course they do not.

Later, it's Aoife who says, "Killing Morris isn't going to save the Nation, is it? I mean, if there really are other gates anyway . . ."

Anto doesn't want to hear that, because what else can they do now? And Morris . . . Morris has to die, he just has to. This one purpose is holding Anto together. And Taaft too—that much is obvious.

He knows closing the gate, all three gates even, won't fix things. The Sídhe can find other "kings" to revoke the treaty. All it takes is somebody willing to have their wildest dreams come true. Age can be reversed. Wounds can be made whole! Anything! Anything at all!

Why, they even made Nessa fireproof.

He remembers her triumphant return from the Grey Land. Impossibly alive. Impossibly happy. And he was so happy too, especially the day he kissed her in the hospital tent and she made plans for a future for both of them . . .

"What's wrong?" asks Liz Sweeney. He's breathing hard. "What is it?"

It's Nessa of course. She collapsed into his arms that day, her legs even weaker than usual after her Call. *Why?* he thinks. *Why didn't she ask for her limbs to be straightened as part of the deal?* Isn't that what a real traitor would have done? Maybe not. His own uncle, Paddy Cluxton, profoundly deaf, had been offered some kind of implant once that would have healed him. Or so Mam said. And he'd refused it. Angrily even! "There's nothing wrong with me!" he'd said, and that was that.

But others *had* accepted the implant, and there's no getting away from the fact that Nessa's entire life has been a war against her own disability; against other people's impressions of it.

He feels dizzy. He doesn't know what to think. Liz Sweeney's arms are like the branches of a spider bush and he shrugs them off more roughly than she deserves.

"I'm sorry," he says. "I need to get out of here."

Nessa didn't get the enemy to fix her legs because she didn't think of it. Simple as that. The Sídhe are like the devil in an old story. When you sell them your soul they'll give no more than you think to ask for.

Or maybe she is like his uncle after all. Maybe she just didn't want it. Certainly Anto wouldn't have changed a hair on her head. He loved her. Loves her. That day in the gym is the most glorious time he can remember, both of them survivors and destined to be together for eternity.

He finds himself leaning forward, wanting to throw up. But when Liz Sweeney finds him again to ask what's wrong, Anto straightens and says, "The Sídhe upstairs told me where Morris is headed. Come on. Let's get after him."

And so it is that on the evening of the third day of the pursuit, just as it's becoming too dark to cycle any farther, on a distant hillside they see a dozen bonfires light up simultaneously. They smell the Atlantic on the chill breeze and Anto thinks he might have spotted it on the horizon before the sun went down. But now he has eyes only for his enemies.

How many of them are over there? How many can he kill? It doesn't matter. He can only do his bit and get Morris, because otherwise what use is he? What use has he ever been? If he can achieve this one thing, then he and his evil arm can go to the grave and be at peace.

They leave the bikes and their packs behind a wall. Mitch hesitates, looking at the metal of the spokes gleaming in the moonlight.

"Shouldn't we cover them with soil or something? What if they're found?"

Everybody else stares at him. Liz Sweeney actually snickers.

"Oh," he says, when understanding hits him. Nobody will be going home after this. Nobody will have a home to go to.

In the distance the music starts.

It's beautiful. The hands playing it have honed their skills over thousands of years. The sound travels up through the cold air, jaunty and fast. Joyous whoops and the rhythmic stamping of a hundred pairs of feet can be heard.

Anto nods to the others. No need to say it aloud; they all know it's time to go. They run in a crouch, shielding themselves with walls and bushes and trees. As if sensing their approach, the music grows wilder, the stamping harder, the shouts more exuberant. And soon Anto's squad has reached the top of a lesser, tree-crowned hill in the shadow of the first. There they halt, stunned by what they're seeing.

A thousand of the enemy are on the facing slope. They lie about in groups, pointing joyfully at the stars. They dance with such perfect grace, such ecstasy! They form circles that merge and swirl, eddying around rocks where individual athletes throw themselves carelessly into the air, diving yards downhill, knowing with complete certainty that their fellows will catch them with an easy laugh. And the colors! Bronze bangles; green jewels; astonishingly tooled garments of scarlet human leather and gleaming bone; hats made from the bark of the Grey Land's most dangerous trees; living cloaks woven from a dozen unfortunate exiles to the hell from which the Sídhe have only now escaped.

In the center of it all, perched on a magnificently decorated horse—this too made of a human being—is Morris. Every now and again the horse cries out, "Morris! Morris! Lord of the Battle Kingdom!" And the man himself, smugly resting on top, waves to the uncaring crowd, as though he is their master and not the other way around.

Aoife whispers, right next to Anto's ear, "I don't see a . . . a gate, do you?"

"You wouldn't," says Liz Sweeney. She sounds as if she needs to throw up. Of all of them, she alone has been in the presence of such a door. "It's too small to see if . . . if you approach it wrong."

"Yes." Anto nods. "Nessa told me all about it."

"That Crom-twisted, diseased sow!"

Anto stiffens, almost biting his own tongue. Liz Sweeney notices and pulls away from him.

"I'm sorry," he says.

"It doesn't matter. I know you don't love me, Anto, but I thought . . ."

"I don't love *her*. I can't. She betrayed us. She's nothing to me."

"By Crom, you can't even scratch without thinking of her." Liz Sweeney is angry. Upset.

"That's not true! Look, can we talk about this later?"

And they both know there is no later, but even if there were, they are no longer a couple.

Everybody else pretends not to notice.

Taaft sets up her rifle. It has a scope she found in Longford, and a bipod mount to hold it steady. It points down the hill to where Morris saunters about on his "horse."

"I'm sure to hit him from here," she says. She hasn't touched a drink since they set off on the hunt. Nor has she shouted a single order. All she seems to care about is seeing Morris die. But a vestige of her former duty returns for just a moment. "Listen up, boys and girls," she says. "The rest of you shouldn't be here when I pull this trigger. They'll come swarming up here like ants."

"That's exactly what we want," says Anto. "It's what we always wanted. To be on top of a hill with automatic weapons while they charge us." Even Aoife agrees. Even she would rather kill than run.

Taaft grins and leans into the scope of her rifle. Everybody else gets their weapons ready too, except for little Mitch, who says, "You know, lads, this hill . . . it's perfectly round. I mean, the trees sort of disguise it, but still."

They all realize at the same time that he's right. They're in a cluster of Fairy Forts. Sitting, in fact, right on top of one and looking across at the next, where their enemies dance. But what difference can that make now? Morris has to die.

"For Froggy," Taaft whispers, and with no more warning than that, pulls the trigger.

The terrified horse rears at the sound of the shot. "My king!" it cries. "Oh, my king!" Morris tumbles to the ground, one leg caught in a stirrup made from his mount's own flesh, and it drags him around the rocky hillside, through flocks of dancing Sídhe . . .

They applaud! That's how the enemy responds to this loss of their vassal. They laugh! And Anto feels no relief that the traitor has died. He sees no sign that a gate has closed or that a gate ever existed here at all.

Instead the music grows wilder, and suddenly all of those large, gleaming eyes are staring across the space that separates the hill of the Sídhe from that of the humans.

A single hero steps forward in armor of bronze, gleaming in the light of the nearest fire.

"You have been foolish, thieves!" he cries into the night. "We have more of your number nearby. We will fulfill our promises to them now."

"What's he on about?" asks Krishnan.

Taaft doesn't care. She's staring down the barrel at the hero. "You're next, big boy," she mutters.

Anto senses something is terribly wrong. Why aren't the Sídhe afraid? They don't want to die here, but now they're just standing there, looking up at their enemies' guns. They should be running. They should be defending themselves.

They are.

The air shimmers.

"I feel . . . ," says Mitch. "I feel . . ."

"Me too," Liz Sweeney whispers. Behind her, Krishnan is doubled over, as though in pain.

And suddenly Anto is throwing up onto the grass of the hill. They all are, their heads spinning, and he remembers the horrible sensation he experienced at the Fairy Fort in Boyle, just minutes before his Call, as though the whole world had expanded around him. As though he were turning inside out.

Somewhere the Sídhe are cheering, but the humans can spare it no attention. That perfectly round hill they're lying on *changes* . . . In an instant, it has become a mountain. The slope gets steeper and steeper and Anto has to cling on as pebbles become boulders and bushes surge to the height of ancient oaks. Krishnan is screaming; little Mitch babbles prayers. But to no effect, because all at once they are tumbling down what is now a cliff, their guns and packs with them. A door appears before them, large enough to take an elephant, and they all know *exactly* where it leads.

"No! Nooooooo!" "By Crom!" "By God!" "Please! Please . . . !"

And through they go! Tumbling onto another slope on the far side, while above them silver spirals replace the glory of the stars.

Dizzy, terrified, halfway down the hill, Anto finds his feet, ripped by slicegrass, his lungs heaving in the acidic air, his eyes stinging, watering. Way below him is some kind of arena, where two people are fighting. But what does that matter? How can anything like that matter? He's *here*. He's back! Oh, Crom! Oh, Lugh! And his bladder lets go; he can't help it. Who could? Who can bear to see the Grey Land a second time?

"Pull yourself together!" cries Taaft. "The door! It's still open! Come on! Come ooon!"

And it's true. The way home stands clear for them at the top of the hill, the sky of the Many-Colored Land visible just beyond it.

A fairy host is moving now to block their escape. He has no idea how many there are, but they surely outnumber their remaining bullets.

"Let's kill them!" shouts Krishnan, his voice wavering with terror. "Let's kill them all!"

And Anto realizes he would like that. He would like it very much.

THE ALTAR

Nessa has no idea how there can be guns in the Grey Land, but she is aware that fighting has erupted on the slopes up near the doors. A number of Sídhe are lifted from their feet by what might be grenades. Gunshots crack and more of the fair folk tumble away.

But others, many, many others, swarm up the hill and must soon cut the intruders off from the door through which they entered.

Dagda looks delighted. "Some of your friends pay us a visit. Sadly, they will not make it down here. I would enjoy their company when you are gone."

He comes at her again, grinning with joy. He kicks one crutch as she tries to pass him, causing her to stagger so that she almost falls. And the spear licks out to bite her in the back of the leg. *Oh, Lugh, that hurts! That hurts!* But then she's clear, and now the skull at the base of the hill is right before her again.

"You'll never reach your friends," Dagda calls happily, "if that's what you're thinking." He's right about that: Nessa's arms have no strength to carry her up that slope to where the humans have come in. Her breath is like the engine of an old bus, and a foul, stinging mix of sweat and blood has almost blinded her. She props herself up against the giant skull. *An altar,* she thinks, *and I'm the sacrifice.*

The same two men from before are behind her like commentators at a football match.

"I say he kills the cripple slowly."

"She lasted a good while though. Didn't I say she'd last?"

And suddenly Nessa laughs. Dagda pauses in his advance, his mighty head cocked to one side.

"Yes," she tells the god. "Yes, I'm going to die. But not alone. Not for nothing."

Her grin is wide enough to match his, savage enough to open the cuts on her face. Oh, why didn't she think of this before? She turns to the crowd.

Standing there, right at the front, are two glitter-skinned human men. The commentators. Here they are, she thinks, immortal. Passing horrific endless lifetimes until the Sídhe keep their promise to send them home.

Nessa extends a hand and burns them both to a cinder.

Everything stops.

The door above slams shut.

There must be a thousand in the Sídhe crowd, but all at once, like at the flick of a giant switch, their manic grins turn to looks of shock and horror.

A promise kept, Lassair said, is powerful, but a promise broken can shake the very worlds in their orbits. And Nessa feels the ground shaking now, she really does, like laughter in a giant's belly.

One of the men she killed was wearing clothing. It's burning and Nessa gratefully drinks her fill. She sees a human woman nearby. Another person awaiting the fulfillment of a promise.

"No!" cries Dagda, recovering all of a sudden. "No!"

Nearby Sídhe try to throw themselves in the way, but the human woman dies anyway and the entire crowd wails.

Nessa doesn't get to gloat—the shaking of the ground throws her from her feet. The very walls of the Cauldron tremble, spilling silvery liquid over the sides, and nobody needs to tell Nessa what's happening: The two worlds, the Many-Colored Land and the Grey Land, artificially held together by the magic of a thousand promises, are trying to go their separate ways again.

This is not Ireland's last day, but it is the end for Dublin.

On a pier in Dún Laoghaire, sticking out into the ocean, a few dozen defenders crouch behind sandbags. Sleet hampers their vision. It freezes fingers to the barrels of guns, even through the wool of their gloves.

A few of them still have regimental patches on their uniforms: a cow with spider's legs, a tree-sized fox.

"They look pretty childish now, eh?"

"Indubitably," Karim responds. She yawns as though she hasn't a care in the world, as though she hasn't lost a score of friends between Roscommon and here. She'll probably join them herself sometime over the next twenty minutes.

Behind them, the sea surges against the old stone. Waves roll in from . . . well, nowhere. If Ryan were to look back—of course he can't afford to do that right now, but if he did—he would see how the water flows right into the fairy mist that hasn't cleared in twenty-five years. He remembers how it used to be on the coast. How the family would stop for the night in a parking bay looking out over the Irish Sea and the horizon seemed to stretch away forever.

But all his attention is focused forward. He squints out over a carpet of dead so thick he knows he could walk from here to Cabra without ever touching the soil. He's seen worse, hasn't he? He's felt worse. A hand pushing into his flesh as though he were made of nothing but damp clay and pain.

The shudder runs through his entire body.

"Dearest Ryan." Karim sighs. "Rest easy. It will be over soon. They're coming."

"There's no way you could see them yet!"

"No need to. I feel them."

The last two members of the North Leinster Infestation Squad are crouching beside each other in a line of soldiers. Some are middle-aged. Others, who have yet to see their thirteenth birthdays, have lined eyes and shriveled hearts. But their outsized rifles come up as quick as anybody else's. Quicker maybe, having more to lose.

"Faraz?" Ryan hasn't used Karim's first name in years. Not since the last of their children was Called and her mind seemed to . . . "Retreat" is the only word he can think of, even if it sits poorly with such an excellent soldier and leader as she is.

She sights down her rifle, as though the name he has spoken belongs to a stranger.

"I . . ." What could he possibly have to say to her now? Or she to him? *You did an amazing job. I'm glad I followed you.* What comes out instead is a muttered, "I love you, Faraz."

All she says is, "They're coming."

She's right. Ryan can feel it now too.

There's nowhere to retreat to after the pier. All over Dublin, little pockets of resistance waver and go under. Already armies of freshly made monsters are marshaling to march on Belfast and Derry, while the entire population of Galway cowers on the Aran Islands with nowhere else to go.

Karim lowers her eye to the rifle sight, obscuring the tattooed names of their children. Her finger rests lightly over the trigger. And that's when Ryan sees the enemy too. Time to get to work.

This last attack starts with a wave of "claws." Men and women barely altered from the normal human form. The only difference is that their hands have been turned into spikes and their minds have been changed just enough to make them eager to kill their own people.

"Jolly quick to make," Karim mutters.

Easy to slaughter too. Down they go by the dozen, falling over the ones in front, as two hundred expert shots scythe through their ranks. *What a waste!* Ryan thinks. Even for the Sídhe. Don't they want these people for their attacks in the north? Why the rush?

But then screams come from where the wounded lie at the end of the pier as larger monsters swarm up out of the sea, all plates of bone and long, suckered limbs.

Suddenly Karim swings up into the air, clutching at the tentacle wrapped around her neck. Ryan cries out, tracking the thing that's taken her, looking desperately for a gap in its plates of bone—

And then . . .

Everything stops.

Like years ago, when a video game would glitch and freeze on a single frame.

The earth rumbles—Ryan can feel it in the soles of his feet. The very walls of the pier shudder, spilling seawater over the sides. And the strangest thing happens: The sun is out.

It's not that it has emerged from the clouds. It's that there are no clouds. They are simply gone. The sea is as calm as a bath, and behind the monster holding Karim by the neck is a ship so large a dozen buildings could fit inside of it.

"A . . . a cruise liner," somebody breathes.

Gently the monster lays Karim down to where she can catch her breath.

"Shorry," it says. "Don' want hurtch youuuu."

And Karim laughs. Everybody does. Shocked, trembling. Happy. She turns to Ryan, and in her normal voice, the one he hasn't heard in years, she says, "Me too."

But then the sun disappears. The clouds, the sleet, the roaring waves are back, and all the monsters scream and return to the attack. It's as though the defenders dreamed all that beauty and must pay for it now, with their lives.

Nessa pulls herself up from the ground as it begins to steady again.

"You think that's enough, thief?" Dagda cries. He hasn't left the center of the arena. His face is a mask of fury but also confusion. "You think three broken promises can undo an eternity of work? We are granting wishes now! Dozens of them! Building up the power again. And there is one more promise . . . the one I myself made to Conor, that will now be kept."

He strides toward her.

Nessa throws herself aside, but she is weaker now and Dagda's shield batters her to the ground. He stamps on her crutches. *Snap! Snap!* Here comes the spear, straight for her belly! Nessa rolls away, but comes right up against his heroic calves, his sandals of human leather.

"And now—" he says.

She hits him in the legs with the last of the fire she drank from the burning clothing of her victims. She gives it every drop of heat she has, until the stench of cooked flesh is powerful enough to make her gag. The pain! Even one such as Dagda howls with it and crashes to his knees. He'll fall into shock. He must do. Anybody would.

But this is no human. This is a god.

"At last . . . ," he says. "It's gone . . . yes? The fire? All used up?"

She tries to crawl away from him, but he has her by the ankle and pulls her close. His grip moves up to her neck and he lifts her like a rag doll.

His feet are nothing but smoking stumps. Sweat covers his face and his clothing twitches in distress. But Dagda's smile returns.

While the gunfire on the hills continues, he takes the spear from the ground beside him and holds it up for her inspection. At the tip, she sees now, lies a fragment of charred, sharpened bone, no larger than her thumb.

"Conor," he says. "What's left of him. Only he has harmed you today."

This is a sacred moment and everybody in the small crowd that remains knows it. They hold their breaths, waiting for the sacrifice that must come, that will stabilize the doorway between the worlds.

Nessa is no longer afraid. At least she is not to be twisted. Nor will she have to stay here forever. *Alone.* For her it will be over soon. All those years fighting for the right to live. Why didn't she just spend more time with the people she loved? Training every day when she could have sat in a warm kitchen with her books. Learning more songs maybe. But would she have met Anto then? A few kisses is all they had, and she remembers her shortness of breath at those times, the mad beating of her heart. Struggling to hide the grin in the refectory; staring into a cup of tea so her eyes wouldn't betray her.

Anto. Mam. Dad. What is to become of them when she's gone? It's not for herself that she's asking, not that! But how she wishes she had more fire, more . . . more heat to strike a blow for the ones she loves.

Then she realizes that she does. She reaches up to touch Dagda on the arm. How warm he is! His entire body is full of heat, and Nessa sucks in as much of it as she can.

He cries out. Drops her at once.

"I thought you knew me," she says, grinning a Megan grin.

She has weakened him, but not fatally. His skin is pale as snow; even his lips are white and he shivers uncontrollably.

"You didn't take that much," he gasps. "Not enough to kill me."

But she doesn't need that much, not at all. He shoves the spear right at her face and Nessa releases all that stored heat into the tip. The sharp point flares once, and then . . . it drifts away, nothing but a cloud of ash.

"Good-bye, Conor," she says.

For five slow heartbeats nothing happens. As though the universe itself can't believe what she has done.

Then the ground doesn't just shake: It *bucks*.

Like a wild horse, like a hooked fish, it thrashes, flinging each of them in a separate direction. Everywhere are screaming Sídhe. Some claw at each other, or at their own faces.

On the nearest hill, the door opens and closes, opens and closes. She imagines that the enemy, whether in the Many-Colored Land or

here, must be fulfilling all the promises they can, but it's not enough—
it's never going to be enough. The worlds should never have clung
together so long. The pressure to split has been building for a
generation.

A number of the enemy have the presence of mind to run for
the last door, hoping to jump through to the beauty beyond before
it's too late.

But the guns throw them back.

Nessa crawls to the base of the hill. The crocodile thing is waiting for her, all alone in the midst of the trampled, shuddering earth.

"Kill me," it says, the words barely recognizable through its
long muzzle. "Burn me. Please."

"I will," Nessa replies. "If you carry me to the top of that hill."

THE LOST

The students fight to escape the Grey Land. With bullet and knife. With the last grenades.

Anto goes down under a pair of "dogs," his giant arm trapped beneath his own body. Fingernails rake his skin in stinging lines. Their hot breath is on his throat as human teeth struggle toward his jugular.

Not for the first time, Liz Sweeney saves his life: *crack, crack*— one shot each as ammunition runs low.

He comes up swinging, punching a Sídhe warrior hard enough to make him fly, snapping the skinny legs of a spiderlike horror that's running toward Krishnan.

Something has panicked the Sídhe. Just a short while ago they were all down in that arena thing, watching some kind of fight. Gouts of fire are chasing them up the hill and—

The ground lurches. Anto trips and down he goes again. He's face-to-face with Mitch in the muck. The boy's eyes are glazed over, the life draining out of them. Does Krishnan know?

But Anto can't tell him; the door is still fifty yards away at the top of the hill. It's none too stable either, flickering like a fading light bulb. Something is wrong with it, and the Sídhe feel it as much as he does. They're all charging for the door too. Piling over each other, trampling, floundering, scrambling.

Anto has never seen such a panic. It's as though this is the last lifeboat. As if they'll never be able to open another door once this one closes for good.

Here a princess with flowing locks stamps on a fallen man; there a hero in glittering bronze rides full tilt into the crowd on a panicking man-faced horse, until somebody in there cripples the creature with a touch of the hand, so that rider and mount drown in a sea of milling limbs.

Mere humans will never shoot their way through that!

As one, the group comes to a halt.

"No!" cries Aoife. Anto feels it too: the gut-wrenching terror that he might never leave this place again. And then, with no explanation at all, a jet of flame from the other side of the hill engulfs the Sídhe. Those who can't get to the door are turned to ash. Others reel away, burning as they go.

"Run!" Taaft shouts to the squad. "This is our chance." Anto obeys; there's no time for anything else, let alone thought!

Krishnan gets to the door first even as it flickers closed. But it flashes open just as quickly and he dives out of the Grey Land. Taaft bundles through after him, cursing and gasping. Aoife stumbles at the threshold while Liz Sweeney howls at her. But Anto picks Aoife up with his giant's arm and all three tumble together out onto the other side.

"Oh, God! Thank you, God!" Anto wants to kiss the icy ground. He drinks the pure, sweet air in massive gulps.

"Up," cries Taaft. "Everybody up! We can't let them through after us!"

Only now does Anto notice that it's daytime. The gate has dropped them far from Sligo, onto a road some place with the sea behind them. The peeling red paint of a postbox suggests it's Northern Ireland.

"Guns ready," Taaft shouts. "Pointed at the door!"

They obey, although nobody has more than a clip left. Here they stand: Liz Sweeney, Aoife, a weeping Krishnan; a boy with a giant's arm and a stocky snarl of an American soldier. It's a pathetic, battered group. But a deadly one.

Before them, a hole in the world shows burning Sídhe stumbling through the slicegrass and a sky of silver spirals. Yet, even as they watch, the door begins to fail. A space once large enough for an elephant and its rider could barely hold Anto himself now.

"I see one!" cries Liz Sweeney. Her gun is up, but Anto shoves it aside, although at first he has no idea why he did that, because one of the enemy is standing there now. A girl of the Sídhe. Except . . . except she's not really one of them, is she? Or wasn't anyway.

———————

Nessa is just as beautiful as Anto's fevered memories of her. More so, maybe. Her body quivers with exhaustion. Every muscle—he remembers them all! Oh, Crom! Oh, Lugh!—they tremble like chicks fallen from the nest, and her glittery skin, cut to ribbons, bleeds everywhere. She's only two steps away. It will take less than a second to cross the gap, to feel her in his arms, to smell her skin and hear her laugh. *We'll go to Donegal*, she'll say. *We'll get some dogs. You'll see. Let me tend to your cuts first. Let me kiss you. Let me forget everything.*

So close . . .

However, Taaft is even closer. She stands right at his shoulder. "The girl's a traitor, kid. You see that, don't you? She's become one of them. She has to die."

"She's poisoned you, Anto," says Liz Sweeney.

Yes! That's the word. *Poisoned.* How else to explain the tearing pain in his chest? That feeling like a fist pressing against his throat?

The door has continued to shrink. Now it's chest high so that the weeping Nessa seems a child. She knows they won't allow her through—she knows that. It doesn't matter that it must have been her who saved them by driving the Sídhe away from the door with fire. It doesn't matter that she could still burn the entire group where they stand. All that counts is that she's one of *them.*

Or is she?

"Out of the way!" Taaft insists.

Anto remembers the Sídhe woman in the park. He remembers what she said when she thought Liz Sweeney meant to eat her food. "You think if you look like us we will spare you after the conquest?"

And that's the moment Anto knows that Nessa's no traitor. It's just the food that makes her look like one. She could have burned Aoife in the Grey Land too, but never touched her. Of course she's innocent! She was always better and stronger than him in every way. Fierce in her love, so that nothing the enemy did would allow her to hurt him, or her parents, or her beloved Donegal! Nothing!

She couldn't look at him the way she is now if she were guilty: a swaying, wounded knot of love and sadness. Not pleading, as a coward would, as a traitor would. Because she knows, she does, that those who eat in the Fairy Realm can never go home. It's in all the stories.

Even if the squad did let her through, the authorities wouldn't believe her. They couldn't suffer her to live. Nor could her old comrades. Taaft will shoot her the second Anto gets out of the way, and Liz Sweeney might open fire even if he doesn't. There simply isn't the time to persuade them otherwise, before the door is gone away to nothing.

Nessa, therefore, will stay in the Grey Land, paying for sins she never committed. Hunted forever in an eternal Call by the vengeful Sídhe.

Anto's comrades shift positions, looking for an angle.

I could kill them all, he thinks, *with this arm of mine. Then Nessa could come home.*

But the old Anto is waking now. The one from before, who was horrified by the suffering of animals. Who, a lifetime ago, stood between the infestation squad and a giant wounded bull. That Anto was worthy to be loved, even by a creature as magical as Nessa.

He can't harm his friends.

So instead he knocks them back with a sweep of his arm and dives in through the portal.

And then, with a final flash, it's gone.

The survivors gawp at what is now nothing but a garden wall, unable to believe they're all still here. Nobody speaks. Nobody moves. Each has suffered appalling losses, yet if this thing is over now, if it's really over, shouldn't they be celebrating? They've earned the right.

There's a hint of spring in the air. The birds know it, arguing noisily, gathering twigs for nests. Here and there, a snowdrop blossom raises its shy head above the grass.

Eventually Taaft clears her throat. "Come on, kids. Let's find some food." But then, Aoife spins around and shouts in alarm. She points a shaking finger out to sea, where something monstrous looms on the horizon.

"What . . . ?" she asks. "What is that?"

For a while Taaft just stares, a look of shock on her face. "That," she says eventually, "is Scotland."

It's the loveliest thing anybody has seen in twenty-five years.

AMONG THE DEAD

Before their banishment, the people of the goddess Danú loved Ireland so much they called it "the Many-Colored Land." It's easy to see why on summer days like this, with roses flowering among the headstones and grass of the deepest green that can be imagined on this earth.

Aoife watches foreign tourists wander among the graves of what used to be Boyle Survival College. How strange they'd want to visit, she thinks, because outside the country, nobody believes in the events that happened here. Or so they say.

Even now, decades after the Sídhe invasion, they reach for explanations as to how the population of the island as well as the buildings, the machinery, the trees . . . aged twenty-five years in a single day. They'll say anything. Scientists pepper their speech with words like "wormholes" and "dark flow." They'll call it a cosmic fluke. They'll *prove* it will never happen again. It couldn't.

Yet, strangely, almost nobody migrated into the country afterward to take up the rich, empty farmland.

But the tourists come. Aoife has met makers of entertainments in search of gory details; she's heard of monster hunters, tracking down legends in the hills and bogs to which they fled, and more normal people, who tour the ruins and the graveyards like this one, giggling at the stories of the guides and taking selfies in front of Fairy Forts.

"Granny?"

Aoife looks down to Mary's black curls, to cheeks red enough to hide in a pile of ripe apples.

"You *said* you'd listen to my story."

"I will, pet, I will. Just let me sit down. By Crom, my hips! Just you wait. Aaah, that's better. By Lugh!"

Aoife never particularly liked children, but Mary, her wife's grandchild, is a constant delight. "Here, just give me a minute to catch my breath, kid."

"Kid! Who even says 'kid,' Granny! I'll be back!" And she adds, cheekily, "Don't go away!" And off she runs, giving Aoife a chance to get her flask out and pour herself a shaky cup of tea. Who'd have thought she'd ever grow old? Around her are the final resting places of those who didn't.

Nearest her seat, under a carved moon, lies Nabil. It was Sergeant Taaft who recovered his bones from Longford, and now she lies beside him.

On the far side of them both, beneath a great plaque to explain her place in history, Alanna Breen is buried, still getting flowers after all this time. The hunt master isn't so lucky; his accommodations— a narrow plot, a rusting marker—are much more modest. Nice man—what was his name? Doesn't matter now. It's all so long, long ago. Once upon a time. Like the fairy tales people still tell in every country in the world that isn't Ireland.

"Mary?" she calls. "Mary? Help me up."

The child skips over to help Granny stand. "Bring my flask too, pet. You're a star."

They walk over to the student area of the cemetery, where, as is her tradition, Aoife makes a point of looking away from Conor's grave. Although she does remember that bizarre night when she spotted the Sídhe here, digging it up, stealing his bones. Nobody has ever been able to explain that one to her. No doubt the reason will be lost forever now. But, oh, never mind. For here lies another peaceful stone, all grown over with wild roses in early bloom.

"Give me the flask, pet. Ta."

"Ewww! Granny! Why're you pouring tea on a grave!"

"I think she'd like it. We never had any of the real stuff growing up. And she was my first love, you know? You never forget that. Never. Maybe someday, you'll bring me a cuppa too."

"Ewww! Come on. Let's go to the ruins. You promised. And I'll tell you my story!"

"Sure, kid. Sure."

It's another one of those "glitter people" tales that scare the living daylights out of anybody old enough to remember the Sídhe and the Call.

A few of the enemy remained behind in the Many-Colored Land when the last of the doors closed behind them, but within a week their skin and eyes had turned normal. They no longer had power in their hands, and anyway, they spent most of their days, when not fleeing for their lives, staring at the sky and trees and suchlike.

But stories among the younger generations persist.

"I didn't see the magic people myself," Mary says. *Thank God,* Aoife thinks. "But Alexandra in my class did. She got lost in the woods and two of them guided her out."

"They . . . uh, they didn't try to kill her, then?"

"Oh, no! They smiled and showed her the way home."

"Uh-huh. And what did they look like, exactly? Beautiful, I suppose? Perfect?"

Mary shakes her lovely little head so that the curls bounce. "Not perfect at all, Granny. The man had this big arm. I mean huge! And the woman walked funny and—Granny? Are you all right? Granny?"

Aoife wipes a tear away. "It's just a story, pet. I'm sorry I don't believe it. But it just . . . it just reminded me of people I knew once. This whole place does."

Could they really have found a way back, those two? In all her long life, Aoife never met anybody as determined as Nessa. It wouldn't surprise her if she ended up ruling the Grey Land, or if she found other doors out of the place into whatever worlds lie beyond it.

"But she saw them, Granny! Lots of people have seen them. They rescued—"

"Enough, kid. Look, we're here!"

On the far side of the trees around the graveyard, the ruins of the school lie choked in ivy. Even the gym, which survived Conor's fire, has been allowed to decay. A dozen tourists stand around it, while a guide tells them the story of the attack, a tale that has now become known as "Traitors' Night."

"Can we listen, Granny?"

"*You* can, pet. I want the rest of that tea."

"Already?"

"Why not? I'm exhausted."

Mary runs over to the tour guide and squeezes in among the foreigners.

Aoife rests against the trunk of a tree, drinking in the scent of it. *Still alive*, she thinks. *Thank you, God, or gods, or whoever.* She's had an amazing life, and now, with a new generation rising that never knew terror, the whole country is starting to blossom again, with youth and beauty everywhere. Time for laughter. Time for gardens and cuddles at midnight under the magnificence of the sky.

Aoife doesn't know why the invasion died when it did, the gates shutting down so suddenly. *Who saved us?* she wonders. *Who saved me and gave me my life back?*

Whoever you are, I love you. Wherever you are, I wish you a happiness as deep as mine.

Bored with the old stories, Mary is already running back.

ACKNOWLEDGMENTS

Most sequels are written in response to reader enthusiasm, so, first place in these acknowledgments must go to anybody who made it through *The Call*. You are magnificent. You kept me going, kept me interested. The five-star reviewers who loved the book; the one-star reviewers who feared their grandchildren might read it—all of you made me want to write *The Invasion*. You have my big, nay! My *monstrous* thanks.

The staff at David Fickling Books supported me every step of the journey. Especially Bella, who made me face reality, and David, who dragged me the other way into poetry. Caro fed me. Rosie encouraged me. Bron and Phil, Simon and Anthony oiled the clanky bits that nobody sees, while Emma Draude pushed and pushed.

In America, Scholastic floated me everywhere on a carpet made entirely of love. They put in so much enthusiasm that it triggered a world shortage. They were all heroic, but for now I'd like to single out Jennifer, Nick, Lori, and Nancy for their welcome and their kind treatment of an Irish waif blown to them across the sea.

As always, I owe debts of blood and tears to my beta readers: Carol, Doug, and Iain. It's not nice to be brought down to earth with a bang, but they do it with extreme tact and the bruises heal eventually.

In a similar vein, I want to thank Talya "The Eagle" Baker, who returned to us as our special guest star line editor. Many blushes were spared!

And what about all those booksellers and librarians out there who pushed *The Call* onto people who were just trying to mind their own business? I've met dozens of you, but not once did I do the right thing and kiss your feet. Without you I am nothing.

I am also nothing without family and friends. Much love to the BwB, who always turn up, as well as to the organizers of conventions like TitanCon, where people buy books to read or to use as missiles.

Finally, let me express my appreciation and love for the entire population of Australia and New Zealand. I won't tell you why, but if any of my other readers ever meet anyone from Down Under, please buy them a coffee and tell them I sent you.

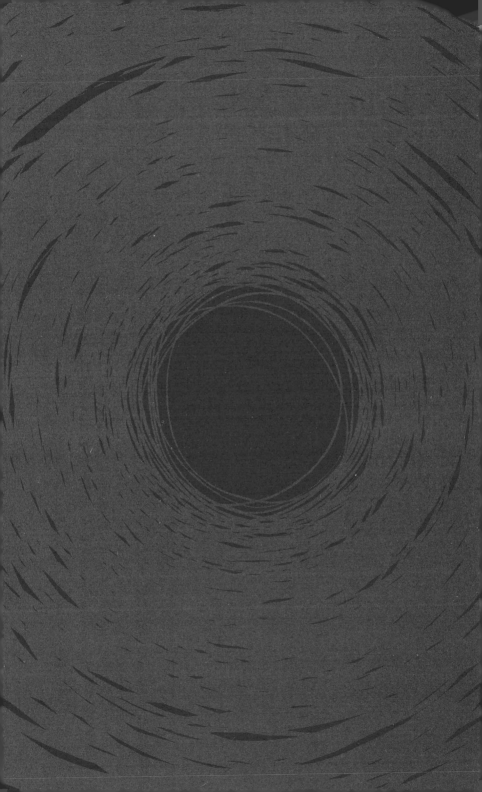